A SECRET IN THE FAMILY

When Lady Frederica Drummond falls pregnant with another man's child while her husband is away at war, she knows she must give up the baby to keep her marriage. In despair, she turns to her old nanny, Robbie, and begs her to bring Sarah up as her own in her cottage at Kirby Hall, where Frederica can watch her grow up.

It is years later that the troubles start. Noticing a friendship developing between Sarah and her son, David, Lady Frederica sends Sarah to Paris, but as World War Two threatens, Sarah soon faces other dangers.

A SECRET IN THE FAMILY

A SECRET IN THE FAMILY

by

Rose Boucheron

Magna Large Print Books
Long Preston, North Yorkshire,
BD23 4ND, England.

British Library Cataloguing in Publication Data.

Boucheron, Rose
A secret in the family.

A catalogue record of this book is
available from the British Library

ISBN 0-7505-1658-5

First published in Great Britain in 2000
by Judy Piatkus (Publishers) Ltd.

Published in Large Print 2001 by arrangement with
Piatkus Books Ltd.

Magna Large Print is an imprint of Library Magna Books Ltd.

Printed and bound in Great Britain by
T.J. (International) Ltd., Cornwall, PL28 8RW

Chapter One

1998

The evening was fine and warm as Sarah Harper held court from her *chaise-longue* in the garden awaiting the arrival of her children and grandchildren. Today was her eightieth birthday, although she found it hard to believe. Out here on the terrace the tubs of geraniums and blue lobelia sent up a dry breath-catching perfume as she looked across at the ploughed fields and the faint blue mist in the distance. The garden was at its best on this September evening, being laid out with great taste by William Harper's great-grandmother in a bygone age, when to design a beautiful garden was considered an achievement becoming to a lady.

Sarah had come as a bride to Falmouth Grange just after the Second World War, having married William Harper, a squadron leader in the Royal Air Force. In those days the house had been surrounded by five hundred acres, but now, owing to death duties, it was down to fifty acres, and even that needed some keeping up as she well knew. Now the house was held in trust for her eldest son, Edward, which was as it should be, she thought, while Hugh, her younger son, would inherit the Home Farm. A man should inherit land, for there was nothing more worthwhile as a legacy except perhaps birth and breeding and her children had that. She could just see the roof of the farmhouse from here while the little lake shimmered silver in the distance and cows grazed in the far field where Hugh had already had his machines out to cut and stack the corn way back in July. Now, the fields shone golden in this dry spell.

Over her head to protect her from the evening sun Sarah held a small lacy Edwardian parasol, a gift from her granddaughter, Lisa. Everything was so elegant in those far-off days, she thought, although she herself had been a child of the Twenties growing up after the First World War.

Looking back now, she remembered the Drummonds, that wonderful family with whom she had spent a lot of her childhood, in that house on the Berkshire downs which stretched endlessly as far as the eye could see. The Drummond children, Joanna, Candida and David – she could conjure them up at will, see them now. She could remember so many things from long ago.

She sighed. Memories from the past. They returned now unbidden, from way back when you often couldn't recall what you had done the day before.

In those days, of course, old ladies of eighty might just as well be dead. Usually widows, they had probably been on their own for a long time, life for them having ceased when their husbands died. But times had changed, she knew elderly widows who went on cruises, jogged, worked out at gyms, took up new hobbies, even in their nineties.

Losing William had been the worst thing that had happened to her five years before. Dear William, the mainstay of her life, not only her lover and her friend, but a true companion. How she missed him... Still, there were consolations, there always were; she had her lovely family: Laura her daughter, and Laura's daughters, Lisa and little Francesca, her sons Edward and Hugh and Edward's daughter Catherine – but here was Lisa, looking so elegant, just like her mother, coming towards her hands outstretched.

'Gran! Happy birthday!' Lisa bent down

to kiss her.

'Darling, how lovely to see you–'

They kissed, and Lisa laid a posy of tiny pink rosebuds on her lap. Sarah buried her face in them. 'Oh, they're lovely! The scent!'

'I know,' and Lisa pulled up a chair beside her. 'Well, it's a bit quiet – where is everyone? Aunt Ida was in the kitchen when I came through with Mrs Manson working like a Trojan – I must say the cooking efforts look wonderful.'

'We're having drinks out here as it is such a fine evening, but eating inside, I think.'

Lisa put her head on one side. 'You don't look a day more than sixty-five, honestly, Gran,' she said, seeing the elegant legs stretched out on the *chaise-longe,* the simple silk suit, the pearls which she was almost never without, and her diamond pendant earrings worn for a special occasion.

'Flatterer,' Sarah said, but she was pleased. 'Ah, here they come now.'

Edward came first, carrying bottles of champagne, followed by Hugh, the younger by two years, and Nancy, his wife. Then Ida, Edward's wife, following carrying a tray of delectable goodies, Sarah was sure, for among Ida's many accomplishments, she was an excellent cook. Then came Mrs

Manson, the housekeeper, with a tray of glasses.

Sarah wished she was forty again…

Glasses and plates were put down on the garden table, while everyone kissed her and wished her a happy birthday. She took time off to wonder where Catherine was, and a small sigh escaped her. Catherine was Edward's daughter by his second wife, Ida, and Catherine had a boyfriend much disapproved of by Sarah, who considered him to be highly unsuitable. He worked on the farm with Hugh and was apparently a good worker, but she had heard tales from the village of his prowess among the girls and didn't trust him. She just hoped that Catherine would not have asked him to the celebration dinner – surely Ida would not have given her approval.

But here was Laura with her other daughter, the afterthought, as she called her. Pretty little Francesca was ten years old – and doubts about whose birth and father Sarah kept to herself.

Francesca looked delightful, in a pretty party dress of blue organza. How different she looked and what a change from those everlasting jeans and shorts. She looked quite happy in her new outfit, although

Sarah knew she had made a fuss when Laura had told her she was to wear a dress.

'Darling! Give me a kiss,' Sarah said, as Francesca dimpled and gave her a small posy and a little parcel done up prettily in coloured tissue.

'Why, what's this? For me?'

Francesca's eyes shone. 'Happy birthday, Gran.'

Sarah kissed her. 'May I open it now?'

'Yes, of course,' and they all watched as Sarah undid the wrapping to reveal a small box inside which was a tiny blue enamel brooch, a lover's knot; she swallowed hard.

'Mummy let me choose it,' she said proudly.

'Oh, darling, it's lovely!' Sarah leaned forward and kissed her. 'I shall put it on – will you help me?'

Then it was time for popping the champagne corks and there were drinks all round, and presently Catherine emerged from the house, followed by a tall handsome youth, dark eyebrows almost meeting above black wicked-looking eyes.

Ida threw her mother-in-law an apprehensive glance then went forward to Catherine to greet her.

'Ah, there you are, darling! And–'

Catherine kissed her grandmother, and, taking the young man's hand, led him forward.

'Gran, this is my friend Julian Stockwell.'

The young man held out his hand, but his eyes held a gleam as though to say, well, I'm here – what are you going to do about it?

'For you, Gran,' Catherine said, and put a small parcel on Sarah's lap.

'Thank you, Catherine.'

She found herself quite hot and bothered inside at the very thought of it. Ida must have been mad to encourage the friendship and it was difficult to imagine what a lusty young man like this Julian – and what kind of name was that for a young man? – saw in Catherine, a quiet, shy little thing, with no go in her.

True, he was fine-looking, in a swarthy kind of way, and she had heard he had been to agricultural college. Still what did that count today when everyone went to university? You would have thought he would have courted a village girl; there were enough of them about and after him. No, he was after Catherine's money, there was no doubt about that. Not an unwelcome inheritance for she was hardly the wife for a lusty young man like Julian Stockwell.

Sarah rose gracefully from her chair, and it was Julian who held out a helping hand.

'Thank you,' she said graciously, and stood tall, elegant for her age, and beautifully dressed. She had style, had always had it, and it stood her in good stead in old age. She linked her arm in Edward's while the others collected her presents and made their way into the house. Her hair, which had been so dark in her youth, had gone white early on, a silvery-white, which she had cut by an expert cutter, while her olive skin – not without its lines these days – supported a good bone structure, her teeth were still her own, and her eyes dark and deep-set.

Lisa looked around. Almost everyone was here now, except Tony – but then there was no reason why Tony should be here. After all, Gran wasn't his true grandmother, only by marriage.

When her Uncle Edward had married for the first time he had wed Giovanna, a beautiful Italian widow with a small boy named Tony. Giovanna was only twenty-four, while the boy, Tony, was just five years old. She died only two years after marrying Edward, and for two years Edward had lived the life of a recluse, never going out and meeting few people. His mother despaired, but then one day after church, he suddenly appeared with Ida, and what a shock! For Ida was as different from Giovanna as it was possible to be. But they had married and she had taken little Tony to her heart as one of her own, and in time given birth to Catherine. Tony and Lisa had played together as children until Tony went away to boarding school, then they seldom met except in the school holidays, and by the time they had both grown up, there was a kind of self-consciousness, an awareness. They had gone around together for a spell, and Lisa thought she might be falling in love with him, but they had lost touch when she went to Paris for two years to study. When she returned she saw him briefly, and at times Tony seemed almost hostile. But although their paths separated, for Lisa there was always the power Tony seemed to have over her of making her apprehensive. Now, it seemed that he was not here and she felt a mixture of disappointment and relief.

What a perfect setting! Lisa had brought her camera and was busy photographing the scene from all angles. Gran had a fine sense of occasion, thought Lisa, who adored her grandmother. Uncle Hugh in his dinner jacket looked quite handsome – she was so used to seeing him in outdoor casual clothes. His curly hair was plastered down as flat as it would go, but already curls were escaping in the heat. His wife Nancy stood beside him, smiling, dear Nancy, in a flowered cotton dress. Everyone liked Nancy, she was so pretty, warm and nice, so right for a farmer's wife, and she also sculpted and painted, had a small studio at the side of the big barn where she sold some of her home-made pottery. So artistic, but without the one thing she wanted most of all in the world – a child. Grandmother was very fond of Nancy.

Philip, Nancy's brother, a weekend visitor, was with her now, and there was no mistaking the likeness. He was blessed with the same charm as Nancy and now came over and greeted her.

'Hi, there, Lisa – nice to see you again.'

'You too,' Lisa said. 'I'm glad you could make it. Quite an occasion.'

They had come to the edge of a small water-lily pool where a girl was sitting, dressed in cool yellow – and Lisa's heart missed a beat.

'Hi, there, Daisy,' she said.

'Hallo, Lisa, I'm just waiting for Tony.

He's on the telephone – again.'

'Oh, is he here?' Her heart now was beating fast. 'I'm so glad you two could make it.'

On the fourth finger of Daisy's slim white hand, clasped around the glass of champagne, was a beautiful antique ring.

'What a lovely ring! May I?'

'Of course.' Daisy transferred her glass to her other hand and held out her ring for inspection. 'It's Georgian, and belonged to Tony's maternal grandmother.'

'It's beautiful.' Lisa eyed the ring enviously. Was she covetous of the ring, or its donor? Daisy was a nice girl, charming, warm and friendly.

She sat down beside her. 'When is the wedding?' she asked casually.

'Oh, we've no plans yet to marry. As you know, modelling takes me all over the world, and I'm not ready to settle down just yet. I'll honour all my commitments for a year, and then we'll see. Perhaps by then I'll be happy to settle down.'

She gave her beautiful smile and stood up as she saw Tony, and Lisa felt a heavy heart. It was a pity, she thought, that she apparently still nurtured feelings for him, and faced the knowledge that she had never really forgotten him. Now, seeing him with this delightful girl at his side, perhaps she would forget the bonds that had seemed to tie her to him. Now, acknowledging her feelings, it was as if she were absolved. Thank God she wasn't really in love with him, that their distance apart had not strengthened whatever emotion she felt for him.

'Hi, Tony,' she smiled. 'Glad you could make it, and congratulations.'

'Thanks.' He looked into her eyes briefly then transferred his gaze to the lovely Daisy.

No doubt about his feelings for her, Lisa thought, getting up. 'Well, I must go and give Aunt Ida a hand; I've been abominably lazy up to now.'

Philip caught up with Lisa and, closely followed by the others, went into the cool dining room. Once more the splendid room had come into its own. Bowls of flowers were displayed down the centre of the table which was laid with precious china and cutlery. It looked magnificent. The lights from the great crystal chandelier caught Sarah's diamond earrings, sparkled, moved, and sparkled again; they were the most brilliant things in the room.

The wine flowed and the dinner was

excellent, served by Mrs Manson and a girl from the village. From her position at the head of the dinner table Sarah surveyed her family from dark eyes filled with gratitude and pride.

Edward lit his cigar, and Sarah knew that he was about to get to his feet and make a speech. He usually did this at a family gathering, it was expected of him and he did it very well. How she wished that William could have been here – but she had much to be thankful for – this lovely family – there might be a few problems, but they were all well and happy. Her eye fell on the newcomers to the family, the additions, and her brow darkened as she saw the handsome face of young Julian Stockwell, and she sighed.

She must be fair, not be too hasty to judge. Wasn't old age supposed to bring tolerance? She had a nasty feeling that one became more intolerant as one got older, suffered fools less gladly.

Afterwards in her bedroom, she sat at the dressing table and removed her pearls, a wedding gift from William, then her diamond earrings, a silver wedding gift, and laid them in her jewellery box. From her right hand she slid off the magnificent opal ring surrounded by diamonds, and placed it gently in its red velvet box, then picked up the red enamelled Cross of Lorraine, one of her most treasured possessions, from the Second World War ... and closed the jewellery box as a tap came at the door.

It was little Francesca coming in with her mother to say good-night.

'Well,' she said fondly to her. 'Did you enjoy my birthday party?'

'Yes, Gran, I did,' and the little girl's eyes shone. 'Did you really like your pressie?'

'What, my brooch? I should think I did!' Sarah said heartily. 'It is lovely, and you know blue is my favourite colour.'

'I know,' Francesca said proudly, and her glance went to the mantelpiece where stood the small figure, a cheap plaster figure wearing a sun bonnet, her demure cheeks rosy red and her skirt lifted as she presumably was about to step into water. It was a pretty thing and of all Grandmother's possessions, Francesca's favourite.

Laura pulled back the bedclothes and Sarah climbed in. When she got settled, she smiled across at Francesca.

'Would you like to hold her?'

'Oh, yes please, Gran.'

'Get her down, Laura,' Sarah said. 'Let

Francesca hold her.'

Francesca held her gently.

'Did you always have her? When you were a little girl?'

'Ever since I can remember,' Sarah said. 'Isn't she pretty? I think she looks a bit like you,' and she smiled.

Francesca looked pleased.

'Now, let's put her back,' Laura said gently, 'and leave Gran to sleep. She must be exhausted.'

'I've had a whale of a day!' Sarah said.

Laura tucked her in.

'Eighty,' she said. 'Not bad, eh? You know, sometimes, Mother, I think you should write it all down. You've had an interesting life, haven't you, and once you've gone there will be no one to tell us–'

'Yes, I suppose I have,' Sarah agreed, and lay awake long after the door had closed behind them.

She took a glance up at the little blue girl before switching off the bedside light.

You are as old as I am, she thought, even older, and saw her on a very different mantelpiece…

Chapter Two

1918

Kirby Hall sat in some fifty acres deep in the Berkshire countryside, not far from the village of Allington. Built of stone, four-square and solid, it had many windows, and an impressive front entrance up a flight of steps, where great gargoyles sat on either side of the front door. The lawns sloped gently down to a drive, which led to the village, past First Lodge, so-called because it was nearest to the Hall, down to Gate Lodge, which nowadays was unoccupied, although at one time the gatekeeper had lived there in two tiny rooms.

The Kirbys had lived in the house for generations, but now the Drummonds lived there, the last Kirby, Sir Edward's daughter, Frederica, having married Sir Richard Drummond, Bart.

On this cold March evening, in the main bedroom, Lady Freddie sat now, eyeing her reflection.

'How's that, Milady?'

Robbie stood back regarding her ladyship in the dressing table mirror, which reflected the lovely face in front of her. She had just dressed her hair, abundant fair hair, drawn away from her face into a heavy chignon, seeing also the lack of expression as Lady Freddie sat still, hands listlessly in her lap, staring at herself and showing not the slightest interest.

'Well, say something!'

With the freedom of long acquaintance Robbie softened the words with a swift smile. She was privileged, having been long in service with the family, and knowing her ladyship from a baby, she knew one sometimes had to be sharp with her, spoiled as she was.

The lovely face reflected in the gilt-edged mirror wore a frown, brows drawn together, beautifully sculpted mouth downturned – all at variance with her upright figure, for part of her beauty lay in her bearing, in Robbie's opinion, her gracious carriage. At the moment her ladyship could not have looked more depressed.

'Robbie, don't go on at me – I'm miserable!'

'Yes, we know all about that. A lot of us are and have a lot more to complain about than you do, Milady. Some women have already lost their husbands in this terrible war. At least Sir Richard is still alive, well, we hope so, and you have a lovely little boy upstairs – you don't know when you're well off, Milady.'

At the mention of her little son, the frown eased and the semblance of a smile touched her lips.

'Yes, I know I should be thankful.'

'Yes, you should,' Robbie said, picking up the brush and comb and removing the cape from around Milady's shoulders. 'Count your blessings, that's what you want to do. There, you look lovely; and where are you going this evening? Another cocktail party? Too many of those going on seems to me. I don't know what's got into young people – you'd never think a war had been going on.'

Lady Freddie peered at her face in the mirror, so used to her reflection that she hardly saw it for what it was, fair-skinned with beautiful contours, full rosy lips and blue eyes. Sometimes it seemed to Robbie that she had it all.

'Well,' she said at length, regarding her. 'I must say you look tired. You don't get enough sleep for a start,' for there were faint blue shadows around the deep blue eyes, and a general air of listlessness about her. Usually she was full of beans, dancing the night away up at the Hall where sometimes social evenings took place for the officers who were recuperating at the local hospital and were well enough to attend before they went back to the front.

'Well, I'd better be getting back,' Robbie said, returning from the bathroom. 'The boys will be wanting their supper.'

Her mistress stood up abruptly.

'I'm sorry, Robbie. I always forget you have another home to go to,' and she smiled with a trace of her usual good humour.

'Yes, I have, Milady! But you be careful now. I hope you'll have a nice evening. Wrap up warm – the nights are chilly and don't stay out too late.'

'I won't, Robbie,' Freddie promised.

'Is young Master David all right? Is Lucy with him?'

'Yes, giving him his bath I expect.'

'Well, I'll pop in and see him on my way out. Good-night, Milady.'

She had got almost to the door when a sudden movement came from Lady Freddie. 'Oh, Robbie–' It sounded like a call for help, Robbie thought afterwards.

'Yes, Milady?'

'Oh, nothing. Nothing. I'll see you later – tomorrow, perhaps?'

'I expect so. I've got the Red Cross knitting bee down at First Lodge tomorrow.'

'Oh, well–'

'Good-night, Milady.'

Goodness, she was in a state, Robbie decided. She thought she knew all Milady's moods, and it wasn't often that she looked as miserable as she did today. Well, she supposed the war was finally getting to her. After all, she was only twenty-four, married almost four years, with a little boy of three, and in that time she had hardly seen her husband. Parted two days after their wedding day, when Sir Richard had been called to the War Office, and seeing him only a few times since. He had now been overseas for six months without leave – of course she was feeling down.

Not that she lacked consolation, Robbie thought grimly. There were enough young officers to console her, she was the bright star of any gathering; she knew there was no harm in her, she adored her husband, and was just trying to make the best of a bad situation. For she did help out at the hospital, and sewing bees, and at the Red Cross.

Robbie buttoned up her coat, put her hat and scarf on and prepared to brave the cold March wind, leaving the Hall by the back door and making her way down to First Lodge.

Edith, as she had been christened, had lived in First Lodge all her life, had been born there, for her father was groom and stable man up at Kirby Hall. Old Sir Henry had been alive then, it had been in the Kirby family for generations. Edith had been fifteen when Lady Freddie was born; when her mother, Lady Kirby, suffered complications in childbirth, it had seemed a natural thing for the family to ask if Edith would be prepared to help Nanny Foster when she left school.

She had been overjoyed, there was nothing she liked better than to be up at the Hall, she felt part of it, especially to help look after this adorable baby whom they had christened Frederica.

She had stayed with the family even after Lady Freddie had grown up and her mother had died, becoming a sort of lady's-maid. But time brought changes, Robbie's own mother died, and Robbie married Tom Roberts who gradually took over her father's duties, her father becoming older and more frail; he then applied for the job as general groundsman to Freddie's father at Kirby Hall, and had been there ever since.

When her father died, Robbie took over the Lodge. Of course with two sons her days were full, but she always found time to go up to the Hall to help them in any capacity – she felt so much at home there.

When Sir Edward Kirby died, Lady Kirby inherited the Hall and the estate, and soon after Lady Freddie married Sir Richard Drummond, a wealthy baronet some ten years older than his new wife. As for Lady Freddie, Robbie, as Edith became known after her wedding to Tom, adored her, there was nothing she would not do for her especially after Lady Kirby's death. Of course, Tom's duties were not the same as her father's had been. Sir Edward kept several horses then, but now the stables had been pulled down to make way for a tennis court, although they did keep a pony and trap.

The dreadful toll taken by the war was a problem for every family. There was no one who had not been affected. Robbie was lucky that Tom had a safe and secure job. He had done his bit for his country, and being left with a limp was a small price to pay even though it slowed him down.

The boys looked up when she came in, so pleased to see her. She was like a rock, their mother. Strong, capable, she did everything, their dad too, but he was almost always outside the house. Now, Robbie took off her coat, pulled the curtains, put her apron on, and began to get the supper. The coal fire in the range burned brightly, for the boys knew they had a job to do when they came in from school every day, to get the coal from the coal cellar and fill the hods; they were good boys, Robbie had trained them well.

Still, she couldn't help fretting a little over Milady. She didn't like to see her looking so down, but she had been right, she had a lot to be thankful for, and she had been right to say so.

In the scullery Robbie saw that the boys had cleaned their boots ready for school the next day, they gleamed as brightly as Robbie's range. They were good lads, both of them, and if little David up at the Hall grew up half as fine, her ladyship should be pleased.

She was frying bubble and squeak on the top of the range when Tom came in. Despite his physical strength, he was a quiet and kind man, although no one should underestimate him. He was strong, yet gentle as a dove, but it was Robbie who ruled the roost.

Now, she heard him take off his boots outside, heard him at the tap sluicing, before coming in to wash his face at the kitchen sink. He nodded to the boys when they looked up, words were fairly scarce in that family, but they all knew what the others meant.

Tom sat down at the table, joining the boys, while Robbie pushed a plate towards him of bubble and squeak, crisp bacon, egg and sausages, home-made from home-killed meat. They did better for food than people in towns. They ate in silence, all of them, Robbie thinking over the events of the day, the boys quiet at the table, as they were made to be. Asking permission to get down, they took their plates to the sink in the scullery then went upstairs to their room.

When they had gone, Robbie pushed her plate to one side.

'What have you been doing today?' she asked Tom.

'Clearing out the ditches in the lower field.'

'Dry weather looks set to last,' Robbie said, scraping the plates and taking them over to the sink.

After supper, Robbie went outside. The nights were growing lighter and she looked to see if any bulbs were through – she had planted lots of daffodils. She loved flowers and grew some fine roses and cottage flowers, while Tom kept her well supplied with vegetables in the summer from his own patch. It was a small garden but all theirs, not to be confused with the great lawns and flowerbeds and vegetable garden up at the Hall which Jim Hardy, the gardener, kept. But now it was too dark to see.

It was towards seven-thirty when she heard a knock at the door. All callers at the Hall had to report to First Lodge now that the Gate Lodge was unused. Opening the door she saw the telegraph boy standing there, and her heart missed a beat. Everyone hated telegrams even though just occasionally they could bring good news, it was bad more often than not.

He wordlessly showed her the telegram addressed to Lady Frederica Drummond – please God that it wasn't Sir Richard. The fighting had been so bad of late they said half a million men had died in France alone. Of course, Sir Richard was not in France but in Egypt, for his father had been

Consul there, but a war was a war, after all was said and done.

She waited by the window, the curtain pulled aside, until she saw the telegraph boy cycle past again on his way back to the Post Office. It was some time after that that she heard the clip-clop of the pony and trap hurrying down the hill, and she felt sick inside as she saw Lady Freddie with the reins in her hand.

She hurried outside as the pony came to a halt.

'Milady! Whatever is it?' For she was as pale as death itself. 'It's not Sir Richard?'

'Sir Richard – he's coming home, he has two days' leave–' she was almost in tears as she brought the pony to a halt.

'Robbie, could you spare a moment to come up to the Hall? Please–'

The last word was whispered in anguish, and Robbie glanced back at the Lodge.

'Please, Robbie,' and her beseeching tone decided her.

'I'll just get a coat and tell Tom.'

When she returned, Lady Freddie made room for her on the seat, and spurred the pony to action.

Neither spoke until they reached the Hall, then Freddie tethered the pony and ran up the steps into the house and into the big stone-flagged hall, followed by Robbie.

'Come on,' she said, running up the stairs to the first floor, and waiting for Robbie to join her in her room. She closed the door firmly and stood looking at Robbie as though she had seen a ghost. She was breathless.

'Milady? Whatever is it? Come and sit down, do.'

'My husband – he's coming home, tomorrow or Thursday – he has two days' leave–'

'Well, that's wonderful – and he's all right, not wounded?'

'No, no,' Freddie was breathless, her face a mask of terror.

'Robbie, Robbie – I'm pregnant!' and she fell forward on Robbie's shoulders, a dead weight.

Robbie stood still, taking her weight, mouth open, then snapped it shut. Pregnant! Well, she might have guessed by the look of her, but Freddie's husband had not been home for six months…

'Oh, my God,' she said slowly. 'How far are you?' the words came out harshly.

'Just gone three months,' Freddie wailed.

There was a long silence, then Robbie said

the first thing that came into her head.
'You silly girl, Milady!'

'Well,' she said at length, 'you'd best tell me all about it,' and half led Lady Freddie to a chair, where she collapsed. Then she went over to the carafe of fresh drinking water and poured her a glass.

'Drink this,' she said.

Freddie did so, as if she could hardly swallow, but she was quieter now as if she had got the worst of it over.

Robbie's face was expressionless, although inside her thoughts were in turmoil. How could her ladyship have let things get so far – let alone a village woman – and her with so much at stake.

'Now take it easy, Milady, and begin at the beginning.'

'Well–' but the words just didn't seem to come.

'One of them young officers, I suppose,' Robbie prompted.

'No,' Freddie said slowly. 'But it doesn't matter now, does it?'

'If you say so, Milady – does he know, this – er – gentleman?'

'No, no, of course not!' Freddie was shocked. 'Oh, I love him so, Robbie.'

Robbie had not much time for that, undying love was not something she could get het up about, especially if you were married and had a child.

'Well, who was it then?'

Freddie was suddenly at her most haughty. 'I refuse to name the man,' she said. 'It is of no consequence now–' and her lovely young face assumed a kind of pathetic dignity. 'He has gone away, I shall never see him again,' and suddenly she wept.

This was worse than Robbie thought.

'Now, Milady, pull yourself together. There's Sir Richard due back; when does he arrive?'

'Tomorrow or Thursday, the sixth or seventh, the telegram said. Oh, what am I to do, Robbie? Help me–'

Robbie was practical. 'Well, Milady, there's not much you can do now – not even time to have – er–'

'How dare you suggest such a thing!'

Freddie sat up straight. 'Remember your place, Robbie,' her nostrils flaring like those of a young mare.

Robbie got to her feet. Her mouth was grim.

'I'm sorry, Milady. I was only trying to help.'

And Freddie burst into tears again. 'Oh, Robbie, I'm sorry. Of course you were trying to help. I need you, don't you go back on me now–'

Robbie went over and put an arm round her. 'Of course I won't, but we have to do what's best – and in a hurry.'

Freddie dabbed at her eyes.

'There's no doubt about it, you'll have to act as if nothing has happened.' Glancing down at her pregnant mistress where she could see there was little sign of the pregnancy yet, perhaps just a little roundness, but there was a look about her that couldn't be denied. She might have known or guessed, but then Sir Richard wouldn't know that – that was something that only a woman would see.

'You mean – but he'll want – to–'

'Yes, of course he will,' Robbie said agreeably, 'but that's a small price to pay, isn't it? If you can get away with it. I mean, we have to be practical, Milady.'

Freddie's face was a study in horror. 'I couldn't,' she said.

'Now,' Robbie said reasonably. 'What else can you do? Say you are out? Gone away? You wouldn't want that – in any case, it's all too late now. Face up to it, Milady, act as if nothing had happened, and after he's gone back, we'll have a think. After all,' she said, taking Milady's hat off and removing her cloak as she stood up automatically to be waited on – 'He will be so pleased to see you he won't have time to–'

'Oh, don't, Robbie, I can't bear it!'

'Well, you're going to have to, Milady,' Robbie said equably, 'whether you like it or not.'

'Will it harm the baby? Bring it away?'

Robbie turned and faced her. 'Now, Milady, have some sense. Will you really mind if it does?'

'But I want it, I want this baby – I don't want anything to happen to it.'

For perhaps the first time in a long career of serving others, Robbie realised that not only were the gentry born without any know-how, but they wanted it all. Still, poor young thing, she was only human.

'Look, never you worry,' she said now, hanging the clothes in a wardrobe after brushing them, and closing the doors. 'You have a nice bath and get some rest, and Milady – look forward to seeing your husband. Remember, welcome him – he's been fighting out there – he needs your love and support.'

And for once Freddie looked conscience-stricken.

'Oh, I know, I know, Robbie, that's what makes it so awful!'

'Now you get some rest, I'll be away now.'

Freddie stood up, a slight, pretty figure, her face flushed, eyes red from weeping, her long hair having come loose in all the excitement. What man could resist her, Robbie wondered?

'Good-night, then Milady–'

Freddie suddenly came to life.

'Oh, take the trap, Robbie, tell Tom to bring it back in the morning.'

'Thank you, Milady, I'll walk,' Robbie said. She needed time to think.

It was dark outside, but there were lamp-posts down the drive to see by. As she made her way down to First Lodge her mind was in turmoil. She opened the front door and saw Tom sitting by the fire; he looked up when she came in.

'Everything all right up there?' he asked, taking the pipe out of his mouth.

She smiled reassuringly.

'Yes, she's all right. You know how she is, getting worked up about things with Sir Richard coming home and that,' taking her coat and hat off and hanging them behind the kitchen door.

She hated to lie to Tom – Tom was such a good man, and she felt a surge of warmth towards him. She didn't suppose Milady felt like that about Sir Richard, otherwise she wouldn't have done what she did. She had a sudden mental picture of Lady Freddie dancing, smoking, laughing, being made love to by all sorts of handsome young men, but thrust the thought aside. No, whatever else she was, selfish perhaps, thoughtless, certainly, she wasn't a hussy, a bad girl. But she'd certainly got herself into a mess. What would they do? For she was in no doubt that she would play a big part in the answer.

Her heart bled for her mistress; she would do everything in her power to assist her, yet the obvious answer was to get rid of the baby, and she didn't like that idea much. Being messed about, surely you were never the same afterwards. She knew a lot of village women who got rid of their babies and she didn't blame them. Unwanted pregnancy after unwanted pregnancy, often with several little mouths to feed and no money coming in, and the husbands not giving a damn except to enjoy their pleasure, and she shuddered. She'd been lucky with a good man like Tom, although she had never had the problem of unwanted babies. She would have loved more children, but they didn't seem to come her way, and she was getting on now. Besides, she thought the world of her boys and there was enough to do to find the money for them in these hard times.

Tom knocked out his pipe.

'That's good,' he said. 'About time, too, she's had a rough ride, her Ladyship.'

You can say that again, she thought grimly.

Chapter Three

While the gods of war were busy making plans for a final onslaught that they hoped would bring the war to a speedy end, ordinary people were going about their lives with their own problems, not the least of whom were Lady Freddie and her devoted lady's-maid, Robbie.

For Robbie was in a fine old state herself, knowing that whatever the outcome, it was going to be fraught with trouble. With the captain arriving home soon, and him such a nice man. He adored his wife, and her pregnant by another man, it didn't bear thinking of. And what of Tom? She would have to tell him, and he would be so upset; he thought the world of Lady Freddie, a real lady, he always said. If only she weren't so far along the line – past three months, she'd said – soon she'd be unable to hide it.

She spent a sleepless night, tossing and turning, Tom asking her once if she was all right.

'Yes,' she had said. 'A touch of indigestion, I expect.' But she looked awful in the morning, you could tell she hadn't slept.

There was a light frost that morning, covering everything with that salty look as she called it, and she saw that the boys had their mufflers on when they went off to school. Tom had already begun his day helping the gardener up at the Hall. She could remember the time when there were four gardeners up there, but now there was only old Jim Hardy who was glad of a helping hand.

She tidied and dusted the living room, and set out the chairs for the Red Cross Knitting Bee which the ladies took in turns to have in their own homes. They knitted blankets and socks and repaired sheets for the local hospital. There was always plenty of work to be done. She put the large sewing box on the kitchen table, the mound of knitting yarns in a basket, assorted needles and patterns; she always liked to be ready in advance for the ladies did not arrive until two o'clock.

She was busy making cakes for afternoon tea, and had just taken a batch of scones from the oven when she saw the large black car go past on its way up to the Hall. Two uniformed men were in it, the driver, and Sir Richard sitting in the back, but it passed speedily on its way and Robbie found herself praying that all would be well. What must her Ladyship be going through?

If the Knitting Bee ladies thought Robbie was on edge that afternoon, they said nothing. They thought highly of Robbie, of her integrity and the way she worked so hard. Never a word of gossip passed her lips, although many's the time they would have liked to know just what she was thinking. This afternoon, she was not her usual self, but they knew better than to ask questions. Whatever the reason Robbie would keep it to herself.

Tom found her quiet that evening, and it did pass through his mind to wonder if everything was all right up at the Hall, recalling that her Ladyship had come down for her the evening before and that Robbie had spent a sleepless night, but he thrust the thought aside. She would tell him when she was ready, and not before.

It was the late afternoon of the next day when she saw the black car pull to a stop outside First Lodge and the driver get out and knock on the door. He touched his cap when he saw her.

'Just calling for the captain, Ma'am,' and at her brief nod, got back into the car and drove swiftly up the hill.

In half an hour it was back again and Robbie put down the curtain which she had pulled aside, taking a deep breath and praying that everything had been all right…

It was when Tom came back down the hill having knocked off for the day that he gave her the message.

'Her Ladyship says will you go up some time this evening, if you can spare a moment, otherwise first thing in the morning.'

'Oh, I'll go up after supper,' Robbie said as casually as she could. 'I have to go into the market in the morning.'

Wild horses wouldn't have dragged her through another sleepless night.

Once the supper things were cleared away she closed the door behind her and walked up to the Hall, making her way to the back door.

She found the housekeeper, Mrs Carstairs, at the sink in the kitchen and called out to her.

'Evening, Mrs Carstairs!'

'Evening, Robbie,' as Robbie hung her hat and coat behind the kitchen door.

'I've just taken her supper up, she said she was starving,' and she laughed. 'Captain went back. You'd have thought they'd have given him a bit longer, and him not well, poor man.'

But Robbie wanted no news from Mrs Carstairs and hurried up to Lady Freddie's room and tapped on the door.

'Come in!' and her Ladyship's voice was light and pleasant as Robbie opened the door.

Her Ladyship sat up in bed against blue satin sheets and pillows, a small supper tray in front of her, golden hair spread round her shoulders, her vivid blue eyes sparkling back at Robbie seeing the concern on her face.

'It's all right, Robbie – it was all right – oh, dear, don't look so worried – here, take this away and I'll tell you.'

Robbie put the tray down on the side table and waited. She had to admit there was a great change in her Ladyship, she looked her usual charming self and oozed good health. But Robbie had not got over the shock yet.

'Look, sit down.' Lady Freddie said, indicating a chair. 'That's better. Now, it was all right, I tell you. Poor lamb, poor Richard, he has been quite ill, picked up a germ or something in Palestine so they gave him a couple of days because they are starting – well, I can't tell you, he couldn't tell me exactly, still I know it's something important and time is precious, but he did manage to steal two days. He is not strong yet, so of course he – well, you know what I mean, Robbie, I don't have to spell it out for you.'

'Someone was looking after you, Milady,' Robbie said drily.

'But it was lovely to see him again,' Lady Freddie said dreamily, as though Robbie had not spoken. 'We rested, and talked, and he slept. It was so peaceful–' and she closed her eyes at the thought of it.

But Robbie was cross.

'Well,' she said standing up and putting the chair back in its place. 'Your little problem hasn't gone away, has it?'

Lady Freddie hugged herself, then dreamily smoothed her satin nightgown over the very slight protuberance.

'No, isn't it wonderful? All is well, and I feel fine.' Robbie had to admit she looked a different person, quite her old self.

'Is that all you can say?' she asked. 'Aren't you worried that your husband may be caught up in the thick of it? That he may be killed or wounded?'

'Oh, not him!' Lady Freddie laughed. 'He's like a cat – he has seven lives – or is it nine? Anyway I'll get dressed now, but we have to have a long talk, Robbie darling, because I've thought it all out and I know now what we'll do.'

Robbie began to tidy the room. 'We'll do,' she noticed.

'I'm glad to hear that, Milady,' she said.

While Lady Freddie was in the bathroom, she threw the bedclothes back to air, and shook the pillows, plumping them hard because she was in so much of a tizzy, and why was she so worried, she asked herself? It was not her business; but it was: Lady Freddie had been a part of her life since she could remember.

Now, she emerged from the bathroom,

scented and powdered, in a blue negligée, and sat down by the dressing table so that Robbie could brush her hair.

The face that looked back at her now was smooth and relaxed and she closed her eyes as Robbie brushed with swift clean strokes.

Suddenly she opened them, and swung round in her chair. 'Leave it loose; I'm not going out yet awhile,' then giving Robbie a warm smile she leaned forward and put a hand on Robbie's arm.

'I want you to listen to what I have to say,' she said. 'Sit down, it's quite important.'

And Robbie felt a stab of apprehension.

'I am going to have this baby,' Lady Freddie said, 'and I am going to close up the Hall for the duration.'

And Robbie felt a sight of relief. That at least was something…

'I shall go up to London and stay in Edwardes Square.'

'You're not taking little David up to London! Suppose there are raids?'

'Robbie, I won't take any risks; how could you think that? At the first sign of any trouble I shall send him to his grandmother in Cheshire. In fact I may do that anyway.'

'So what will happen, up here, I mean? Will Mrs Carstairs stay on and–'

'Not if she wants to take on other work, but the outside help must stay on, for after all, we don't know how long this war will last nor when Sir Richard will be home.'

Robbie thought it was time that they got down to brass tacks.

'When is the baby due, Milady?' she asked, and Lady Freddie had the grace to blush.

'September, Robbie – and that's what I want to talk to you about.'

She looked away. 'I shall have the baby in London.'

'But–'

'Now wait; I'm not going to beat about the bush, I would like you and Tom to legally adopt it as your own baby. There! What do you think of that?'

Robbie went as white as a sheet and sat down abruptly on the nearest chair. 'What?'

'I am serious, Robbie. I would like you to adopt it, bring it up as your own – that way I shall be able to see it, keep an eye – I can't let Sir Richard know, it would kill him, and I certainly am not going to put it out for adoption. I want it – oh, Robbie, I wish you could understand, it means so much to me–'

A baby, another baby – and just for a brief moment Robbie felt again the joys of motherhood, the feel of a baby's warm head on her breast.

She shook her head. 'No Milady, it is not possible.'

'Oh, Robbie! Please, Robbie, think about it; I know it is a hard decision.'

'Hard decision! You can't imagine what it would mean to my family! Have you thought of that? Tom, the boys – it is, well, it's out of the question.' Her heart was beating uncontrollably, she was inwardly shaking.

They sat silent, the air was heavy with their breathing.

Then Lady Freddie spoke. 'Perhaps it is asking too much of you,' she said slowly, 'I'm sorry, I thought–'

'Yes, but I am afraid you didn't think, Milady. What on earth do you think Tom would say? He would be horrified, and I needn't tell you how much you would go down in his estimation. He thinks the world of you.'

Lady Freddie lowered her head and bit her lip.

'I know he does. Look–'

'I suppose you had it all worked out,' Robbie said. She felt cold and bitter towards her mistress. Perhaps because the idea of a new baby had caught hold in her heart – and feeling guilty at having such feelings – at her age, she was after all, thirty-nine.

'I thought I had,' Lady Freddie said gently. 'I can see how shocked you are. I shouldn't have asked. It was too much to expect, even of you.'

'Far better to go away and have it somewhere where no one knows you, and put it out to a good family.'

'No! I will not!' Freddie said, and her eyes filled with tears. 'It's my baby and I know what I want for it. How can I make you understand?'

'It is not fair on Sir Richard–'

'Perhaps not. But he will know nothing about it, and in wartime these things happen.'

'He might return home before September.'

'I shall have to take a chance on that and I am prepared to. I shall have to think of an alternative – go away somewhere, America–'

She was certainly adamant about it, I'll give her that, Robbie thought admiringly. But how stupid could you be? What a mess of trouble she was creating for herself.

'Will you think about it, please, Robbie?'

She looked like the little girl Robbie had

looked after all those years before she grew up and became the woman she was today, and she moved forward, close to tears.

'Oh, Milady!'

And Freddie came forward into her arms.

'Oh, my heart bleeds for you, it really does, Milady,' and Robbie herself was near to tears.

'But I am happy to go ahead with it – I want it so much. I can't explain to you – you wouldn't understand. I wouldn't want you to go short of money. There would be a lump sum for you and Tom and I would pay annually for its upkeep and education – you wouldn't have to spend a penny piece on it, I promise you.'

'Oh, Milady, don't – can't you see how impossible it is,' and she shook her head.

'Then will you please – just for me – think it over? I shall be leaving at the end of the week. I've told Mrs Carstairs to hand the keys over to you. Robbie, will you?'

Her Ladyship was mad, she told herself, walking back down the hill. How could she think such a thing possible? It might have been different if she had not a husband and family, but even then – no, it was out of the question; how could she and Tom cope with another baby at their age: Tom was almost forty – besides, they had their own children to think of. Round and round the thoughts went.

But deep down, the seed had been sown. A little brother or sister for the boys, a new baby to care for, no – it was out of the question.

It was after the boys had gone to bed, when she and Tom were sitting by the fire, that she made up her mind. After all, Tom had to know about it sometime; the fact that her Ladyship was going away, why she was going – or should she say nothing? Nothing at all? But the questions beat inside her head.

She almost surprised herself when she suddenly put down her knitting and stuck the needles in the wool.

'Tom, I've something to tell you.'

Tom looked up from his paper and saw from his wife's face that it was something serious.

When she said nothing, he prompted her.

'What is it, Edie?'

She took a deep breath. 'Milady – she's pregnant.'

'Oh!' and a wide smile spread over his kind broad face, to be replaced by a frown. 'But–'

'That's what I mean, Tom. She's pregnant and it's not Sir Richard's baby.'

Tom banged the arm of his chair with his fist.

'Christ Almighty!' he said as he got up to stand with his back to her. She had never heard him swear before.

She was silent. Then he turned to face her.

'What's this all about then? Did she tell you? When did she tell you?'

'The day before Sir Richard came home.'

'Ah, so that's it! Scared, was she? No wonder you didn't sleep. Thrown it on to your shoulders, has she?'

'Tom, imagine what she is going through.'

'Or Sir Richard when he finds out!' he said grimly. 'What a turn-up for the book!'

Robbie decided that least said was soonest mended.

'What's she going to do about it, then? Eh? Did she tell him when he came home?'

'No, how could she?'

'But–'

'He's been ill,' she said. 'And he had no suspicions–'

'Poor bugger,' Tom said softly.

'I know,' Robbie said, and waited a moment or two.

'The thing is, Tom, she wants to go

through with it, wants to have the baby, there's no turning her, Tom. She is quite adamant.'

'And will pass it off as his, I s'pose.'

'Now, how can she? He's not been home for six months.'

'How far is she?'

'Just gone three months, she says.'

She had never seen Tom look so dejected.

'Tom, she's only a young thing – her husband away – it happens in lots of cases.'

'She's a married woman with a child,' he said doggedly, and she knew he was genuinely upset. Like finding out his idol had feet of clay.

'Tom, you may as well know it all; she is determined to have it and she wants us to adopt it – there! I've said it,' and she picked up her knitting to occupy her trembling hands.

He turned to face her, open-mouthed.

'Yes, Tom, that's what she suggested.'

Then in silence he lit his pipe, something he never did in the evening after supper, and took a few puffs, but still said nothing.

Eventually he spoke. 'And if we don't, we'll lose our jobs, will we?' He sounded bitter.

'Oh, no, Tom! It's not like that. Honestly, she's genuine enough, but you know what they're like – gentry–'

'I'm learning,' he said, and she watched him limp towards the window and stand staring out at nothing.

'I hope you told her that it's out of the question,' he said at length.

'Of course I did, Tom. How could she even suggest it? At our age?'

'That's not the point,' he said. 'Bloody cheek, expecting folk like us to step in and help them out.'

She supposed that's what it boiled down to really.

Presently he knocked out his pipe, and came over to her and put an arm round her shoulders.

'No wonder you didn't sleep, Edie,' he said, and she took his hand.

'Tom, I've been thinking, you don't suppose–'

He looked shocked to the core.

'You're not thinking–?'

'She said there would be no question of money; she would pay us a lump sum and pay for everything, the baby's upkeep, school fees–'

'At our age?' he asked her gently. 'Come on, Edie, be sensible – you'd be doing it for her.'

'Well, not only, it did just cross my mind that it might be nice to have a baby around again.'

'If you was meant to have another you'd have had it,' he said.

'But it's Sir Richard I'm thinking of – one of the nicest men that ever broke bread – he doesn't deserve this.'

'How could I hold my head up?' he asked, 'how could I face him knowing what I know, con – condoning a thing like that?'

It hadn't been fair to ask him. 'I know, Tom,' and she bent low over her knitting. 'She wants to know by the weekend so she can make plans.'

'I bet she does,' he said grimly. She had never seen Tom like this before.

He looked at her suspiciously.

'You're not thinking,' he said slowly, 'you wouldn't want – the truth, now, Edie.'

'Well,' she said. 'At first I couldn't believe what she was suggesting, but now I keep thinking – a baby – an unwanted baby – and she's determined to have it, Tom, and she'll give it to someone else. Little Freddie's baby – oh, Tom, I can't bear it, she's like one of my own…'

They talked well into the night, and the

result was that when a baby girl was born to Lady Frederica Drummond, on 9 September 1918, Edith Roberts made a special journey to London a month later to take her home.

The baby was christened at the village church in Allington as Sarah Jane Roberts, and her address was given as First Lodge, Kirby Hall, Allington, Berkshire.

Chapter Four

Robbie laid her plans well.

One sunny day in August when she had taken the boys on a picnic to the local woods, she spread the cloth on the ground and laid out the bread and cheese and tomatoes, the fruit cake she had made that week, the home-made fruit juice and milk, and waited for them to return from their quest to find wild fruit, blackberries, and whatever else young boys look for on expeditions like this.

They returned full of excitement, emptying their pockets, Donald as the eldest carrying the jam jar full of early blackberries, Laurie with his catch of snails and caterpillars; they were country boys, both of them, with no sign of Tom's earlier Cockney origins.

Robbie looked at them fondly – her boys. Donald, so dark, like herself, slim and wiry; Laurie, fair-skinned and fair-haired, taking after Tom's family and his blonde sisters. He was a stocky little boy, and given to jokes, where Donald was more serious.

Having talked about their finds, they lay back on this hot sunny afternoon, eyes closed, arms behind their heads, the warm earth beneath them as enticing as a featherbed.

'Boys,' Robbie said, without a trace of the excitement in her voice that she felt inside. 'How would you like a baby brother or sister?'

She lay relaxed with her eyes closed in order to play down the immensity of her question. They both sat up at once, Donald's face as rosy as a tomato, Laurie's mouth open.

'Mum!'

'You mean–?'

Donald, at twelve years old, shot a quick glance at his mother's figure, and away again, while Laurie stared at her face.

She opened her eyes and looked at them both. 'What do you think?' she asked.

They stole a quick glance at each other.

'Well–'

'It would be funny, wouldn't it, Mum?' Laurie said at length, 'I mean, to have a baby in the house,' he looked nervous. 'Will it be a boy or a girl?'

'No one knows that, silly,' Donald chided his brother. 'You don't know until they're born. I suppose a boy wouldn't be bad–'

'Oh, not a girl!' Laurie wailed. 'She'd get in the way of all our things!'

'When will it be born?' Donald asked.

'Some time in September,' Robbie said.

And Donald flushed again. 'But–'

'I'd better explain,' Robbie said. 'It wouldn't be my baby, it would be ours – to love and take care of.'

And they waited.

'Someone I know, a distant cousin of mine, her daughter is having a baby, and her husband has just been killed in the war–'

God forgive me for embarking on this lie, she thought, but it has to be, and I will stick to this story whatever happens, 'well –' and their eyes were glued to hers – 'this young woman does not want to bring up the baby without her husband, and she wants to make a fresh start in Canada after the war, so rather than put it out for adoption, which some young mothers do, she asked me if we would take it, adopt the baby, and give it a home–' and waited for the story to sink in.

'So it wouldn't be our baby,' Laurie said, and sounded quite disappointed.

'Of course it would!' Robbie explained. 'It will be one of our family.'

'What does Dad say?' Donald asked, the practical one.

'He thinks it would be nice to give a home to an unwanted baby. It is a kind thing to do.'

'Then that's all right then,' he said and sat thinking. 'It would be a kind of relative, a distant cousin, sort of,' he said at length.

'That's right, Donnie,' she said.

'And when do we get it?' Laurie asked.

'In September, sometime.'

'Where will it sleep?' asked Donald.

'In a cot in our bedroom, until it grows a bit.'

'It won't sleep in our room, will it?' Laurie looked anxious.

'No,' smiled Robbie, thinking, I'll cross that bridge when I come to it. Oh, I hope I am doing the right thing, I wouldn't upset these lads for the world, but who knows – perhaps it will turn out to be a blessing.

'Well, I've told them,' she said to Tom later that evening.

'I still don't like it, Edie,' he said.

'Oh, Tom, but I've said we would!' Edie cried.

'Oh, I'll not go back on my word, but it's not something I go along with – you know that.'

And then the same story had to be put about, to all her local friends, her sewing guilds, the Red Cross ladies, and she kept to her story of its being her cousin's daughter's baby.

'Oh, Edie,' the said. 'You've got some pluck!'

Having sown the seeds, she waited.

In September came a letter for her from Lady Freddie – the postwoman would not have been surprised at that, there was no telephone at First Lodge. Her ladyship had given birth to a daughter, and it was followed by another letter telling Robbie and Tom that a bank account had been opened for them in a nearby town and the sum of five thousand pounds had been deposited there. In future, payments would be made into the bank, and they could collect money as they wished; a cheque book would be sent to them and the bank manager would explain it all.

They had never had a bank account, and Tom's eyes darkened when he read this.

'We don't want the money,' he said, but Robbie soothed him.

'Look, Tom, we can't afford another baby – it's only right and proper that she would pay for its keep.'

A little girl, Robbie was thinking, a baby girl – would she look like Lady Freddie?

Tom said no more, but one day early in October Robbie received another letter, asking her to go to London to collect the baby, who was four weeks old.

It was a great day in First Lodge. The boys had gone back to school after the summer holidays, and instead of following her instinct to run after Tom and find him to tell him the news, she was so excited that she waited until he came in at dinner time, and told him then.

He had not the heart to be churlish about it, for she couldn't hide the glow in her brown eyes and, despite misgivings and not being a religious man, he prayed that all would go well now that it had finally come about.

'I'm to go early tomorrow, Tom, by the eight-fifteen train,' and she held a hand to her heart as if she could not contain her excitement at the prospect. Going to London was rare enough, but to collect a baby – their baby! It was almost more than she could bear.

Once in the train she tried to keep calm. She was to bring no luggage, and to take a taxi to a London hotel; everything would be made clear then. She wondered if she had left everything at home as prepared as she had hoped, the small cot brought down from the loft and scrubbed clean by Tom, a new mattress and cot blankets.

She and Tom had gone to the small town and seen the bank manager who explained everything to them. Tom had then returned to the Hall while she had shopped. Her Ladyship said she must not stint on anything, to buy just what she wanted. Piles of baby napkins, tiny baby clothes; she went from department to department, never had she had such a day in her life, and all to be delivered with not a thing to carry!

If the thought was there that she wished it was her own baby she was preparing for she stamped it down. A baby girl. The name Sarah – Sarah Jane – had been her Ladyship's wish.

On arriving at the hotel in Bayswater, she

was to ask for a Mrs Barrymore. It sat in a row with other hotels, although there was a uniformed porter at the door, who opened it for her when she told him whom she wished to see. A young page-boy took her to the lift and escorted her to the door of room number twenty-eight.

The door was opened by a uniformed nurse, her face beneath her starched coif kindly and warm in greeting.

'Good morning; I am Nurse Barrymore. Do come in, Mrs Roberts,' and she led the way to a small drawing room.

'Sit down,' she said. 'Would you like some tea?'

Robbie shook her head. 'No thank you.'

'I expect you're longing to see the baby,' she said. 'I'll take you to see her presently–'

'Is her Ladyship here?' Robbie asked. She had never envisaged that it would finally come about. In her mind's eye, Lady Freddie had handed over her baby and wept, while Robbie took the baby and walked slowly and carefully out of the door…

But here she was, with a strange white-uniformed nurse, who now sat opposite her, appraising her.

'Her Ladyship is not here, quite simply because she was very upset at handing over the baby. It is always a traumatic time,' she said, speaking from obvious experience.

Robbie was so disappointed; she had hoped to see Lady Freddie.

'I have had this task to do so many times during this dreadful war, and it is never easy, never easy indeed to hand over a much-loved baby, but there it is.'

She looked up and smiled at Robbie.

'You will come to realise that it is for the best – a clean break, as they say. Her Ladyship will grow used to the idea that Sarah is with you, and she is fortunate that she will be able to see her daughter grow up, although my personal instincts are that it would be better not so. However,' and again she smiled, 'I am sure you are longing to see her – come this way.'

With rapidly beating heart, Robbie followed her into a small bedroom set aside for Mrs Barrymore's own use, where in the corner lay a small crib. Robbie tiptoed over and saw there the tiniest baby, sleeping peacefully, with a fuzz of dark hair and a sweet little face; her small rosebud mouth was pursed, eyes closed, and Robbie caught her breath as her eyes filled with tears.

'Oh! The little love!' was all she could manage.

Nurse Barrymore took her arm. 'She's a good little thing, or she has been up to now. I will give you her baby food and all the instructions for its use. You will be able to carry that and a change of nappies if you need them. I have it all ready and it is not heavy. A taxi to the station, and you will be fine. Her Ladyship seemed to have no doubts as to your ability to look after her ... I expect you breastfed your babies, but there – Sarah's baby food suits her, and I have no doubts that you will make an excellent mother from what her Ladyship has told me.'

Robbie felt she was back at school.

'Now I have written down all the things I think you need to know, there is no point in your hanging about while I explain, I have put my instructions in the envelope inside the holdall you will carry.'

With her precious burden in her arms, her handbag and the small holdall over her wrist, Robbie made her way across to the lift escorted by Nurse Barrymore, who had obviously done this sort of thing many times before. The nurse escorted her to the front entrance, where she bade the porter call a cab to take her to the station.

Robbie couldn't help feeling she was in a

dream looking down at the sleeping baby, cosily wrapped in its shawl like a cocoon, who seemed so tiny. She had forgotten how small new babies could be. Once at the station, the cab driver came to help her out with her holdall, and she paid him, and he peeked at the baby.

'Little girl?' he asked, and Robbie nodded.

'Good luck, mate,' he said, and Robbie made her way into the station, where she looked up at the departure board and found the time of the train. Half an hour to spare. She made for the ladies' waiting room and sat down. She could not have described how she felt, to be holding once again a newborn baby – the feeling was nothing like she felt after the boys were born, for then there was such relief that the pain was over. She studied the little face and knew that never in a million years could this little scrap of humanity be said to be like her Ladyship, which somehow made it easier. There might have been complications if she had been the image of Lady Freddie. But she was going to be dark-haired, of that Robbie was sure, and dark-eyed, Robbie suspected; her skin was peach-coloured rather than fair. Robbie couldn't wait to unwrap her and see those little hands and toes.

She was glad when the train came in and they were on their way. It was not a long journey and she stared out at the view from time to time, then looked at the baby – what have we done, she wondered? But there was no time for reflection, now, the stage was set.

Before she knew it she had arrived at the station, and to her astonishment saw Tom waiting there with the pony and trap. She was so relieved to see him and felt so emotional that she almost burst into tears.

'Tom! What are you doing here? Oh, you don't know how glad I am to see you – how did you know which train?'

'I didn't,' he said, 'but I was determined to wait all day if necessary–' and he looked down at the bundle in her arms. 'Is she all right?'

'Oh, Tom, she's lovely – look at her,' and she moved away the shawl so that he could get a closer look.

'Hold on,' he said. 'I'll take her while you get set.'

And she looked down from the trap and saw Tom holding little Sarah, an expression on his face that she would never forget.

'Here you are,' he said gruffly and handed her back to Robbie.

Taking the reins, he spurred the little pony to action, and as she pranced along down through the High Street and out towards the countryside Robbie sat beside Tom with her precious bundle.

She was taking her baby home.

Once inside the house, Tom held Sarah while Robbie washed her hands.

'Oh, London was so dirty, Tom, crowds of people and uniformed men everywhere; it's lovely to get back into the fresh clean air,' she said as she tied on an apron.

She removed the shawl and sat on the old oak nursing chair that Tom had retrieved from the loft, a soft towel over her lap, and was surprised to find that coping with a baby came back to her naturally; it was like undressing a little doll, for she had never held a baby girl before. Sarah stirred and opened her eyes, dark eyes, looking up into Robbie's own dark ones, so trustingly.

Robbie smiled down at her, talking softly all the while. She had relined the large baby basket in pink and white which held the safety pins and baby powder and cotton-wool and the pile of fresh nappies.

'Oh, you little dear,' she said softly, seeing the tiny nunsveiling nightgown with the little bit of embroidery, the soft white knitted matinée jacket, the thin little legs and tiny fingers as Robbie picked her up and held her to her breast.

Sarah had had her feed and had been put down to sleep in the pram which had belonged to Lady Freddie. Tom had been up to the Hall and unlocked the door to the top floor attic and brought it down. It had been covered with dustsheets ever since David had been born. Cleaned and polished, the coachwork gleamed like glass, and it now held a pram mattress and white hand-knitted blankets, the china handle gleamed and the storm cover had been scrubbed.

Over in the corner of the big kitchen Sarah lay sleeping while Robbie awaited with increasing excitement the arrival of the boys from school. She found her heart beating wildly when they arrived, anxious to see their reactions at the prospect of a new baby in the house.

They tiptoed over to the pram and stared at the sleeping child, Laurie moving away first towards his mother, looking at her with a frown.

'She's so little,' he said. 'Is she all right?'

'She's fine,' Robbie smiled. 'She's only four weeks old, remember.'

Donald stayed longer.

'She's not like us, is she?' he said eventually. 'I mean, she doesn't look like us – is she like your cousin's family?'

What a sweet, serious boy he was, Robbie thought fondly.

'Well, a bit–' she said noncommittally.

'And you went on a train,' Laurie said enviously.

'Yes, I did, and do you know what I thought? We could go up to London at Christmas time, to the shops, just you and Donnie and me – on a train–'

Laurie's eyes glowed. 'Could we really?'

'Of course, why not?' Robbie said.

'But who'd look after–' his voice tailed off.

'Sarah?' Robbie said gently. 'Well, by then, Dad could, or we'll think of something – and by the way while I waited for the train, I bought some chocolate for you from London.'

She saw their eyes glow.

That's that hurdle, she told herself.

The autumn leaves swirled about the courtyard as October wore on, and sometimes Robbie pushed Sarah round the gravel paths surrounding the gardens to the Hall, sometimes left her outside in her pram if the weather was nice. But now it was growing colder, towards November, and Sarah slept either in her cot or her pram, only disturbed to be bathed or fed. She was such a good baby, for which Robbie was more than grateful; things might have been a lot harder if she had cried a lot. The boys went straight over to her pram when they came in from school, but Sarah slept on, only occasionally opening her dark eyes and fixing them with a look.

'Can she see us?' Laurie asked, taking one of her tiny fingers in his.

'I'm sure she can,' Robbie said. 'She's taking it all in, I am sure.'

There had been a rather strange atmosphere abroad in the last few days, almost, Tom said, like the calm before the storm, and that is exactly what it turned out to be.

For after all the rumours and counter-rumours at last it had come about, the day everyone had been waiting for. The war was over. The eleventh of November was declared Armistice Day, and there were celebrations everywhere. People went wild and cheered until they were hoarse before some kind of stability returned and they set about facing their new world. For so many the loss of loved ones and a stark economy would affect everyone, for someone had to pay for the war; the country was heavily in debt and it would take the greatest effort on everyone's part to pick up the pieces.

Robbie's family had suffered privation less than most, and Robbie's first thought was for Sir Richard, Lady Freddie's husband, and whether he was safe. Surely they would have heard, but there had been no message from Milady since Robbie had gone to collect baby Sarah.

It seemed an odd state of affairs…

Half-way through December there was a letter from Lady Freddie to say that the Hall would be opened up again in time for Christmas. No mention was made of the baby. Tom was to cut down a Christmas tree and a new housekeeper had been engaged to get the house in order for their arrival a few days before Christmas.

They returned as a family, Sir Richard, Lady Freddie and young David, but it was two days before Robbie was sent for and that on a Saturday morning when Tom could keep an eye on little Sarah.

Robbie walked up the drive with fast-beating heart; it seemed so strange not to see Mrs Carstairs working in the kitchen, but the log fire in the hall burned brightly as she made her way upstairs and knocked on her Ladyship's door.

Even her voice didn't sound like her when it came. 'Come in.'

Lady Freddie was sitting at her dressing table, and even from the door Robbie could see how thin she was. Her shoulderblades stuck out under the silk blouse, there seemed to be nothing of her. Robbie's instinct was to rush forward and take the girl in her arms, for that's all she was, but at that moment, her Ladyship turned bright blue eyes on Robbie, eyes that glittered, brittle eyes, thought Robbie, the cheek-bones standing out in the thin face.

'Milady–' Robbie was close to tears.

'Ah, Robbie,' and Lady Freddie's voice was cool, as she turned back to face herself in the mirror. 'Happy Christmas. It's nice to be back–' and Robbie stood, at a loss for words.

'Happy Christmas, Milady.'

'Is your family well?' asked her Ladyship, patting powder round her nose.

'Very well, Milady,' Robbie said. So that's how it was to be. Sarah was not to be referred to. Well, and she thought rapidly – she had got the message – perhaps after all it was better this way, but what she must have suffered to have given baby Sarah up. Who knew how deep the wound had gone...

She picked up a scarf from a chair automatically, and folded it.

'Is there anything I can do, Milady?' She was on her dignity now.

'No, Robbie, thank you, but perhaps tomorrow you can do my hair if you've time.' The meaning left unsaid. 'We are going out to dinner.'

'Very well, Milady–'

'And you might pop along to see David – you know how he loves to see you.'

'I will, Milady.' She turned to go.

'Oh, and Robbie – thanks–'

Robbie closed the door behind her, her eyes full of unshed tears.

She walked down the path towards First Lodge. Robbie, who never swore – had never found it necessary.

'Bloody war,' she said softly.

Chapter Five

Today was Sarah's birthday, and she was eleven years old. The post always arrived after she had gone to school and there were several birthday cards waiting on the mantelpiece for her return, to say nothing of a rather splendidly wrapped parcel, flat and slim, which Robbie guessed had been sent by Lady Freddie and looked as if it might be an article of clothing, a dress or something that she knew Sarah would love.

Lady Freddie always remembered Sarah on her birthday and at Christmas, sending her gifts via Robbie or through the post, and it would not have been thought untoward as a gift to a treasured servant's child. Robbie, who still acted as a part-time lady's-maid, had close touch with the Hall and its occupants, as did Tom, for he still held his job, despite a bout of rheumatism the previous winter which had set up in his injured knee.

Robbie sat at the kitchen table, the teapot in front of her, finding it hard to believe that eleven years had gone by since that fateful day when she had gone to fetch Sarah from London. So much water under the bridge, the years seemed to have flown by.

Two years after her return to the Hall, Lady Freddie had given birth to a daughter, Joanna, followed later by a second daughter, Candida, both as fair as their mother and with her good looks. The little girls, together with David, constituted her family.

Her days were well occupied; she had a nurse to look after the little girls, and a nursemaid, which made Robbie's task of bringing up Sarah much easier. Only once in that time had there had been an anxious moment when Sarah had taken a tumble on her new bicycle and hurt her head. Only then did Lady Freddie relax her rule and come down to First Lodge to visit her and bring gifts of sweets and fruit.

For First Lodge had undergone some changes since the early days. The loft, which housed all their surplus possessions, ran the entire length and width of the house, and Robbie suggested that it ought be made into a bedroom to house their growing family.

Lady Freddie readily assented since she owned the Lodge and its environs, and could see the sense of it, so the two boys moved upstairs to their own room, and Lady Freddie had a washbasin installed in the room as well which delighted them. They felt quite grown up with the floor to themselves. Sarah moved into their old room, and part of the stables was closed off and given doors and locks for their belongings.

Having more space made life so much easier, particularly since last year Donnie had moved away and married his childhood sweetheart. On leaving school, he had taken an engineering course offered by a local factory, and was now a qualified instrument-maker. He had gone to school with Ginny, a farmer's daughter, and when they were both twenty-one they married and moved into a workman's cottage on her father's land, and Robbie was pleased for both of them. But she missed Donnie, his tall dark figure about the house, and knew that both Laurie and Sarah did too.

For Sarah adored her two brothers, had been bridesmaid at Donnie's wedding. With Ginny's three sisters, the four bridesmaids, wearing pale blue copies of Victorian dresses which Ginny's mother had made, were very pretty as they carried their tiny posies of pink roses.

Robbie glanced up at the mantelpiece where the little figure of the 'Blue Girl', as Sarah called her, had pride of place. Robbie couldn't remember where it had originally come from, she only knew that she had brought it with her from her old home when she married, and now it was Sarah's favourite possession, for Robbie had given it to her. Sarah had looked just like the little blue girl at Donnie's wedding.

Thinking back over the years, as she did every birthday of Sarah's, she knew she wouldn't have done anything different. Despite the qualms she and Tom had had they didn't regret a moment of it. For Sarah was like her own daughter, and although Lady Freddie's attitude had seemed hard to take at first, it had all been for the best. Everyone had got used to Sarah as Robbie and Tom's adopted daughter, and with a new family for her Ladyship to look after, everything had worked out rather well. If Robbie had any misgivings, they had to be about David, for he and Sarah behaved just like brother and sister. They were so alike in every way except looks, liked the same things, loved rambling in the woods near their home, exploring, finding things. Sarah was even allowed to ride Joanna's pony which had been bought specially for her, and which, since she was not keen on riding, Sarah took over. It was a usual sight to see both David and Sarah cantering across the fields.

It would adjust itself in time, Robbie thought, everything did, especially now that David was at Eton where his father had been before him.

Robbie fingered the box addressed to Sarah, and imagined it would hold a beautiful dress. Lady Freddie had excellent taste.

She heard the sound of the village bus stopping outside, and hurried to the door to greet Sarah, who flung her school satchel down and hugged her mother.

'Happy birthday, Sarah; did you have a good day?'

'Yes, it was lovely. I got some cards, and even a present from Lizzie–'

'Oh, that was nice–' but Sarah had caught sight of the cards on the mantelpiece and the parcel on the kitchen table, and her dark eyes shone.

'Is it from Lady Freddie?'

'I expect so,' Robbie said. How pretty she was with those great brown eyes, her dark hair shining, almost black, tied back now with a black ribbon according to school rules.

She opened her cards first, which pleased Robbie, and smiled over every one before she turned her attention to the parcel. She took her time opening it; the brown paper wrapping disclosed a flat box tied with pink ribbon. Inside the box, folded in tissue paper, was a dress, and Sarah took it out reverently. It was of pink silk, in the new short length, but it was straight, with the waistline lower than usual, and from the waist was an overskirt of fine lace held at the centre with a tiny posy of lace and rosebuds and two slim ribbons of black velvet.

'Oh!' Sarah breathed, dark eyes shining.

'Go upstairs and try it on,' urged Robbie, knowing beforehand how lovely she would look in it. A party dress, she thought, and hoped she would get the chance to wear it...

Sarah came to the bottom of the stairs, knowing that she looked at her prettiest: the pale pink suited her colouring, and the dress was so fashionable, smart enough for the most sophisticated London child.

'It's lovely, Sarah,' Robbie enthused.

Sarah looked down at it, feeling the soft material. 'It's beautiful,' she said. 'So soft – could I keep it on to show Dad?'

'Of course you can!' Robbie said. 'It's your birthday – and you can wear it for your party on Saturday.'

Sarah's eyes glowed, then darkened over. Robbie knew what she was thinking: that her friends would have nothing like this to wear, and she was not a girl to gloat, realising that she had more than most girls at her school, her parents working up at the Hall, and being the only daughter with two big brothers to take care of her, while her friends mostly came from large, poorer families.

'Well, anyway,' she said at length. 'I can wear it next week to David's back to school party, can't I?'

'The very thing,' Robbie said. 'We were wondering what you were going to wear.'

'I wish he wasn't going away again,' Sarah said presently. 'I shall miss him–'

Robbie sighed deeply. 'Well, Sarah, it was bound to happen – boys grow up – and–'

'Oh, I know, I know,' Sarah said.

'What did Lizzie give you?' Robbie asked, to change the subject.

Sarah dived for her satchel again – 'Look, some cards – and this from Lizzie.'

Inside the small packet was a tiny box of assorted coloured cottons, a thimble, needles and a tiny pair of scissors.

'That's nice, and very thoughtful.'

'She knows I like to sew, and you can't always get the colours of cottons you want.'

That was true, Robbie thought. Sarah did like to sew – was always making something – she loved colours and materials, and had a doll which she dressed – although she wasn't a girl who played with dolls. She liked to read, her school work was satisfactory, but it was at painting, and reading, and handiwork that she excelled. The kitchen was full of the things she had made, iron holders, kettle holders, teacosies – and there was nothing she liked more than delving into Robbie's box of material scraps. Give her a piece of brightly coloured cotton or silk, more rarely, and she would sit quietly for hours.

When Tom came in she jumped up to greet him, and twirled around in her new dress to show it off.

The love in his eyes was something to see, Robbie decided. Proud as he was of his sons, it was Sarah who was close to his heart. His little girl, he called her; perhaps all men at heart wanted a little girl, she thought, much as a mother wanted sons.

Sarah looked so lovely, Robbie could

swear Tom's eyes held tears.

'Look what I brought you,' he said, lifting his basket up from the floor.

'Eggs – oh, Dad, she's started laying again!'

And there they were; three large brown eggs from Cassandra, the black hen that was Sarah's favourite.

'She knew it was my birthday,' she said solemnly, and they all laughed.

'Do you want to wear your dress for tea, then?' Robbie asked.

'No, I'll go and take it off, and save it – don't want to get it marked, after all, it is very delicate–'

When Saturday afternoon came round, the day of her party, Robbie was surprised to see her come down in the dark velvet dress she had worn the previous year, which Robbie had made for her.

Seeing Robbie's raised eyebrows for an instant, Sarah knew what her mother's thoughts were.

'No, I thought I'd save it for next Saturday,' she said. 'It's a bit too – dress-uppy – no one else will have a dress like that, I should feel silly–'

'That's all right, my pet,' Robbie said.

'That green dress suits you beautifully; it is such a pretty dress, even though I say it myself.'

She had made lots of cakes and jellies for tea, there was Lizzie and little Gwen and Jessie, Alice and Mabel – two of the girls had lost their fathers in the war – and another father was an invalid. Goodness knows how their mothers managed; Robbie often took produce and eggs down to the Village Hall for distribution to the poor.

Now they played games, and laughed and shrieked, and giggled and whispered as young girls do while Robbie sat knitting in her corner, and after tea, Tom took them all for a ride in the pony and trap which was a real treat.

Then it was over and time for them to go home. Sometimes on occasions like this, Robbie sat and pondered. It was a strange situation, unusual, but then strange things had happened during the war – goodness knows how many illegitimate children were born or how many men had died not knowing they were fathers and, not for the first time, she thought fleetingly of Lady Freddie's lover and who he might have been.

Certainly Lady Freddie was not letting on;

she had never mentioned the whole affair from that day to this.

When the day came round for David's party, Robbie made a special effort. She loved doing Sarah's hair, it was so thick and strong and had a mind of its own. She brushed the dark locks until they shone, then wrapped them round her finger where they hung in long curls, while the soft new hair at the hairline grew in tendrils. With it tied back with a big pink ribbon, and wearing her new pink dress, Robbie examined her hands to see that her nails were clean. She never knew how closely Lady Freddie looked at Sarah, and was anxious that she would approve of her guardianship. The round brown velvety eyes were soft, their expression warm, the brow clear with marked dark eyebrows. Long lashes fanned her cheeks, and although the two Drummond girls were fair and as pretty as a picture, Robbie knew that Sarah was beautiful.

'Let's get your coat,' she said, 'then Dad will take you up.'

Sarah loved the drive to the Hall, and now there was the added thrill of seeing David again – although she was saddened to think he would be going away – she would not see him again until Christmas – perhaps not even then if they went up to London.

She arrived on the dot of three as requested, and Tom said he would call for her at six-thirty as arranged. He waited until the door was opened by the housekeeper, Mrs Owens, then Sarah was inside. Tom secretly hated these rare occasions when Sarah was up at the Hall; if he had his way there would be no contact whatsoever, but he knew that that was unreasonable.

Sarah was shown into the drawing room where the boys and girls had gathered. On seeing Sarah, the two Drummond girls shrieked with delight and ran over to her. 'Sarah! Sarah!'

Lady Freddie came towards them. 'Careful, careful, you'll knock Sarah over,' she smiled, giving a kind glance at Sarah, and looking at the dress.

'You look very nice, Sarah,' she said and the blue eyes held that strange gleam that Sarah had often noticed before.

'Thank you, Lady Freddie,' Sarah said. 'It's lovely.'

'I knew it would suit you as soon as I saw it,' Lady Freddie said.

'Why can't I have a dress like that?' Joanna asked.

'When you are older,' Lady Freddie said. 'Now I think you have met most of the children here, Sarah.' She turned and Sarah looked at her, seeing the slim figure in the very latest outfit. Her fair hair was cut short, close to her head, and her dress was satin and chiffon, in pale grey, sleeveless with narrow straps, and the hemline dipped to one side, ending in a little flutter of chiffon, and her shoes had been dyed to match. The bodice of the dress was embroidered with tiny gunmetal beads. All this Sarah absorbed in an instant, so conscious was she of fashion and colour. On one shoulder was pinned a pink silk rose. Oh! thought Sarah, how wonderful Milady looks...

And then David came towards them, straight and tall, very like his mother with the fair colouring, in well-tailored grey flannels and tweed jacket, hand outstretched towards Sarah.

She took it, her heart fluttering, he looked so grown up, which indeed he was, three years older than herself, and quite the young man.

'Glad you could come,' he said, eyeing her and the dress.

She was glad she had worn it, and not the old velvet dress. She looked quite different in that, so much younger.

Lady Freddie clapped her hands.

'Well, I think we're all here,' she smiled. 'What about some games: postman's knock, hunt the slipper – Nurse Radlett will start you off.'

At some point she disappeared away from the scene, and Nurse Radlett took over. There were three boys of David's age, and two sisters of the boys, and friends of Joanna and Candida, all aged between nine and fourteen. Just before tea Sir Richard appeared, a large, warm and comfortable man, who said on their behalf they wished David a successful term at Eton, and everyone clapped. Then tea was announced and Sir Richard spent a few moments with them before disappearing, but not before he had spoken to most of the children, including Sarah.

'Hallo, young Sarah,' he said. 'Nice to see you–' and passed on.

The tea was a tremendous success, so many wonderful things to eat; after tea, while waiting to go home, David came over and sat beside her.

'Are you sorry to be going back?' Sarah asked, seeing his familiar face, the blond cowlick of hair, the vivid blue eyes, and knew that she was going to miss him more than she dare tell anyone.

'Yes, sort of,' he said, 'but I'm also looking forward to it.'

'Even having to wear that special suit and a strawbarge?' she said grinning at him.

'It's not funny,' he said, but he smiled, and looked at her. 'Don't forget to ask to ride Cindy, you can, you know, my parents really won't mind.'

Her eyes shone.

'Could I?'

'Why not? Joanna's not going to bother, and you know how Cindy likes a run.'

'Thank you,' she said. 'Perhaps we'll see you at Christmas,' she suggested, suddenly feeling tongue-tied. He somehow seemed so grown up today.

'Maybe,' he said. 'I don't know what the family are doing – what about you this term?'

'Doing my eleven plus, I suppose,' she said. 'I'm not looking forward to it – I'm not brainy like you.'

'Me – brainy?' and he laughed. 'You've got more brains in your little finger than I have in my whole head.'

He was her very special friend; she had lots of friends, but David was different, and she knew that being away at school was changing him – it was bound to. She would just have to get used to it.

She said her goodbyes and thank yous and drove home alongside Tom in the trap. Tom cast an eye at her from time to time, but she said nothing. He thought he knew how she felt – and in his heart was glad the boy was going away.

When she arrived home Laurie was there, and he seemed to break the spell. She grinned at him, he was so different from anyone else she knew, broad, stocky, handsome, all the girls loved him, they were all after him, she thought proudly. Sometimes he brought one or other home to Sunday tea, but the friendships never lasted.

'He's enjoying life,' Tom said. 'I don't blame him – plenty of time for him to settle down–'

'So how was the party?' he asked.

'Lovely,' Sarah said, eyes shining.

Laurie secretly thought it was bad for her to mix with the Drummonds. No good would come of that. He knew enough about the working class and the gentry to know that never the twain shall meet and he didn't want his little sister to get hurt wanting things she could never have.

It was a long time before Sarah saw David again, for the Christmas holidays came and went, it seemed the family had gone to France to stay with friends, and when they did return to the Hall, little contact was made.

In the meantime Sarah had her school exams at which she did passably well, but failed to gain a scholarship to the grammar school. Then her teacher asked Robbie to come and see her, as she did all mothers of children who showed a certain aptitude, and it was with some trepidation that Robbie set out.

She had no qualms about Sarah, knew she was a sensible girl, and thought in her heart that it was a pity she could not have received an education at a private school. Although they could have afforded it on the money given to them by Lady Freddie, it would not have been at all suitable that Sarah should attend such a school. She had to take her chances like the boys.

Miss Woods welcomed Robbie. She had been at the school when Robbie was a child, and had been young then. Now, surely retirement age, Robbie was still in awe of her.

'Well, Edith,' she said. 'You have a lovely

daughter there – but I expect you know that.'

'Yes, Miss Woods,' and Robbie beamed.

'She is a nice child,' Miss Woods went on, 'good-natured and helpful, and I did not expect her to win a scholarship – her talents lie in quite another direction. I am sure you realise that she is very artistic and good with her hands and I wondered what you thought of the idea of sending her to a trade school.' Edith's face fell.

'Now, there is nothing to be ashamed of in attending a trade school, there she will receive great advantages in the field that she is so good at, and I personally think she will go a long way.'

Robbie looked thoughtful.

'I don't need to tell you what a good little seamstress she is, and she paints and draws well, although of course there is no future to be had as an artist.'

'But dressmaking...' and Edith's face was a study of disapproval. 'I was hoping she would learn more, like history and geography, even French – like they do in good schools.'

'That will come, all in good time,' Miss Woods smiled.

'I know she hates arithmetic,' Robbie said.

'I did too.'

'Yes, lots of children do. I sometimes think it is the way it is taught, but we are not concerned here about her arithmetic, it is what we are going to do for her in the future. You know, Edith, things have changed since the war, women are demanding more than your or my generation, and we realise now that it is a good thing for a young woman to be trained to do something with her life other than marrying and having babies.'

Robbie was shocked. 'Well, I hope she does!' she said. 'Get married and have babies, I mean.'

'Of course she will, but what do you think of my suggestion? If you are agreeable I will put her name forward.'

It was no good asking Tom, thought Robbie. He wouldn't know much about a girl's education. He would happily leave it to her to make decisions as she had done with the boys.

'Well, if you think that's right, Miss Woods,' she said at length, picking up her gloves from her lap and beginning to put them on.

'Yes, I do,' Miss Woods said. 'So leave it with me – and thank you for coming in to see me.'

Quite often mothers don't, she thought sadly. Either busy with too many other children, or too tired to make the effort. But she knew Edith Roberts – she had been one of her favourite pupils. Imagine, she thought, as she saw her to the door. I was only twenty-five when she was here as a tiny girl, she was one of my first pupils, and I was slim and blonde.

She tucked a grey hair into her bun and pulled her grey cardigan down. Where had the years gone?

'Goodbye, Mrs Roberts.'

'Thank you, Miss Woods.' And somewhat disappointed at the turn of events, Robbie made her way home.

'So what did Miss Woods say?'

Sarah had hurried home from school anxious to know what had been decided.

'Well, Sarah, Miss Woods thinks you should go to a trade school because you are so good with making things; she said you are very artistic–'

Sarah was quite well aware that going to a trade school was not exactly education at a higher level, but tempered with that was the thought that at least there it might mean that she could make things to her heart's content. It might turn out to be quite good.

‘Oh, well then,’ she said. ‘When would I start?’

‘If they take you, next September.’

Sarah looked up to the mantelpiece where sat the Blue Girl, and touched her rosy cheek – something she did quite often.

‘I will be twelve next September,’ she said dreamily. ‘Golly, twelve–’

Chapter Six

By nineteen thirty-six, Sarah had been at Debenham and Freebody’s for almost two years. Apprenticed as she had been, and the period coming to an end, she was ready to think about finding a position in the fashion trade. It had been apparent to her teachers from the start that she was exceptionally gifted in drawing and design, and she was a favourite pupil as well as being the best of the little bunch taken in in nineteen thirty-four.

Sarah’s own wish was to work for a designer, but that was perhaps a little too ambitious for a girl who had been to a trade school, even if she had finished her training at Debenham's, but she lived in hope.

She lived in the store in the building reserved for trainees, sharing a dormitory with six other girls, and going home every weekend. She knew that her mother missed her, especially now that Laurie was married – but that was another story.

For Laurie had brought home a girl who was quite different from his usual young ladies. They had all been smart, almost cheeky, bantering with him, giving back as good as they got, blonde or brunette. Sunday afternoons were always fun when Laurie brought a girl home to tea.

But this time, it was different. He brought no girl to Sunday tea for three weeks, and when he did, it was shy, quiet little Hilda. Robbie couldn't have told you why, she had misgivings from the start. For this shy girl, plain as a pikestaff who wouldn't say boo to a goose, had completely enslaved handsome Laurie. He held her hand as if to give her courage, waited on her, looked at her adoringly – and Robbie sensed that Laurie, fun-loving and mischievous, smart and clever, had been completely bowled over by this violet of a girl, and knew then that she had to accept Laurie's choice. They were married within three months of meeting, and set up home in Allington where Laurie was a garage mechanic. They had a flat over the garage premises and a baby boy was born exactly nine months later to the day; they called him Thomas, after his grandfather.

Robbie had plenty of time to reflect on this, Sarah being away and Donnie and his young wife beavering away at their studies, for both had resolved to improve their education, Ginny even going to shorthand and typing classes in the evening, while Donnie studied for an engineering degree. She was so proud of them, although wishing for a grandchild in that direction seemed useless, at least for the time being.

Still, she had Tommy, and he was a dear little chap. Like Laurie to look at, and Robbie couldn't help thinking, thank God, for Hilda was such a plain girl, with her broken front tooth, her pallid skin. Sometimes she wondered what Laurie had seen in her, but after a time came to realise that he cherished her, wanted to protect her, for she came from a poor family with a none too savoury reputation. What her past life had been Robbie had no idea, but she felt intuitively that Laurie had rescued her, and he thought the world of her. She came round to First Lodge on the bus to see Robbie every Wednesday, bringing a basket holding snow-white nappies, and while Robbie made tea, would knit tiny white garments, the pristine knitting falling from her fingers as though untouched by human hand. She said little, but looked up shyly at Robbie every time she was spoken to, biting her lip to hide her broken tooth, almost, Robbie thought, as though apologising for being there.

She was always glad when Sarah came home at the weekend.

This weekend she was particularly anxious and somewhat excited, for Sarah had an appointment with a prestigious small house in Knightsbridge. Her name had been put forward by Mrs Delany at Debenham's and she was to take samples of her needlework and some of her designs. Robbie knew that she was anxious to grasp this opportunity because it would be such an honour to gain experience at the House of Gallen whose proprietor was French.

Robbie's one worry was that if Sarah were fortunate enough to secure a position there, whether she would be able to live on the premises, for the wages were very low, certainly not enough for her to afford a room in London, and Robbie did not like the idea of her spending so much time travelling between London every day and First Lodge.

By the time Friday evening arrived and Sarah burst in, there was no need to ask how she had got on. She hugged Robbie, her dark eyes shining like stars; she had hardly been able to sustain her excitement coming home in the train.

'I am to start in two weeks' time, so I have two weeks off, and we shall go to the seaside for a day, and I'll take you to London and show you where M. Gallen's premises are – oh, I'm so excited–'

Robbie was pleased for her – and proud. Wait until Milady heard the news…

For Milady could not help but be interested in Sarah's future. As she grew into womanhood Lady Freddie was able to observe where others could not just where she got her beauty from. Not from herself, that was for sure, but that dark beauty was like a knife in Freddie's heart whenever she saw her, which was not often these days. Her own two daughters, blonde and pretty, so like herself when young, took up most of her time, although they were both away at boarding school, but now it was coming to the end of the school holidays and they were preparing to go back to school.

She was pleased at Robbie's news, glad that Sarah was making progress in her world, and more pleased than she could say that things had worked out. If she had any misgivings it was to do with David and Sarah, but she so arranged it that they took their holidays either in Cheshire, or sometimes abroad, and a lot of the time in London.

Sarah looked forward to her two weeks' break, and she and Robbie went by coach to Bournemouth for the day, where they sat by the sea, and paddled in the shallow water, followed by a short excursion in a boat, getting off laughing at the end of it, and more than ready after their day to return home.

But it was London that intrigued Robbie, for it was in a part of London where she had never been before, Knightsbridge, and the little streets around it, the tall narrow houses that Sarah told her were so expensive where many famous and titled people lived.

'But they are so narrow and go up for ever,' Robbie said. 'There can't be room to swing a cat.'

'Ah, but it's London, you see,' Sarah

explained. 'The hub of the Empire – isn't it exciting? I love it.'

Robbie stole a glance at her, and seeing the dark eyes glow, she supposed it was only natural with her background that Sarah would be impressed.

'Well, I would like to see where you are going to work.'

'That's where we are going,' Sarah said, and half-way down Montpelier Street she stopped outside a very circumspect house with glass windows as a shopfront and a doorway, above which was written in small discreet letters: THE HOUSE OF GALLEN. Above were two floors with long sash windows, and yet above probably attics, Robbie thought, where Sarah might live, but there was little to be seen in the window other than crushed wine velvet on the floor and a dress of palest grey on which carelessly hung pearls.

'Is this it?' she whispered.

Sarah nodded. 'Mmm, let's walk on – see, here is a famous antique shop and further on, an interior decorator. It is one of the most famous streets in London – this part of London anyway.'

Robbie sighed, she had imagined something quite different, but the House of

Gallen was so unostentatious that she realised she knew very little about the world of fashion as it was in London and Paris.

Sarah, of course, was absorbed by the shops and their window displays, and took her mother down Bond Street, which was a real eye-opener to Robbie. Such elegant ladies, dressed in the latest fashion, windows full of expensive clothes – it was another world. The clothes were nothing like she saw at home, long dresses of mid-calf length, with narrow belts and pretty designs of flowers and stripes. The sleeves often billowed out at the wrist, and the models wore large flat hats or tiny bowler-like hats, and sometimes there were suits, with tartan jackets and plain skirts; with this sort of thing they wore velour hats, quite mannish-looking, which dipped over one eye. Altogether Robbie felt she was in another world. She went home with mixed feelings. It was all so strange to her, to her way of life, to her upbringing, but then she recalled the true nature of Sarah's background and realised that if Sarah had been her own daughter, things might have been very different.

On that last Friday before she started work in London, Sarah began to pack her things, for she was to go up to London on the Sunday. Having been fortunate to find a room on the premises with another girl, she was anxious to make a start.

It was a lovely warm September day, and Robbie had left the kitchen door open to let in the warm air while she went down to the village to shop.

Sarah was upstairs when the knock came at the door, and going downstairs, she saw outlined against the sunshine the tall figure of a man, and knew immediately who it was.

'David!' she cried, running down the stairs, and he smiled up at her in greeting. It was all she could do not to throw her arms about him, so pleased was she to see him.

'David,' she smiled.

'Sarah,' he said, 'I saw the door open–' and there was no doubt how pleased he was to see her. Tall and fair, he looked so handsome, she was momentarily nonplussed.

'Come in,' she said. 'Mother has gone shopping and Dad's in the park somewhere.'

'I know, I saw him in Bottom Field. He said you were home.'

She led him to a chair at the kitchen table and sat down opposite him.

'Have I changed as much as you have?' she

smiled at him.

He grinned back. 'I don't know – have I? You're quite the young lady, eighteen, aren't you?'

'And you are twenty-one,' she said, suddenly at a loss for words. 'Would you like tea? The kettle's boiling.'

'No thanks. I wondered if you would like to come for a stroll around the park – I have to be home by four – I'm going back this evening.'

She knew he was at Oxford, and hoped she didn't look as disappointed as she felt.

'Oh. Yes, sure – I'll just get a jacket.'

They walked out of First Lodge like old friends, talking nineteen to the dozen.

'It would have been nice to have had a canter. I see Cindy's still here–'

'No time,' Sarah said. 'We've left it a bit late.'

'I didn't get back from France until yesterday,' David excused himself.

'And I was going up for my appointment – I'm going to work in London.'

'Yes, Mother said.'

They walked across the fields to the nearby wood, a place where they had often played as children. It was instinctive, the place they always made for. Beneath the great oak tree their names had been carved out by David, long long ago, when they were mere children.

'Look at it,' he laughed. 'Weatherworn isn't it?'

'You can still see what it is, D and S,' Sarah said.

They sat down on the broken log as they had always done in the past.

'Funny how it all stays the same, when so much has happened in between,' he said, casting a surreptitious glance at her, seeing the lovely face and dark eyes, the way her hair grew back from her forehead, short now, but thick and fashionably cut.

Sarah, glancing sideways from time to time, thought how handsome he had grown, what a very presentable young man he was. He must be almost six feet tall, and with those blue eyes and fair hair, just like Lady Freddie–

'How are the girls?' she asked.

'I don't see much of them,' he said. 'They've been staying at Gran's for most of the summer.'

'Joanna must be sixteen now, and Candida thirteen.'

'Yes, I don't know what they will do when they leave school.'

Not that it mattered. Sarah thought. They didn't have to work – as lady's daughters, the question didn't arise.

It was a strange thing, but she felt more at home with David than anyone else she knew. There had always been something special between them – they instinctively sought each other out, and she hadn't felt like this with his sisters. They were nice girls, both of them, but she felt nothing special for them; perhaps it was because they were younger–

'Have you got a boyfriend?' he asked presently.

She looked shocked, and laughed out loud. 'I've no time for boyfriends!'

'But you are very pretty,' he said, looking at her.

'What about you – do the girls in Oxford run after you?'

He reddened. 'Of course not. I've too much work to do for that – I'm in my last year... Also, but I haven't told Mother, I've joined the Flying Corps–'

'Oh, David, you haven't!'

'I have – I wanted to. If there is a war–'

'Oh, don't talk about it – we were both born in the last war – you at the beginning and me at the end of it. We don't want another one – I feel very strongly about wars–'

'Do you?' He looked at her curiously.

'Yes, I do. I suppose if I were a man I would be a pacifist.'

'Then it's a good thing you are not,' he laughed.

They looked at each other, silently, and presently he took her hand.

'Sarah–'

She felt disconcerted as the flush stained her cheeks, and drew her hand away.

'I think we ought to get back,' she said. 'We've walked quite a way.'

'Yes, all right–' and the moment had gone.

They walked back almost in silence. When they reached First Lodge, they stopped and he looked at her searchingly.

'We've never written to each other, have we?' as she shook her head.

'Shall we?'

'What – write to each other?' She seemed amused. 'If you like.'

'We don't want to lose touch, do we?' he asked. He seemed very anxious.

'We won't,' she smiled. 'How can we? We live so near each other.'

'But it's ages since we met. I've missed you,' he said.

Again that tell-tale flush.

'But you will give me your address,' he urged. 'Look, I have a pencil and my diary.'

And she gave it to him; care of the House of Gallen in Montpelier Street.

'And now yours,' she said, as he tore a page out of his diary.

'David Drummond, just St John's, Oxford,' he said.

'Thank you.' And she folded the slip of paper, as he put the diary in his pocket and held out his hand.

'Good luck, Sarah,' he said.

The touch of his hand was electric, as she stood momentarily nonplussed.

'You too,' she said, as he turned and walked away.

Robbie was in the kitchen making tea, not unaware of the little drama being enacted outside.

'I've just seen David,' Sarah said. She seemed a little breathless. 'Gosh, he is so handsome–'

But Robbie busy at the stove, seemed to have her mind on other things.

'Guess who I saw in the village?' she said. 'Little Jessie Truelove…'

Back at the Hall, David found his mother in the drawing room where she was busy embroidering a chair seat.

'Hello, Mother,' David said. 'I've just seen Sarah–' as she raised her eyebrows – 'Sarah – down at the Lodge.'

'Oh, Sarah – yes–'

'Gosh, she is so pretty!' he said. 'Quite the young lady! And so grown up–' but Lady Freddie was intent upon her sewing.

'I was thinking–' and he stood with his back to the fireplace and when she didn't look up – 'Mother?'

'Yes, darling?'

Lady Freddie turned round blue eyes to his.

'You know we agreed to postpone my twenty-first celebration until Dad got back from the States? Well, I was thinking, why don't we have it in London?'

'Why not?' Lady Freddie said casually.

'I mean – couldn't we ask Sarah – Robbie's Sarah? She works in London–'

'Oh, I don't think so, darling,' Lady Freddie said gently. 'It wouldn't be–'

'What?' David asked, the light of battle in his eyes.

'Well, not fair on her, darling.'

'In what way?'

'Well, it'll be family, and your Oxford friends, and some of the local girls you've played tennis with, gone to dances with – you don't think she might feel a little out of place–' her voice trailed off.

'I don't see why she should,' he looked belligerent. 'I can't imagine Sarah being fazed or intimidated by–'

She interrupted him. 'Ah, do I hear the girls?'

David, who had not heard a sound, knew it was his mother's way of ending the conversation. Well, fair enough – but he had no intention of losing touch with Sarah…

Sarah's training was to last for two years, and she settled down to hard work, learning that the work she had done at Debenham and Freebody's was nothing compared to this. She shared a room with Emily, another talented student, and although Emily came from a different background, her family were well-to-do, and strong socialists, she and Sarah got on well together.

The work was quite hard, M. Gallen being a strict taskmaster. Perfection in all things was his criterion, from the colour of a reel of cotton to the tacking of a toile. He knew that both these girls had talent, perhaps Sarah a little more, and was anxious to see them give full rein to their ideas, something he found young ladies a little loath to do in the beginning, but time would tell. He encouraged them in the drawing and designs, and some of the most tedious tasks fell to them – the fine hemming round the bottom of a voluminous ball gown – but it was some time before they graduated to actually sewing a dress. Everything was hand-sewn, of course, but Sarah was used to that. She found the time went swiftly, but she and Emily often walked in the park on summer evenings. It was wonderful to get out into the fresh air after being cooped up all day in the dark basement.

Mme Gallen, a small, tightly corseted Parisienne, who always wore black satin, served her time in the shop, dealing with clients whom Sarah and Emily hardly ever saw, shut up as they were in the workroom. Four other women worked there, two English and two French women, all brilliant at their jobs. The embroiderer was responsible for all the wonderful beading on the dresses, the expert cutter, whom M. Gallen looked after like a treasured piece of china – the cutter, he would have said, was the most important part of the business. Two seamstresses made up the Gallen workrooms, and as time went by, Sarah was proud to be there, and delighted that she was having first-rate tuition. One day, she knew, she would go to Paris – there would be nothing she would like more than to see the home of fashion. Working for Gallen's had given her a taste for high-class couture.

After all, she now had just a smattering of French – you couldn't help but pick it up working as she did alongside two Frenchwomen, and Mme Gallen spoke only French to the staff, although she could speak English quite well to clients.

Sarah resolved to learn French. In the winter, at any rate, there were good LCC evening classes.

The next two Christmases she received cards from David, and sent him cards in return.

In the summer of '38 she received a letter from him asking her to meet him for lunch as he was coming to London for the day. He would pick her up outside the House of Gallen, he said, he knew where Montpelier Street was. Sarah put on her best suit, and a small fur stole around her neck for the day was chill, and tilting her Tyrolean hat with its feather over one eye and making sure her seams were straight, went out to meet him.

Her heart leapt when she saw him

standing there, with his dark suit and bowler hat and his rolled umbrella. She was so proud to be seen with him.

'Sarah–' and he held out his hand.

She took it and smiled up at him. 'Hallo, David.'

'I thought we'd go across to the Hyde Park Hotel – that suit you?'

'I just have an hour,' she said. She had never been inside the impressive hotel, but she had passed it enough times. And what a wonderful spring day it was, and it wasn't even her birthday…

They sat facing each other beside the low table, David looking as pleased with life as Sarah.

'Well, Sarah, how is life treating you?' he asked her.

'Wonderful,' she said. 'I love it, everything about it, London, the work–'

'Do you get home often?'

'Most weekends, just occasionally I don't–'

'Are your parents well?'

'My father has had a bad winter: arthritis and rheumatism, the cold seems to affect his war injury – and what have you been up to?'

'Well, I left Oxford.'

'And what are you doing now?'

'The City like my father. I'd rather be in the Air Force.'

'David, you're not still–'

'Yes, I go flying at weekends – sometimes I go down to Croydon or Biggin Hill. I flew to Paris the other day – it was absolutely wonderful! With a co-pilot, of course.'

And she saw the enthusiasm in the blue eyes.

'Sounds wonderful.'

'And what are you going to do next?' he asked. 'Isn't your two years nearly up?'

'Yes, at the end of September. Of course, M. Gallen could keep me on – if I'm good enough, or I can go somewhere else – I'm not sure yet–'

'You'll be good enough,' David said.

An hour passed, during which they ate an excellent lunch after which Sarah had to get back to the shop, and he took his leave of her outside, saying he would be in touch again.

'We must do this more often,' he said, smiling into her dark eyes.

That weekend, at home, he told his mother he had lunched with Sarah.

'I took her to the Hyde Park,' he said, smiling at the remembrance of it. 'She's quite stunning, Mother, knocks all the other girls into a cocked hat.'

It was at the mention of that hotel that, heart beating fast, Lady Freddie decided that the time had come to have a talk with Robbie. And not too soon, she thought grimly…

Chapter Seven

When the telephone bell rang, Robbie jumped.

A new innovation, it had been installed at Lady Freddie's request, since she decided that contact between the Hall and the Lodge would be that much quicker by telephone and useful in case of emergency.

Robbie picked up the receiver. She expected it to be Lady Freddie, since no one else ever rang, except the one occasion that Laurie had phoned from the garage, and that more of a joke than anything.

Now as instructed, she spoke into the instrument.

'First Lodge–'

'Ah, Robbie–' and Lady Freddie sounded a little breathless.

'Is everything all right, Milady?'

'Yes, Robbie, it's just that I would like you to come up to the Hall when you can – this morning? I have a free day for once.'

'Yes, Milady. This morning, around eleven?'

'That's fine, Robbie. See you then–' and Lady Freddie replaced the receiver.

Things had come to a head, as she might have known they would, and heaven knew what Robbie would say, but there was no point in worrying about Robbie's reactions now. Things had gone too far for that.

Walking up to the Hall Robbie couldn't help but think what a blessing the telephone was. Hitherto, someone had to come down from the Hall, or it was left to Tom to pass messages.

She walked more slowly nowadays; almost sixty, her figure heavier, she no longer hurried back and forth to the Hall. Her skin was lined and suntanned, her eyes dark and kindly, her hair more grey now although she had never changed her hairstyle, her hair being dragged back tightly into its bun. She had never had the slightest desire to have it cut – Tom, she thought, would have gone through the roof at the very idea.

She opened the door to the kitchen, seeing

Mrs Owen busy making pastry at the large scrubbed kitchen table.

'Nice morning, Mrs Owen.'

'Yes, it is, a touch of autumn this morning I thought. Her Ladyship is in the drawing room, Robbie.'

Robbie hung her coat behind the kitchen door, and, tapping on the double doors of the drawing room, waited to be told to enter.

'Milady–'

'Ah, Robbie, I'm glad you could come. Sit down – I think there is something we need to discuss.'

She could see Milady was pale, and somewhat het up, judging by the set of her shoulders, and the way she was gripping her book, her knuckles showing through the skin.

'Best then, to get it off your chest, Milady,' Robbie said quietly, trying to hide her own apprehension.

'I'm not going to beat about the bush: did you know that David and Sarah have been meeting in London?'

Robbie felt the blood ebb away from her face – it sounded so blatant put like that.

'No I didn't, Milady, although Sarah hasn't been home for two weekends – she is due home on Saturday–' and wondered why she herself felt guilty. 'It must have been during the last two weeks,' she added.

'Why do you say that?' Lady Freddie asked shortly.

'Because I think she would have told me if they had met before; it is not like Sarah to keep secrets, and she would see no reason why they should not meet.'

'Exactly,' Lady Freddie said. 'That's the point I am trying to make.'

And suddenly her guard fell, she almost collapsed against the back of the chair, her handkerchief at her mouth. 'Oh, Robbie – what have we done?'

A surge almost of dislike surged through Robbie, followed swiftly by pity.

'Milady – please be calm. No good getting yourself in a state about it.'

'But we must stop it, we can't allow it–'

'Short of explaining the situation to them, there is not much we can do, is there?' she said drily. 'I do see that it is unwise, of course it is, but they are only friends – it's natural they would want to see each other, they grew up together, like brother and sister, you might say.'

'Oh, Robbie, don't!' Lady Freddie cried. 'You are blinding yourself to the possibilities here… Suppose I tell you that David is in love with Sarah?'

Robbie paled. 'Nonsense, Milady!' she said to hide her fear.

'You don't believe me, do you?' Lady Freddie said bitterly. 'But I am his mother, and I know it. He has always been soft on her, and now – well, I can tell, he can't wait to see her again. He even wanted her to come to his twenty-first birthday celebrations in London, until I put my foot down.'

Poor Sarah, Robbie thought. 'She didn't tell me anything about that,' she admitted.

'Of course not, because I nipped it in the bud before it went any further.'

Robbie looked at her. She had never felt so alienated from her employer.

'It takes two to make a love affair, Milady, and I don't think Sarah – well, she's very keen on her job, is very good at it, and quite an ambitious young lady–'

Lady Freddie took a deep breath and sat up straight.

'Dear Robbie,' she said. 'I expect the answer is that I know a great deal more about the world than you do, you've led such quiet blameless lives, you and Tom, you are the salt of the earth – but real life is not always as simple as it might look to you. I am afraid you and I together, must step in here and try to find a solution. I think I have it, but I shall need your help.'

'What is it?' Robbie asked, dreading the answer.

'Sarah must go away,' Milady said.

'Go away!' Robbie almost shouted. 'What are you saying, Milady? Send her away? My daughter? You must be mad!' and now she was past caring what she said.

'Robbie! Robbie!' and Milady was almost in tears. 'I didn't want this any more than you do, but don't you see – it could be dangerous for both of them? Suppose Sarah loves him too, why shouldn't she? It is not beyond the bounds of possibility, is it? He is a very attractive young man. They meet – how many times we may never know, and grow more and more fond of each other–'

'Sarah would have told me,' Robbie said stubbornly.

'Look, as I said, I think I have the solution, the best way out for everyone. Do you want to hear me out?'

Robbie sat stiffly, staring in front of her, and it was a Robbie Lady Freddie had never seen before.

Now she was entreating her, urging her to

see the sense of it.

'I have given this a lot of thought, believe me, and I am only trying to do the best for the children,' she said, as Robbie made no answer.

'It came to me last night, while I couldn't sleep thinking about it. I have a dear friend in Paris – she owns a salon on the Rue Faubourg St Honoré – my mother used to shop there for clothes when we went to Paris. She was more like an aunt to me – they had a château in the south of France where we used to go and stay in the summer, and it seems to me, since it is such a prestigious Paris house, that Sarah would do well to have a spell there, always supposing that Aunt Lisette would be prepared to take her–'

'Go to France!' Robbie opened her eyes wide in disbelief, 'to Paris, Milady – abroad? How would she live – she cannot even speak French; how would she manage? My little Sarah–'

Her eyes filled with tears, so unlike Robbie that Lady Freddie almost felt ashamed – but not quite – and held on to her one hope.

'She would love it,' she said enthusiastically. 'The chance to have a training in Paris, and live there; it is a wonderful place, and I can assure you Madame Lisette is the kindest of women – she would be like a mother to her–'

And that's something you've never been, Robbie thought bitterly.

'Her father wouldn't hear of it,' she said at length.

'Tom? Oh, I am sure he would agree – especially when you tell him of my fears. He will understand – he is a man–'

Robbie stood up and pushed back her chair.

'I think you are worrying unnecessarily, Milady,' she said at length. 'If there was anything in it at all, Sarah would have told me. She is coming home this weekend and so we shall see if she tells me about their meeting – I shall know, Milady. I know Sarah,' which implied that Lady Freddie did not, but she couldn't resist the dig.

Lady Freddie blushed and got to her feet.

'Very well, Robbie. We'll let it ride for a day or two, but I am serious about this. Will you bear that in mind?'

They took their leave of each other as strangers, so upset were they both, so alienated by their feelings.

'Goodbye, Milady,' Robbie said, and made her way back down to First Lodge, her mind in a turmoil. She wouldn't say anything to Tom until Sarah had been for the weekend. She couldn't think straight at the moment.

A pretty pass ... who'd have thought it would come to this?

When Sarah arrived home on Friday evening, Robbie could see she was bubbling over with good news.

'I couldn't wait to get home!' she said. 'To tell you–'

'Tell me what?' Robbie couldn't stop the pang of fear that shot through her.

'I've done so well in my tests that Madame Gallen says Monsieur Gallen is thinking of giving me another year!'

'That's wonderful,' Robbie said, relieved.

'He says I am very good at design – and he thinks that's where my future lies.' And she stood leaning back against the kitchen table as proud as a little peacock, Robbie thought.

Well, so she should be. The girl was talented and she wondered what she would say when she mooted Lady Freddie's idea to her, but she would say nothing at the moment, just bring it up casually during the weekend.

How smart she looked, her dark eyes

shining, her hair cut in the new style, smooth with almost a page-boy bob. She had taken off her beret, and was wearing a tailored navy and pink tweed suit, with a pleated skirt and fitted jacket, a navy blouse, the cuffs of which were turned back over the jacket sleeves. She had on navy court shoes.

She twirled round. 'Like it?' she asked.

'It's lovely,' Robbie said. 'Did you–'

'Of course I did,' Sarah smiled. 'I make everything; you won't catch me buying shop clothes. In any case they're so far behind the fashion–'

She didn't add that she was making Robbie a dress for her birthday. Her mother so seldom had anything new she knew it would be a grand surprise.

'And wait until I show you some of my designs – M. Gallen said they are as good as anything that came out of Paris. I'll show them to you later ... have you seen anything of Laurie?'

'Yes, he and Hilda came to tea last Sunday – oh, that small chap is a dear little boy, and the image of Laurie.'

'I can't wait to see him again,' and Robbie heard her singing as she went upstairs.

What a pity that this ugly cloud hung over their heads.

It was Saturday morning before Sarah broached the subject of her lunch with David.

'I saw David – David Drummond – a week or so ago, he took me to lunch, and guess where?'

'I can't imagine,' Robbie said, busy at the sink.

'The Hyde Park Hotel!' and waited for it to sink in. 'What about that?'

'That was kind of him, and what was it like?' Robbie began stacking the washed dishes in the drainer.

'Oh, wonderful! Not only the food, but the atmosphere – so luxurious, you can't imagine–'

'And how was he? David?' Robbie asked, sticking her neck out.

'Oh, he's fine,' Sarah said. 'It was lovely seeing him again, he is such a nice boy. And would you believe, he has joined a flying club, and flies sometimes at Biggin Hill – that's in Kent. I'm not sure Lady Freddie knows, so best not say anything.'

'No, of course not,' Robbie said, relieved that Sarah's attitude was scarcely like that of a young woman hopelessly in love. Now, she thought, was the time, casually to mention Lady Freddie's offer.

She turned, drying her hands.

'By the way, I saw Lady Freddie on Thursday, and I don't know what you'll think of the idea, but she said she has a friend in Paris, an elderly lady who has a couture house – is that the word? Anyway, a fashion business, a fashion house she called it, and wondered – just wondered, mind you, if you would like to go over there for a spell... She said–'

She was stopped by a whoop from Sarah, who was staring at her, eyes wide, mouth open.

'Oh, she didn't! Really? Did she mean it? Oh, if only I could!'

'You'd really like to go?' Robbie asked, her heart sinking.

'I should say so! What an opportunity – what did she say – was she serious about it, I mean?'

'Oh, yes, she was serious all right,' Robbie said, trying to keep the bitterness out of her voice. 'She said would I mention it to you–'

'What is the name of the house – did she say?'

'No, I can't remember. Apparently her mother used to buy her clothes there and they became very friendly with the family, that sort of thing. Anyway, perhaps she'll tell you about it when you see her.'

'Oh, but I mustn't let an opportunity like that go!' Sarah cried. 'Could I go up to see her, do you think? Would she mind?'

'Calm down,' Robbie said. 'It was only a suggestion.'

'You mean, she didn't really mean it.'

'Oh, yes, I think she did. You could telephone her, ask her if she has a moment to spare – you would like to see her – something like that.'

'Now, do you think?'

There was no holding her, Robbie thought.

'Well, some time over the weekend, I should say–' and Robbie had the awful feeling of a die cast...

Sarah telephoned Lady Freddie just after lunch on Saturday, and at her request made her way up the little slope to the Hall, her heart beating fast with excitement.

The door was opened by Joanna, Milady's elder daughter, who had grown so tall, just like her father. Slim and elegant, with vivid blue eyes, just like Lady Freddie's. She was so pleased to see Sarah, and flung her arms round her.

'Gosh! You look stunning!'

'You too! You've grown!' said Sarah admiringly, secretly wishing she had been taller instead of the five foot five she was.

'I've come to see your mother.'

'Yes, she's in the drawing room, oh, she will be glad to see you.'

Across the huge hall, scattered with rugs, and with a large centre table on which stood an imposing bowl of autumn fruits and flowers, was a fire burning in the huge grate – nowhere would you have found a more warm and pleasing atmosphere.

Arms linked, the girls walked across to the drawing room whose doors were open and saw Lady Freddie sitting on the sofa by the fire, the flames of the fire turning her fair hair into a gold halo.

'Oh, there you are, Sarah.' She did not get up but patted the seat beside her.

'I want to talk to Sarah,' she smiled to Joanna. 'Give us about fifteen minutes, then when you come down we'll have some tea; and close the doors after you will you, Joanna – there's a draught with them open.'

When the doors had closed after her, Lady Freddie turned graciously to Sarah.

'Now, my dear.'

She saw by the stars shining in Sarah's brown eyes that she was agog with excitement, and at the very sight of those dark eyes, twin liquid pools with their thick black lashes, she was transported to another pair of eyes, smouldering dark eyes which had looked into hers – oh, so long ago – a lifetime ago – then pulled herself together.

'Did your mother mention my little idea to you?'

'Yes, Milady,' Sarah said, 'and–'

'Now, it is just an idea at the moment, Sarah, but I wanted to speak to you first to see how you thought about it.'

'Oh,' Sarah cried. 'I should be over the moon if I could go to Paris!'

'Yes, well, I thought it might be a good opportunity – Madame Puligny de Montfort is an old and trusted friend, and her house is one of the best in Paris – Madame Lisette–'

'I have heard of her!' Sarah said with growing excitement, for she knew the names of all the couture houses in Paris.

'Well, then, you will understand when I say it would be a wonderful opportunity for you. I would have to be sure you understand what it means, Sarah, going to live abroad on your own, although I have no doubts about putting you in Aunt Lisette's care.'

A real relation, thought Sarah.

'Of course, I understand to work for a French couturier is very hard work indeed;

their standards are so high.'

'Monsieur Gallen is French,' Sarah said, on her dignity, 'so I am used to French being spoken, and I do have a smattering, but no more than that.'

'Well, I expect Madame Lisette will insist that you take French lessons – it is in your own interests. Are you adventurous enough to go along with the idea?'

'I should say so!'

'It means leaving your mother and your family–'

'I already live away from home.'

'Yes, but you won't be able to get home at weekends as you do now,' Lady Freddie said gently. 'What does your mother say? Is she agreeable?'

'Oh, yes, otherwise I wouldn't have come to see you. She knows what a marvellous opportunity it is for me – and I can't thank you enough, Milady–'

'Well, it is not settled yet, I have to write and I will possibly telephone Madame Lisette to talk it over, so I will let you know.'

'I will need to know fairly soon, because I think Monsieur Gallen is thinking of giving me an extra year, at least that's what Madame Gallen said.'

'Oh, well, I shall get on to it right away and

I expect Madame Lisette will probably wish to contact him. I don't know the exact procedure in these circumstances, but we shall take it step by step.'

She smiled at Sarah, and rang the little bell on the table at her side.

'Now, let us have some tea. Will you stay to tea, Sarah?'

'Yes, thank you, Milady, I'd love to. And thank you again for your kindness.'

Her cheeks faintly pink, Milady smiled. 'My pleasure Sarah', and felt just the tiniest pang of guilt.

Six weeks later, and the arrangements were signed, sealed and delivered. Sarah was to catch the cross-Channel ferry from Folkestone Harbour to Boulogne, and from there she would board the Paris train where she would be met by Madame Lisette or one of the staff.

She had her new passport in her handbag, and a small travelling case so that she would not have too much to carry. Laurie was to see her to the station to catch the London train. Everything was organised.

Only the night before did she have qualms at leaving her parents. Her dear father, who was not all that well, and Robbie. What would it be like in a strange country?

She had packed her belongings. Opening her passport she saw the face of the girl staring up at her, heart-shaped face, dark hair, wide dark eyes.

'Are all passport photographs as bad as this?' she asked. 'Surely I'm not as ugly as that!' and she laughed.

'Who am I like, do you think?' her head on one side. 'Your cousin or her daughter?' and Robbie's heart turned over. It was the first time Sarah had ever mentioned her background.

'Whatever happened to her? The daughter?'

'My cousin died long ago,' Robbie said as levelly as she could. 'The daughter – I don't know – she went to Canada. I never heard again.'

Sarah closed the passport and put it in the purse inside her handbag. Then she took a deep breath.

'I wish you were coming with me,' she said, half tearful and half smiling.

'Can you imagine me in Paris?' Robbie joked and Sarah laughed again.

'No, you stay here and look after Dad, and I'll be home at Christmas to tell you all about it.'

God willing, Robbie thought.

Chapter Eight

1938

And here she was, in France! Across the Channel, her first sea trip, and now Boulogne with its strange French buildings, and hordes of blue-coated porters swarming over the ship; the place even smelt different, of French cigarettes which brought back to mind the little salon in Montpelier Street, and something indefinable, something she was to learn was garlic.

It was magical – but never had she felt farther away from home. She followed all the other foot passengers, most of whom were going to board the train to Paris, for she had spoken to quite a few people on the ship, and soon she was sitting in a corner seat in a leather-seated train next to an elderly English couple who were going to Paris to celebrate their golden wedding anniversary. They longed to see it again, just once, they said, the place where they had spent their honeymoon; the trip had been given to them by their children as an anniversary present.

Fifty years, Sarah thought, it seemed such a long time ... a part of history.

But her eyes followed the train journey, and she fell in love with France from that moment on. Quaint little towns rushed past and sometimes they stopped at places that were famous during the war, places she had heard her father mention. How strange to think he had been here all that time ago. And girls at school would have known those towns, girls whose fathers and brothers had been killed, on the Somme, at Abbeville – all the names she had been brought up with.

And then, she could hardly believe it, was the Gare du Nord. The kindly elderly lady was asking her if she would like help, the husband took her case down from the overhead rack, and they stayed with her on the platform until she saw a young woman waiting for someone, and knew that she must be Mlle Nicole. Madame Lisette had described her, having sent her because she spoke English.

'Mam'selle, bonjour, vous etes – you are Miss Roberts?'

Sarah, relieved and delighted to be met by someone speaking English, smiled back at her. *'Oui* – yes, I am Sarah Roberts, and this is Mr and Mrs Elliot from London, who were kind enough to stay with me until you arrived.'

'And I am Nicole Mallet, sent by Mme Puligny de Montfort.'

There were greetings and thank yous all round until the Elliots left, giving her the name of the hotel where they would be staying in Paris, in the event of her needing assistance.

'We shall be at the George Cinq for three days, my dear,' and raising his hat to them both, Mr Elliot escorted his wife to the taxi rank.

'So you are Sarah; did you have a good journey?' and Nicole looked as if she might be fun, a girl of Sarah's own age, or perhaps a little older.

'I'm just fine,' Sarah smiled, excited that she was actually here in Paris, that the girl looked friendly and spoke such good English.

'Come, let us find a taxi,' Nicole said. 'You have not brought much luggage with you.'

'My mother thought I should travel light,' Sarah said, 'and I'm glad I did.'

'Come on then,' and Nicole hurried them to the waiting taxis, and gave the order to an address in the Place de la Madeleine.

'I thought Mme Lisette's salon was in the Faubourg St Honoré–' Sarah began.

'It is – but we are going home first to the room we will share in the Rue de la Madeleine,' Nicole said.

'Oh,' Sarah said, wanting to talk to Nicole and ask questions, but fascinated by the Paris streets, so different from London, and knew that she would rather be here than anywhere else in the world. It was absolute magic.

The taxicab stopped outside a tall imposing building and, having paid the driver, Nicole led them through swing doors and into an impressive entrance hall, where a uniformed concierge acknowledged them with a nod, and she made not for the lift with its magnificently designed wrought iron gates, but to the side where there were wide stairs.

'Mme Lisette lives on the second floor,' she said. 'Her apartment is–' and she rolled her eyes – 'Oh, magnificent, *tres magnifique*,' she whispered. 'The lift only goes up to the third floor, and we are on the sixth.'

'The sixth floor? Goodness!' Sarah couldn't imagine living so high up in the world.

After a long climb, Nicole opened the

door of a pleasant room with two beds and sparse furniture, and went across to the windows and opened them wide. 'Oh,' Sarah said a trifle breathlessly. 'The windows open inwards!'

'How else?' asked Nicole, flopping on the bed.

'Well, at home our windows open outwards,' she said, and Nicole smiled.

'Never mind,' Sarah laughed. 'It's not important. Is this my bed?'

'Is that all right? I'm used to sleeping near the door.'

'That's fine,' Sarah said sitting down on it. It was hard but had great soft square pillows. The room had brilliantly flowered wallpaper, and yet another exotic design on the bedspread, and the two chairs were covered with bright red and blue cushions. Whatever else could be said about it, it was certainly colourful.

'I say, your English is good,' she said admiringly to Nicole. 'You have hardly any accent.'

'That's because I am half English,' Nicole explained. 'My mother is English, my father French – he works over here, or has done for six years.'

'Do you work for Mme Lisette?'

‘Of course,’ Nicole said. ‘I have been with her for four years, since I was sixteen.’

‘Four years!’

‘But I have only about another six months to do, then I go back to England, for my parents’ time in Lyon is up then – my father works for a French newspaper – and I don’t think about it, because it makes me so miserable to think of going back to London.’

She jumped up suddenly. ‘Sorry, I’m not doing my job. This is your cupboard, I have my own, they are small, but then if you are anything like me you cannot afford many clothes. We share a bathroom on this floor – with others, of course – it is not very nice, but we are lucky to have one at all – the French are not madly keen on bathrooms, you know. There is a basin though, in this cupboard over here – cold water, of course,’ and she opened a cupboard door.

‘Oh, that’s a good idea.’

‘And sometimes the water is not good, so don’t drink it – whatever you do,’ and she pulled a face.

‘I’ll remember.’

‘And this chest of drawers we will have to share. You have the two top drawers and I’ll have the lower two.’

'Oh, that's nice of you – but why don't you–'

'The lower ones are bigger,' Nicole grinned.

Sarah thought she was going to like this girl.

'Now, you unpack; you don't seem to have brought a lot, and tidy yourself up and we will go back to Madame Lisette – OK?'

'It won't take me long, although I'd like a wash after that train journey.'

'Here, borrow my towel, you'll probably want to do a bit of shopping later on.'

'I've brought a small one,' Sarah said.

'Then I'll leave you to it,' Nicole said. 'No hurry,' and stretching herself full length on her bed, began to eat an apple, crunching it between her small white teeth...

Face washed, hair combed, Sarah brushed down her skirt, and stood staring out of the window.

'Sur les toits de Paris,' she said, humming the tune. 'That's about the only bit of French I know,' and turned to look at Nicole who was watching her. 'I can't believe that at last I am here, looking out over the roofs of Paris – it's like a dream come true.'

'This is the nice bit,' Nicole said. 'Wait

until we get back to the salon and the workrooms, you will really learn what hard work is!'

And together they began to walk down the long flight of stairs.

It was more than Sarah could have hoped for to find someone who spoke English so well. It had been one of her fears, and not only that, but Nicole seemed like a fun-loving girl, with an obvious sense of humour, judging by the twinkle in her eye. Sarah decided she was going to enjoy life in Paris.

They walked to the Rue Faubourg, and Sarah stood still, seeing the small blue enamelled name plate up on the wall, open-mouthed.

'Is this it?'

'It certainly is.' Nicole smiled. 'Impressive, isn't it?'

'And the salon is here?'

'Just across the road – see, the name above the doors – LISETTE?'

'Oh,' breathed Sarah. 'It's beautiful–'

'Of course,' said Nicole, taking her arm and crossing the road where a white-sleeved policeman, whistle in his mouth, had stopped the traffic. 'Of course we don't go in the front entrance, you can see that later, but further along, the back entrance, for staff,' she explained. 'Much the same as in London, eh?'

'Yes.' But Sarah had caught sight of the façade, the prestigious gold lettering, the gleaming glass windows, and a glimpse of a blonde mannequin wearing a beautifully tailored black evening suit, with trousers and a stunning white shirt, head tilted provocatively, and carrying a silver-topped cane and a top hat; she was the embodiment of all that Marlene Dietrich, the German film star, stood for.

'Ooh,' she breathed. This was style…

'Through here,' Nicole said, leading the way, and then they were at the back of the premises, in a large workroom where it seemed dozens of girls were working on one stage or another of dressmaking. There were drawing boards, and large tables, ironing boards, the lifelike models, and everywhere swathes of material, draped, hanging, a veritable maelstrom of colour.

Sarah couldn't have felt more at home.

'Wait here while I see if Mme Lisette is in her sanctum,' Nicole said, but no one seemed to be taking any notice of her, getting on with their work as if their lives depended on it, which they probably did,

Sarah thought.

Nicole returned after a few moments. 'This way,' she said. 'And don't look so worried, she's not going to eat you,' and Sarah smiled gratefully.

The room was small, and at the desk sat an elderly woman, older than Sarah had imagined, perhaps in her early seventies. She was small, slim and elegant, her grey hair drawn back from her brow, a small mobile face and dark eyes, and she wore spectacles hanging from a wide black ribbon.

'Ah, Sarah Roberts – welcome to Paris. 'Ow do you do, my dear?' and held out her hand.

She spoke good English, heavily accented, and Sarah felt drawn to her. This was nothing like the ogre she had imagined, but something told her this woman would not suffer fools gladly.

'Sit down,' Madame said. 'I want to have a little talk with you. I want you to tell me about your previous place or employment, what experience you have had, although I have already spoken to M. Gallen, whom I knew a little before he went to London.'

Sarah was pleased; there was nothing like coming with a good reference.

'And Lady Drummond, of course – we are old friends, I knew her when she was a little girl, and her parents. So if you are prepared to work hard, my dear, this could be a great opportunity for you. Of course, as a beginner you will not earn much, but it will be sufficient for your needs. Your room is free, and your expenses small…'

She put on her glasses and studied Sarah closely. 'Stand up,' she said, and when Sarah did so, 'and turn around–

'Did you make your costume?' she asked.

'Oui, Madame.'

'And you have not much French, I understand.'

'No, Madame, I am sorry.'

'That is soon remedied. One afternoon a week you will attend French speaking classes, and I suggest you attend evening classes two or three times a week; Nicole will tell you about them later – but it is important to understand French even if you do not speak it well. You're training will be wasted otherwise.'

'I shall look forward to it,' Sarah said. 'I have always wanted to speak French. I got used to hearing it at Monsieur Gallen's.'

'But Monsieur Gallen does not speak the French of Paris,' Mme Lisette said with the faintest criticism. 'He is from the south.'

That's understandable, Sarah thought. Like Cockneys and people from the North at home – sometimes they couldn't understand each other.

'Yes, Mme Lisette,' she said.

'Now you have seen your room, and presently I will ask Gaby to take you round the workrooms and introduce you to everyone. Gaby is my personal assistant; she has been with me many years,' and she rang the little bell on her desk.

There was a knock on the door, and a middle-aged Frenchwoman came in who nodded to Sarah in greeting.

'*Bonjour*, Mademoiselle.'

'*Bonjour*,' Sarah smiled, anxious to be friends with everyone.

'Gaby, this is Sarah Roberts, who is coming to work with us. Take her into the workrooms and introduce her and show her around. Bring her back here when you have finished.'

'*Oui*, Madame.'

There followed for Sarah a most illuminating tour of the premises at the end of which she knew that what she was doing was the right thing for her. Lady Freddie's offer had been too wonderful not to accept.

She felt totally at home.

She settled in to the workrooms with few problems, except that of language. The House of Gallen, being French, had stood her in good stead when it came to the basics of haute couture, and of course in Paris, nothing but the highest standards prevailed. It was soon discovered how well she could draw, a few rapid sketches creating a figure in a model gown or an outfit were sufficient to show Madame Lisette that here indeed was an artist. A girl after her own heart, and she was reminded of herself when young. Such enthusiasm!

She learned fast because she was absorbed. About the history of French couture, how in the nineteenth century there were high-class dressmakers for the upper classes and royalty who copied styles of the rich and famous using Spitalfields silk or French lace, but they never originated the styles.

'It was a fellow-countryman of yours who started it all,' Mme Lisette explained. 'He came from Yorkshire, a man named Frederick Worth, he had worked in Paris and set up his own design and dressmaking business here in the mid eighteen-fifties, and instead of copying what was the fashion of the day by sending sketches and fabric swatches to his clients, he produced a collection of made-up samples which were shown on live models to individuals or small selected groups. This idea was a sensation, because clients could imagine themselves wearing the clothes that the models wore, so it was an outstanding success – and that,' Mme Lisette concluded, 'is how the fashion shows started.'

Well! Sarah absorbed it all. Flung in at the deep end as it were, she soon discovered that her time with M. Gallen had paid off and stood her in good stead.

After a few weeks, Sarah was used to the idea of leaving home with Nicole early in the morning, and working through the day, shopping in the evenings at the cheap little shops that abounded down the side streets, getting to know Paris; at weekends, strolling along the boulevards and into the Louvre, round the museums, absorbing French culture to her very utmost.

She was completely unaware of the outside world, of the German invasion of Czechoslovakia, of Chamberlain's return to London from Munich waving his little bit of paper, of the threat of the Nazi hordes from

Germany on the very doorstep of France. People were always talking about another war, and she paid scant attention to war scares. More interesting was what the other designers were doing, like Schiaparelli, who had opened a couture boutique on the Plâce Vendôme selling sweaters, jewellery and scarves. Everyone who was anyone, it was said, was dressed by Schiaparelli that year, and Madame Chanel, everyone's favourite for so long, and whose last collection had not been such a success. Sarah lived in the world of haute couture.

She was always pleased though to receive letters from Robbie, and wrote home every week. First Lodge and the Berkshire countryside seemed a long way off now, but she looked forward to going home at Christmas and as the days grew shorter began to think more about buying Christmas presents for the family.

In early December the weather was cold and frosty and by night the city of Paris had never looked more beautiful.

Nicole came home one Sunday evening from seeing her parents for the weekend. They lived in Lyon, and it appeared that her French cousin Pierre was coming to Paris the following weekend, bringing a friend, and he suggested that Nicole and Sarah might like to join them for a night out on the town. Both worked in Lyon in a law firm, Pierre being twenty-three and his friend Louis twenty-two.

Both girls were excited at the proposed visit, dressing themselves up for the occasion and meeting the two young men on the Left Bank of the Seine at a designated restaurant.

The haunting strains of French music, the accordion, the girl singing in the husky voice, was something Sarah knew she would never forget. When the young men arrived, she was instinctively drawn to Pierre, while Nicole seemed quite pleased with Louis, who was fair with blue eyes and a roguish smile.

Pierre was quieter and seemed fascinated by the fact that Sarah was English. He had never, he said, taken an English girl out before for you couldn't count Nicole, who was his cousin, related to him on his father's side.

That explained, they got on like a house on fire, with English and French being spoken and laughed at, while the food at the restaurant was excellent. Later they walked along the Seine until quite late at night, promising to meet the next day, which was Sunday, to explore Paris.

It was a fine winter's day as they walked and discovered more about the Left Bank, the artists' quarter, the Eiffel Tower, stopping for onion soup in the old French flower market, then seeing the Place de l'Opéra before going back with Pierre and Louis to the station where they would catch a train for Lyon.

At the station, Pierre took Sarah's gloved hand in his, dark eyes looking into hers.

'I have enjoyed this weekend – we must do it again,' he said.

'I should like that,' Sarah said, knowing she was more moved by this young man than she had expected to be.

'So you will go home to England for Christmas?' he asked.

'Yes, I am looking forward to that.'

'And after that – who knows?' he said. 'Who knows what the New Year will bring? Do they worry in England about the war?'

Sarah frowned. 'The war?' she said genuinely puzzled.

'Well, the situation is not good,' he said. 'For France anyway, and for the rest of the world, maybe. If there is war we shall have to go, Louis and myself–'

'Oh, but there won't be a war,' Sarah cried. 'Of course not – they are just ugly rumours–'

'I wish I could agree with you,' Pierre said. 'But we must not leave on such a sad note. Perhaps in the New Year–'

'That would be nice,' Sarah said, and he took her hand to his lips and, pushing the glove back from her wrist, kissed it.

So French! Sarah thought, sighing blissfully. To have one's wrist kissed by a Frenchman…

'Bonsoir,' she said, 'Pierre.'

'Au revoir,' he said as they went for the train. The girls waited until the train moved away, the two men waving at the window.

Nicole took Sarah's arm. 'What do you think? Nice, isn't he?'

Sarah found herself blushing.

'Yes,' she said. 'Did you like Louis?'

'Yes, I did – he is so funny – Pierre is more serious, isn't he?'

'Yes, I suppose so,' Sarah said thoughtfully. After all, he talked about a coming war – and she shivered.

There had better not be. She had been born during one war – that was quite enough for one lifetime…

Chapter Nine

Robbie's kitchen in First Lodge had a festive air. Not surprisingly, for the smell of mincemeat tarts and pastry filled the room, the larder was full of Christmas puddings awaiting distribution at the Parish Hall – it just needed the arrival of Sarah from Paris to complete the picture.

She was arriving home that day, and Tom even now was waiting for her down at the station with the pony and trap.

Robbie patted her hair as she had done every five minutes, glancing in the mirror to see she was spick and span – it had been so long since she had seen her beloved daughter. There was so much news she had to give her and she wanted to hear all that Sarah had to say. Would she have changed much? Everyone said she would – Laurie even laughed and sang the old wartime song: 'How're gonna keep her down on the farm, after she's seen Paree?' But Sarah would always be Sarah … and Robbie's hand flew to her throat as she heard the clip-clop of the pony as the trap turned into the drive.

She hurried to the front door, and there was Sarah – and Robbie was so excited she thought she would burst.

'Sarah!' They hugged each other, unashamedly tearful. 'Oh, you look wonderful! So do you!' And Tom stood by watching, a lump in his throat, seeing his wife and his daughter and realising how much they meant to him.

Sarah took off her hat, and hugged Robbie again. 'Oh, I've missed you all, and it smells so good to be back – really Christmassy–'

She was beautiful, Robbie thought. So elegant, smart, just how you would imagine a Frenchwoman to look, she was so proud of her, her daughter … and she gave a great sigh. It was wonderful to have her home again.

Sarah's eyes flew to the mantelpiece where the Christmas cards sat, and she smiled when she saw the figure of the little Blue Girl, then went over and touched her cheek gently. 'Still here, then,' she said, and then it was teatime; Robbie cut some cake, and Sarah laughed.

'We don't have cakes like that in France,' she said.

'What do they have then?' Robbie asked suspiciously.

'Well, light confections, little pastries – you buy them at a patisserie.'

'I make the best cakes ever,' Robbie said. 'Don't I, Tom?'

'You do, Edie,' he said. 'Your mother has won prizes for her cakes.'

Sarah hugged her. 'I don't mean that,' she laughed. 'Of course you do – no one makes cakes like you, I meant French cakes are different, they make good tarts, and small pastries–'

'You mean like those French fancies they sell in Lyon's?' Robbie asked.

Sarah laughed. 'No – well, some are, but they are rich, and full of cream and nuts, that sort of thing, frothy–'

'So you've been on a rich diet, then,' Robbie teased. 'You don't seem to have put on much weight.'

'The food is different,' Sarah agreed. 'But I am really looking forward to Christmas dinner. Is it to be goose or turkey this year?'

'Turkey,' Robbie said. 'Ginny's father–' and stopped. 'Look, let's clear away, and then you can tell us all about Paris, and I'll give you our news.'

'It sounds as if you have lots to tell me,'

Sarah said, eyes twinkling. 'Let's wash up first, shall we, then I'll show you what I've brought you.'

'Oh, not until Christmas morning,' Robbie cried.

'Not Christmas presents,' Sarah said. 'I've brought you some bits and bobs from Paris – French things–'

They huddled round the table while the fire cast shadows round the large kitchen, talking nineteen to the dozen and exchanging news.

'Well, I'll be going up then,' Tom said around nine o'clock. 'It's been a long day.'

And an exciting one, Robbie thought, eyeing him swiftly. He was always up early and needed his sleep. She knew his leg was paining him but he never would have said.

'Good-night, Dad,' Sarah said, lifting her face for his kiss. 'I've missed that,' she said.

'It's grand to have you home,' he said gruffly.

'I'll lock up, Tom,' Robbie reassured him.

'How is he – really?' Sarah asked anxiously.

'Fairly well, except that I think he is in considerable pain with his leg, and it's unfortunate that his work is outside in all weathers.'

'Yes, that can't help,' Sarah said. 'How long is it before he retires?'

'Oh, don't,' Robbie cried. 'We're just so thankful that he has a job – although with the threat of war hanging over us there are more jobs in factories now–'

Sarah was horrified. 'Not you, too,' she cried. 'You can't seriously believe that there will be another war!'

'I'm only going by the signs and what people say; do you know a lot of children have been evacuated already, just in case, and they are putting Anderson shelters in the gardens in London. I know because Mrs Branston, who moved to Tottenham, told me in a letter – and they are going to issue us with gas masks and the children too – can you believe it?'

Sarah could see she was genuinely worried. 'What do the boys say?'

'They think it's on the cards. In fact Donnie thought you shouldn't go back to Paris–' and saw the look on Sarah's face.

'You really are serious about it, aren't you?'

She was genuinely shocked, wondering why she knew so little about it; she had been so immersed in her work that she couldn't absorb what the papers and the people were talking about, and recalled many occasions when the talk had been of war, and she had ignored it all.

'Golly,' she said at length, serious for once.

'And after all, France is probably where it would all begin, they had it worst last time–'

'Mum, you've got yourself into a tizzy over it – now promise – no more about war while I'm home, eh? I'm going to enjoy this break – I only have six days – and it's not like you to worry about things before they happen.'

Robbie felt guilty. 'You're right – I have let it get on top of me. Sometimes it seems only yesterday that the last one finished.'

'Now, tell me about the boys. How are they?'

Robbie looked happier now and embarked on her news.

'Well, Hilda is pregnant again; she wants a little girl this time, so I hope she gets it – and the little boy, young Tommy – he is a lovely baby, laughs all the time, just like Laurie used to, and she keeps him so nicely, knits all his clothes and still brings him over in the pram every Wednesday. I really look forward to that.'

'What are they doing for Christmas?'

'Coming here, of course!' Robbie said. 'We're going to have a real family Christmas.'

Sarah's dark eyes shone. 'And what about Donnie and Ginny?'

'They're fine. Doing so well at their work, and you'll never guess? They're buying a house!'

Such a thing had never been known in the family.

'No! But how can they afford it?'

'Well, they are both working – no family, you see, and this house is on a new estate being built out towards Newbury way. Four hundred and twenty-five they are, ten and fivepence weekly, with a nice little garden and new kitchen and a bathroom. I must say it sounds lovely. Fifty pounds deposit, 'course Ginny says they would have liked one of the dearer ones – detached, but I said all in good time. This is a start – I'm so proud of them.'

And she looked it.

'Ginny's Mum and Dad are giving us the turkey for Christmas – then they are coming over Boxing Day. Now, you've let me go on and I haven't heard anything yet about how you are getting on with your work and how much you like Paris – although I must say judging by your letters, you seem to be enjoying it.'

'Oh, Mum, I am! I love it, everything

about it, France, Paris, the work. I can't thank Lady Freddie enough for giving me the opportunity to go there. Imagine, if we hadn't known her, I might never have had the chance!'

But Robbie had got up to go to the dresser for the key to the front door, and busied herself locking it.

'Yes, well,' she said. 'I am sure she will be pleased that you are enjoying it so much. Did you write to her?'

'Yes, when I got there. I told her how much I liked it and thanked her – I never heard–'

'No, well, you wouldn't,' Robbie said, sitting down again. 'So this Madame – Lisette – is it? What's she like?

'Well…' and Sarah waded in, glad of the opportunity to talk about it all, her work, how she lived, where they lived, she and Nicole – French food – prices – and Robbie made more tea until she glanced at the clock, and saw that it was just gone eleven.

'Come on, my girl,' she said. 'Time for bed. You must be whacked after the day you've had. Now get along upstairs, and sleep well and I'll see you in the morning – there's a hot water bottle in your bed.'

Sarah flung her arms around her mother.

'I've missed you,' she said. 'It's so nice to be home–' and thought as she went upstairs that she hadn't mentioned Pierre.

Well, there was plenty of time the next day.

At first, she had no idea where she was, waking up in her old room without that particular French smell that pervaded everything in France. Instead, she heard the crow of the cockerels and the sound of the farm tractor going over Bottom Field; she stretched luxuriously as she realised she had a few days' holiday – no work for five more days…

In the morning they went to the market. Tom drove them in order to carry the Christmas puddings to the Parish Hall, there were last-minute presents to buy and extra food, and going around the shops Robbie was so proud of this smart pretty daughter who seemed to attract quite a lot of attention.

'Sarah! Home from Paris!' That seemed to be the general greeting accompanied by a swift glance at her clothes and her general appearance. Truth to tell, she did look a little out of place in Allington market, Robbie thought. But everyone was pleased to see her, and there were invitations to call in for a Christmas sherry if she had time or a cup of tea and a slice of Christmas cake.

'I'd forgotten how friendly everyone is in the country,' Sarah said.

'Are they different in Paris?'

'Well, it's a city, Mum, like London – it's the same up there – people are always rushing about, too busy to take time off to say hallo sometimes.'

'I wouldn't like that,' Robbie said.

Then it was home again, and teatime, and the postman had been while they were out, bringing more Christmas cards with two for Sarah.

She opened the unknown one first. It was from her co-workers in the House of Gallen; before she opened the next one, the blush on her cheeks betraying the fact that she knew who it was from, Robbie busied herself with riddling the ashes and emptying coal on the fire from the hod. No need to wonder who that was from – was it a letter or a card?

Sarah crumpled the envelope and stood the card on the mantelpiece.

'It's from David,' she said. 'David Drummond,' as if any explanation were necessary. Robbie glanced at it, a pretty card with Christmas robins and holly. She would read what it said inside later. Sarah seemed to be making no secret of it.

'That's nice,' she said. That evening before bedtime she opened the card. It read simply, HAPPY CHRISTMAS, with love and best wishes from David…

Love, Robbie thought…

Christmas morning dawned bright and cold and clear. Robbie had been up since dawn preparing the turkey and the stuffing and Sarah put in an early appearance to lay the table in the large dining room which was seldom used. It was a combined sitting and dining room with a sofa and easy chairs, but as a general rule it was used for special occasions, everyone in the family normally much preferring the kitchen.

There was a Christmas cracker at each place setting on a snowy white cloth, table decorations made by the Women's Institute, of which Robbie was an enthusiastic member. She had brought out the old Christmas paper chains to hang over the fireplace and from the ceiling – they would give baby Tommy a Christmas to remember – while holly and mistletoe hung from the rafters and Tom stoked the fire with logs which blazed causing him to extricate the fireguard from its hiding place, and he found the bottle of port he kept hidden in the cellar for high days and holidays. It was always a family joke when Robbie had her annual Christmas drink of port and lemon.

Everything under way in the dining room, Sarah went back to the kitchen to give Robbie a hand, but everything seemed to be organised. She fingered the little blue girl's china cheek, smiling to herself, before turning round to see Robbie pulling aside the curtain at the kitchen window.

'What are they doing up at the Hall for Christmas?' she asked.

'Away, I think, her Ladyship said they would probably spend Christmas in London.'

'By the way,' Sarah said idly, and apropos of nothing. 'I met a nice boy – well, a young man–' and saw that Robbie was looking at her, surprised, but pleasantly so.

'French, I suppose–' she said, but not in a critical way.

'Yes. He is a cousin of Nicole's; he lives and works in Lyon studying law. He and a friend came to Paris for the weekend and the four of us went to dinner at a restaurant and then explored Paris – it was lovely.'

And Robbie saw that her eyes sparkled at

the remembrance of it.

'What's his name? How old is he?'

'His name is Pierre, and he is twenty-three, but don't read more than that into it, Mum,' and she smiled. 'It was he who talked about the war and said how he'd have to go if war broke out.'

'Well, yes, he would, one of the first, I expect. Still, let's hope it won't come to pass – and I expect you will meet a lot of nice young men out there.'

But it occupied a lot of her mind while she waited for her guests – the best thing that could happen, she thought, that Sarah would get keen on another young man, but not French – that might mean–

She put it out of her mind as Laurie and Hilda and baby Tommy arrived. Hugging his sister as if she had been away for years, he laughed and cracked jokes, while Hilda stood shyly by holding the baby.

'May I?' Sarah asked, holding out her arms.

And Hilda put little Tommy into them where he opened his big blue eyes wide and stared at Sarah, then slowly began to smile, showing new baby teeth.

'Oh, he's lovely!' Sarah cried. He looked just like Laurie, but she was not going to say so. 'Oh, Hilda, aren't you lucky!'

Hilda smiled, showing her broken front tooth, and Sarah wondered why Laurie didn't consider that she would look a lot better if the tooth was seen to. But no one seemed to mind the broken tooth. Laurie from time to time threw loving glances in her direction as though to give her courage, and Sarah had a thought that plainness grew on you. Once you got used to a plain person's looks you began to see beauty, while sometimes a beautiful person's looks began to pall–

And here am I philosophising, she thought, on Christmas Day of all days – and wondered what Pierre was doing–

Then Donnie and Ginny arrived, armed with parcels, both looking fine like a very well-established married couple. There were hugs and kisses and presently Tom handed round the port while they opened the presents from beneath the brightly lit Christmas tree.

Robbie thought they had never had such a wonderful Christmas dinner with the whole family complete.

Oh, if it could always be like this!

Then they cracked nuts and opened boxes of sweets which no one really wanted, until it was time for them all to go home with promises from Donnie and Ginny to bring Ginny's parents on Boxing Day.

'I'd say that was the best Christmas we ever had, wouldn't you?' Sarah asked, one arm round Robbie's shoulder.

'I am a very lucky woman,' Robbie said, and meant it.

It was the morning after Boxing Day, the day before Sarah was due to return to France, that the telephone rang and a man's voice asked for Sarah.

Robbie thought quickly – she was sure it was David – but knew she couldn't in all honesty say Sarah was not there.

'Hold on, I'll get her–' and she called up the stairs.

'Telephone for you, Sarah.'

'Me? Who is it?' but Robbie either didn't hear or wouldn't answer.

'Hallo, Sarah Rob–' but knew in a flash who it was.

'David! How are you? Where are you?'

Robbie walked into the dining room, she didn't want to hear any more. Oh, why couldn't he leave them alone?

'Did you have a good Christmas?'

'Wonderful! Where did you spend it?'

'In London mainly, in Edwardes Square – that's where I am now.'

'Oh–'

'Sarah, I'd love to see you, is there any chance you could come up to town?'

Sarah frowned. 'Oh, David, I go back to Paris tomorrow.'

'Well, I can't get down, I'm due back at the base tomorrow. I just thought if we could meet – I'd love to see you – for lunch?'

'Well, it's my last day with the family–'

'Right then, if I catch the eleven-forty train, I could be down at the Lodge–'

The hall was probably closed down, Sarah thought, and had the feeling that Robbie wouldn't be best pleased after the excitement of the last two days.

'No. Look...'

'If I don't see you this time heaven knows when you'll be home again,' he grumbled.

'Easter,' she smiled. 'It'll come round soon enough.' Meanwhile she was thinking, I could be in town in an hour, and it would be nice to see London again, and David – I could be home by four.

'Look, David, I'll come up,' she said.

'You will?' He sounded wildly happy.

'Yes. Just for a short time, but I must be home early. I'll be there at lunch time –

perhaps we could have something to eat near the station, say around twelve, twelve-thirty–'

'I'll be there,' he said. 'Take care.'

'Sarah, you can't!' Robbie cried, when she told her of her plans. 'Today – but you go back tomorrow – oh Sarah!'

'Mum, I won't be that long, home again by four, but it would be lovely to see David again and he was so anxious for us to meet.'

I'll bet he was, Robbie thought grimly. Oh, why can't he leave her alone – she couldn't forbid her to go…

'Don't be cross with me,' Sarah said, dashing upstairs to get ready. 'I won't be long, really–'

Was she keen on him? Robbie asked herself. How could she stop her from going? Milady would be furious if she knew, and guessed she had no idea. Oh, what a mess. Now, here Sarah was, beret perched on her short dark hair, raincoat over her arm, looking as lovely as she ever would. Of course he was in love with her, and wouldn't Tom be cross too, when he came in…

'Bye, Mum–' and she was gone, her high heels clacking down the path.

I'm sorry, Milady, she said to herself. But what could I do?

When Sarah got off the train, the first person she saw was David, and he was in Royal Air Force uniform, so tall and handsome.

'Oh, David!'

'Sarah!' He threw his arms round her and hugged her tightly.

'Thank you for coming! You look wonderful!'

'So do you. What's the uniform? I didn't know–'

'I wrote to you telling you I had joined the RAF.'

'I thought it was some kind of reserve, I didn't realise you meant the actual Air Force.'

'Well, it was what I wanted to do, and Mother seemed to go along with it, at least she didn't object. If anything it was Dad who was disappointed at my not joining the firm.'

'You are a nutcase, David! Well, where shall we go? I can't stay long.'

'I noticed a little café over there that's open. I just had to see you–'

He took her arm and led her across the road to the small café, steering her to a corner seat in a booth.

'How long have you got?' he asked.

'Well, I'd like to be home around four, which means catching a train soon after three – but we've time for a chat.'

'Right; let's order then. Oh, it's good to see you!'

Sarah looked across the table at him – why did she always feel she was coming home when she saw David? Even Pierre paled now she was beside David – he was so dear to her, she felt completely at home with him, those lovely blue eyes looking so earnestly into hers, and when he slid his hand across the table to take her hand in his, she knew she wanted to be close to David more than anyone else in the world...

Nothing mattered but the two of them...

Chapter Ten

Back in Paris for the New Year, Sarah got down to work. She was kept busy designing for the autumn show, for the Paris spring and summer shows were well under way. More and more she was being called on to come up with new designs, since that seemed to be her particular forte. The one dark cloud on the horizon was the sense of coming disaster, with the newspapers reporting that the Maginot Line so long held to be a bulwark against the Germans was nothing but a joke, that the French politicians were all too old to know what they were doing.

Paris was held in the grip of winter that first few weeks, and it was all the girls could do to keep warm, for there was no heating in their room and sometimes they huddled under blankets and read fashion magazines, or with scarves wrapped round them against the chilly winds ventured to the local smoke-filled café which was always warm, and full of lively chatter.

Madame Lisette suffered a bad bout of flu that winter, and took some time to recover. When she did come back to the workrooms they could see she must have been quite ill, for she looked a lot older.

She complimented Sarah, though, on her first day back, having been shown the new designs with which she was thoroughly impressed.

'I love those new width trousers and jackets, the edge-to-edge coats and the fur-lined matching cravats, my dear. I am very pleased with you.'

Sarah was delighted; to have her designs approved by Madame Lisette was praise indeed.

A few weeks later, she asked Sarah to lunch with her in her apartment.

'I have been waiting to see how you would settle down, but now I observe that you seem quite at home with us,' she said. 'Come on Sunday next, around twelve, then there will be time for an aperitif, and we shall eat lunch prepared by my faithful Hortense, who like Gaby has been with me for such a long time. It is Apartment Six – you know where it is…'

'Oui, Madame – merci, Madame.'

Sarah's French had improved enormously since she had arrived. She had a natural aptitude for the language, and had been helped greatly by Nicole in her pronunciation as well as attending French classes three times a week.

She was tremendously excited at the thought of going to Madame's apartment, which Nicole had told her was sumptuous, and the moment she set foot inside the double doors she knew that Nicole had not exaggerated.

The apartment was huge, filled with

antiques and wonderful carpets and paintings, large enough to house life-size figures and there were flowers everywhere. The scent from the mimosa and carnations filled the room, and Sarah drew a deep breath.

'They are lovely, are they not?' Madame asked. 'The flowers are from my son – he sent them for my birthday.'

'Oh, Madame – I had no idea–'

'Why should you?' Madame Lisette asked. 'And I will not tell you which birthday it was – I have given up counting. Now come through and take off your coat – Hortense will show you where.'

'Bonjour, Mademoiselle.' Hortense, like most French women Sarah had met, was not given to smiling easily. Very straight-faced, but polite, she took Sarah's coat and hat, hung them up, and led her back to the drawing room. The room had a beautiful rose-coloured wallpaper, and the great heavy curtains were of matching silk, swagged and tied back over draped French voile which covered the windows. The fireplace was of grey marble and there were deep chairs of rose silk and two French sofas covered in a paler silk while the ornate gilt mirrors reflected the splendour of the room.

Sarah had never seen such a beautiful room in her life – imagine it being your home! Such luxury – such taste – there was nothing up at Kirby Hall like this!

'Now sit down, and try this,' Madame Lisette said, handing her a small glass filled with a colourless liquid. On the tray were tiny biscuits and she held out the dish. 'Try one,' she said.

Sarah tasted the small confection and sipped the drink, which turned out to be sweet and burned her throat as she swallowed.

'Oh,' she gulped.

'I can see you are not used to our French ways,' smiled Madame Lisette. 'Now,' and she sat opposite Sarah on the pink curvy sofa. 'Tell me about your home. You live on Lady Drummond's estate – with your parents?'

'Yes, Madame.'

'Have you brothers and sisters?'

'Yes, two brothers: they are both married. One of them, Laurie, has a baby son.'

'Ah, so your mother is a grandmother–' and she looked across at the small table where sat several photographs in ornate silver frames.

'I had a granddaughter, but sadly she died

– she was only two years old.'

'Oh, I am sorry,' Sarah began.

'It was a long time ago. She died together with my daughter-in-law, my son's wife. They were both so ill, it was a terrible influenza epidemic. If she had lived she would be a similar age to you, but it was not to be.'

She turned to the table again, to the largest picture there. It was of a handsome, dark-haired man with smiling eyes.

'That is my son, Gerard,' she said. 'He is a colonel in the army, stationed in Algiers. He never married again, much to my sorrow.'

She turned back to Sarah. 'But I must not make you sad with my history; tell me about Lady Drummond, how is she? Do you see much of her?'

'Not really,' Sarah admitted. 'Hardly ever after I left school and started to work in London.'

'She was a beautiful little girl,' Madame Lisette said. 'I was really quite jealous – I would have loved a daughter – but she and Gerard got on very well, they were about the same age, and our families spent many happy holidays together in Provence.' She sighed. 'No one is there now except a housekeeper. I have not visited it since last year – although, I have to say we may yet find it very useful if there is a war–' and her face looked grim. 'What are they saying in London? Did you find much talk of war when you went home at Christmas?'

'Yes,' Sarah had to admit. 'There was some talk, much the same as here, preparations certainly seem to be going ahead – but I think that is just a safety measure – just in case–'

'Do you now?' and Madame Lisette smiled. 'Are you perhaps an ostrich to keep your head in the sand? Or a born optimist?' She gave Sarah a gentle tap under the chin. 'Come along, let us see how lunch is progressing.'

The rest of the day passed pleasantly enough, and after that an early spring arrived while the talk of war grew ever stronger. Added to that was the departure date set for Nicole who was leaving Madame Lisette's establishment to return to London with her parents. Sarah could not envisage life in Paris without her, but before that happened, the two young men, Pierre and Louis, came to Paris to wish Nicole farewell.

Sarah was pleased to see Pierre again, but

not too pleased to hear his news: that he was to go into the army at the end of June if not before, depending on the war situation.

'Oh, I can't believe it!' she cried. 'I think Madame Lisette was right when she said I must be an ostrich – I really didn't think it would come to pass.'

'Well, it has not happened yet,' smiled Pierre. 'And we pray that it won't, but all Frenchmen are on call, and I am in the reserve, so there it is.'

'Well, let us enjoy ourselves while we may,' said Sarah. 'I am feeling particularly down because Nicole is going away – I don't know what I shall do without her.'

'What will you do if there is war?' Pierre asked seriously, and Sarah's first thought was of David.

'Go home, I suppose; I could hardly stay in Paris. Still, let's not talk about it.'

They relived their previous weekend, and Sarah knew by the end of it that Pierre wanted to continue their friendship, whatever happened. She liked him, enormously, he was handsome, and charming, gentle, clever, too, but the spark was missing. That something that bound her to David, and she thought of the possible war and David flying up there in the clouds in his fighter plane –

and knew that there was nowhere else on earth where he would rather be. She shivered slightly.

'Are you cold?' Pierre asked her, concerned.

'No, just a shiver; do you think we should start back now for your train?'

Nicole and Louis had gone their separate ways on this Sunday, so Sarah and Pierre made their way together to the station.

While they waited for the others they stood talking, and Pierre looked down into Sarah's eyes, lifted to his, those dark brown eyes which had the power to move him so deeply.

'Sarah, you will write to me – promise?'

'Of course,' she said. 'We must not lose touch,' and wondered if she was being unfair. Suddenly he bent and kissed her on the lips swiftly, and startled, she backed away.

'I am sorry,' he was hasty in his apology, 'but I simply could not resist you–' and she had to smile. 'That is to – seal? – our friendship, *n'est-ce pas?*'

She might never see him again, Sarah thought. Who knew what the future would bring?

And then they were joined by Nicole and Louis, and there were more farewells. They waited once again until the train pulled out of the station, then walked slowly back home.

Nicole linked her arm with Sarah's.

'Pierre has got a pash on you,' she laughed.

Sarah blushed. 'Oh, don't be sil–'

'He has! Louis told me, got it bad, Louis said.'

Sarah had no answer to that, just hoped she hadn't led him up the garden path. On the other hand, she did quite like him...

Easter was late that year, and Sarah went back home to England for the Easter break. The countryside looked wonderful, there were primroses in the hedges and the unusual warm spell had brought everything out earlier than usual.

It was lovely to be home again, such a different life, and on Easter Saturday she and Robbie took a trip to London.

Sarah was astonished to see the sandbags outside offices and shops – the precautions being taken everywhere. On the train journey she could see evidence of Anderson shelters being put up, ugly grey corrugated iron things – an insult to the landscape. In towns, air raid shelters were being dug too –

everyone seemed to be intent on barricading their premises.

'Not only that,' Robbie said grimly, 'but we have our gas masks. I've got one for you too; we had to put down how many people lived in the house, so–'

Sarah was shocked; as each day went by now, she realised that not only was a war possible, but it was almost inevitable.

'I did wonder,' Robbie said slowly, 'if perhaps it might be better for you to call a halt to your time with Madame Lisette. After all, if there is a war, I wouldn't want you to be stuck in France.'

'Oh, let's wait until it happens, Mum!' Sarah cried. 'It is so depressing to be always talking about a war.'

'War is depressing, and a lot more besides,' Robbie said grimly. 'Still, you are quite right,' knowing she had lost the issue, that there was no way Sarah would give up her work in Paris unless she absolutely had to.

It was after lunch on Easter Monday when the doorbell rang, and answering it, Robbie saw with a shock that it was David, smiling at her.

'Hallo, Robbie, surprised eh? Well, I'm home for the day and thought I would give

Sarah a call; is she in?'

Robbie's heart plummeted. What could she do? What could she say? Pretend Sarah was out when any moment she would come down the stairs in full view–

'Yes, David – somewhere about – I'll call her. Come in won't you?'

There was no doubt about the pleasure each of them felt on seeing each other, or of David's feelings about her, which were there for all the world to see. Even Sarah, whose dark eyes sparkled back at him looked as though her dreams had come true.

'David–'

Robbie felt like weeping. Oh, Milady! Who would have thought it would come to this? But she pulled herself together.

'Would you like tea, David?'

'No, thank you, Robbie, I thought Sarah and I might go for a walk – it's cold, but such a nice day.'

'Yes, I'll get my coat,' Sarah said.

'I have to go back tomorrow,' she said as she came back into the room.

'And I am due back tonight,' and David made a face. 'Still, we must make the most of it; I am so glad I found you at home.'

They walked up the hill towards the Home Farm.

'And are you still enjoying Paris?' he asked.

'I love it,' Sarah said. 'And what about you?'

'I've never been so busy. It's building up, you know–'

No need to ask what he meant.

'Oh, David!' she said softly.

''Fraid so – that's why I'm glad I am already there in position, as it were.'

'How can you say that?' she asked him. 'Ready to do battle with those awful Germans, and everyone says we haven't enough planes – nor men and tanks and things.'

'Well, I don't know about the army, but we've some wonderful fighter planes, and some rattling good men to fly them.'

'Oh, David, I am sure we have, but not enough, I hear, we are hopelessly outnumbered. What are the chances of beating that mighty Nazi machine? It's all I hear in France, the Germans, the Germans – it's as if they were God himself!'

David laughed. 'Well, you know by now what the French are like – hot-headed, they dramatise everything – it's in the nature of the beast.'

'David, you're just trying to cheer me up –

but seriously, I hate wars.'

He took her hand in his. 'Let's not talk about it. Tell me about Madame Lisette; I've never met her, but apparently our families used to be friends, and Ma says she is a fantastic woman.'

'She is,' Sarah said. 'Apart from being my employer, I like her enormously, and she is very kind to me – I'm such a novice.'

'Still, you must be improving all the time, you were in London before that–'

'Oh, yes, I'm doing quite well, but of course the war has held things up. People are not ordering – oh, there I go again–'

He stood still, and looked down into her eyes, soft brown eyes that held such warmth for him. 'Sarah, I may be able to come to Paris for a day or so in the summer – shall we meet?'

'Oh, that would be wonderful,' Sarah said. 'Have you any idea when?'

'Not at the moment, but I'll give you good notice. June, July, probably.'

They walked on, David with his arm round Sarah's shoulders, Sarah happy for it to be there.

Before they reached First Lodge, in the shade of a newly burgeoning oak tree, he took her in his arms and kissed her. She closed her eyes and gave herself up to his kiss. How different it was from the brief kiss she had had from Pierre. She realised then how much she loved David, how much she had always loved him… Then hand in hand they walked back to the Lodge, and Robbie, looking behind the lace curtains for their arrival, was in no doubt about the strength of their feelings for each other. Her heart felt near to bursting. Oh, Sarah, Sarah…

She busied herself in the kitchen when Sarah came in, and, glancing across at the door, saw David turn and wave on his way up to the drive and the Hall.

Sarah closed the door and stood with her back against it, starry-eyed.

Thank God, she goes back to Paris tomorrow, Robbie thought, and I never thought to hear myself say that.

In the morning, bags packed, Sarah waited for Tom to bring the pony and trap around to take her to the station.

'Now, when will we see you again?' Robbie asked. 'Summer holidays?'

'Of course. I look forward to that,' Sarah said, 'two whole weeks, and when I return I shall have been one whole year with Madame Lisette.'

Time did fly, Robbie thought. That much was true…

'And don't forget it will be your twenty-first birthday in September: is there a chance you will be home for that?'

'Oh, I do hope so! I wouldn't miss that for the world. You see, all Paris closes down in August, so that's when I would be given my holidays, but I could come back for the weekend – it is only a question of the fare, after all, I am sure Madame Lisette would allow me to come–'

'Well, we'll see,' Robbie said, knowing that a lot of water would have to pass under the bridge before then.

As the weeks went by, it was obvious that business of all kinds was falling off. France was preparing for war, and Madame Lisette's order book was nowhere near as full as it had always been. She was forced to dismiss two of the seamstresses, fine workmanship and evening gowns were no longer the order of the day, and the fear everywhere was that France would be overrun by the German army. Despite all the talk by politicians, no one had any faith in them, they saw Germany as a threat on their own doorstep, powerful, determined and ready to walk in.

Any talk of Sarah's summer leave was cut short when Madame Lisette suffered a heart attack at the end of June.

All the staff rallied around her and while she was in hospital Gaby and Hortense between them saw to the running of the apartment and the business. Her illness could not have come at a worse time, when Lisette was having a special late spring and early summer fashion show, among the chosen outfits being two designs of Sarah's.

It had been exciting to see her sketches quite literally come to life on live models. She had gone in great excitement to the silk showrooms to choose the material Madame Lisette had herself suggested, and the fine wool barathea for the pale grey belted raincoat. There was a matching hat and scarf and the young model, hat tilted over one eye, belt pulled tightly round her tiny waist, drew applause from the crowd as she teetered along in her very high heels. Sarah was so excited, her cheeks flushed deliciously pink, dark eyes sparkling, as Madame Lisette, out from hospital and watching from her wheelchair discreetly placed out of view by Hortense, could see.

She had grown fond of this young girl

from England, had discovered early on that she was really talented; how sad that the timing was not right, that she had arrived on the scene just when things were looking at their blackest... But she must look on the bright side. The girl showed distinct promise, she was talented, no doubt about that. That sort of gift would stay with her always – just because she herself was old and ill, it was her duty to guide the girl into her future however bleak it looked at the moment.

She decided it had been a very good day for Madame Lisette when Lady Freddy recommended her.

In the middle of July, one Sunday morning, following a telephone call, Sarah found David waiting for her in the foyer, and her heart leapt when she saw him.

'David!'

'Sarah!' And she was in his arms, totally oblivious of the stares from obviously delighted French people who were passing through.

He stood her away from him and looked at her, drinking in everything about her, that lovely face – if only she could be his for always...

'Sarah darling, it is only to be the briefest visit, I am over here courtesy of the French government. We have been taking part in the Bastille Day celebrations together with our French allies.'

'Oh, how wonderful! Well, we must make the most of it. How long have you got?'

He glanced at his watch. 'Just two and a half hours, then it's back to Le Bourget.'

She took hold of his arm. 'Well, what shall it be? Lunch? A stroll in the Tuileries? The Champs-Elysées?'

'Let's just walk – isn't that what lovers do in Paris?'

Sarah's face was rosy red, her dark eyes dancing.

'Oh, it's lovely to see you! I can't believe you are here!'

'Well, I am!' and he held her arm tightly. 'And I never saw you look so beautiful!'

'And you!' she laughed. 'How proud I am to be seen with you – in your uniform – no wonder all the girls are looking at you!'

He looked down at her, his beloved Sarah, and wished that this moment might go on for ever…

By the Seine, and in the shadow of the Sacré Coeur, they stood as lovers have always done, cheek to cheek, heart to heart, and promised each other that it would always be like this – that no one would ever come between them. Wars might rage, hostile forces be encountered, there could be nothing that could break the bonds which held them together.

And then it seemed as if he had never been there – he was gone.

Chapter Eleven

When Gaby, Madame Lisette's chief assistant, asked for Sarah to report to her office, Sarah imagined it was to do with the date of her summer holidays. Everything had been thrown into confusion because of Madame's illness, and on top of that there was the lack of business owing to the threat of war and the shortage of orders coming in.

Madame Gaby looked very serious when Sarah presented herself.

'Mam'selle,' she began. 'Please sit down. I want to talk to you. I think you should be aware of the seriousness of Madame Lisette's failing health.' Sarah was shocked, not realising that the situation was as bad as that.

'I very much doubt if she will be able to carry on, at least certainly not in the capacity to which we are used–'

It must be very hard for this little Frenchwoman to tell her this, Sarah thought, looking at the straight ramrod figure, clad in its usual black satin tight-fitting frock, the hair pulled back behind her ears, the lacy jabot at her throat.

'I am sorry, Madame,' she said. 'I do realise how serious it is for the House of Lisette–'

'Do you?' and Gaby gave her a dry smile. 'For forty years Madame Lisette has been the inspiration behind this most famous fashion house, and I cannot imagine what we will do without her. Of course,' she hurried on, 'I cannot say for certain that she will not come back to run it in the old way, but whereas the staff, including myself, would take over and carry on as best as we could, things are made somewhat difficult by the dreadful political situation.'

Sarah's heart sank. She was genuinely fond of Madame Lisette, she was like the grandmother she had never known, apart from teaching her about French couture, something many foreigners never learned. She supposed she could apply for a job at another fashion house, but they were all in the same boat – and what more natural than that she would return to England? She could not possibly stay in Paris if war broke out.

'I realise that the last two weeks in August had been reserved for *les vacances,* but unless it is imperative that you return home at that time, I will ask you if you could stay on for a little while until things get sorted out.'

Sarah's hopes rose.

'Of course, Madame,' she said.

'It is just for the next two or three weeks while we see what will happen. The doctor advises complete rest, and Madame is not to be disturbed about anything at all. I have taken the liberty of sending for her son, Gerard – and as luck would have it, he is being posted back to Paris immediately in view of the war situation.'

'Madame will be pleased to see him!' Sarah cried.

'Yes, she will. She adores her son. Also, Hortense and myself would be grateful if you would call in to see her on occasion now that we are not so busy. She likes you, and is pleased when you call. She likes young people around her, and it is good for her.'

'Of course, I would only be too pleased.' Sarah assured her.

'So – it is settled – if perhaps you would postpone your *vacances* until the beginning of September–'

'That would suit me very well,' Sarah admitted. 'It will be my twenty-first birthday then, and I would wish to be home for that.'

'Then it is settled,' Gaby said, looking pleased. 'I cannot tell you what your duties will be in the next three or four weeks, but we must pull together for Madame's sake. Once we know where we stand in the war situation, if it all resolves itself peacefully, then we shall carry on much as usual, with, we hope, more orders coming in. Why do you not call in to see her this evening when you have finished here?'

'Yes, I will, of course I will,' Sarah said, thinking she would take Madame some flowers. That would cheer her up. Perhaps Gaby and Hortense were looking on the black side, but certainly Madame Lisette had not been back to the showroom since the fashion show.

It was a sunny summer evening, the day had been very warm, even the pavements seemed hot beneath her feet, but the flowers along the streets had been well watered which made it seem cooler. It was quiet everywhere, for as elsewhere in Paris most people seemed to have gone to the country to escape the heat of Paris in August. On the corner of the Place Vendôme she bought marguerites for Madame Lisette, a white bowl of white flowers, knowing how much Madame liked them. She often used them in her window displays.

'Ah,' Hortense said when she opened the door, looking pleased at the sight of the marguerites. 'You must not stay long, for we are expecting Monsieur Gerard, Madame's son, some time this evening.'

'Oh. Well, just give these to her, I don't want to intrude,' Sarah apologised.

'No, you must go in and see her – I told her you were coming. She will be disappointed if you go away.'

Hortense closed the door after Sarah, and led the way to Madame's sitting room, where Madame Lisette was resting on a *chaise-longue*. She looked very pale and wan, and Sarah felt a pang of sadness; she could see how ill the old lady was.

Madame held out her beringed hands towards Sarah: 'Ah, my child – and are these for me?' She buried her face in them, and raised deep-set dark eyes to Sarah.

'How kind of you to come,' she said.

'Everyone sends their best wishes, and their hopes that you soon get well,' Sarah said.

'Thank them for me. Sit down for *un moment*,' Madame Lisette said. 'They tell me I must not become excited, but it is *tres difficile* – my son is coming home – home to Paris after all this time.'

Sarah smiled. 'Yes, I heard, that's very exciting.

'He has been three years in Algiers – so long – but now must return to Paris because of the war situation. Is it not dreadful? Still, to see my beloved Gerard again – I am very fortunate.'

'I must not stay long,' Sarah began, sitting in the chair Hortense had pulled up for her next to the *chaise-longue* as she took the flowers and disappeared.

'Now,' Madame said. 'What have you been doing with yourself? You miss Nicole, I expect.'

'Yes, very much.'

'Never mind, you will be going home

yourself soon; let us pray all this talk of war will blow over and you will return to Paris once more.'

'Oh, I hope so,' Sarah said fervently.

Glancing towards the door of the salon, Madame swiftly delved behind a deep cushion and brought out a sketch pad, raising pleading eyes to Sarah's. 'Please,' she said. 'For me – just sketch me something – anything; it would give me great pleasure.'

'Oh, but Madame, you are not supposed to do anything connected with work,' Sarah said. 'You must rest quietly.'

'Nonsense,' Madame said with some of her old asperity, and Sarah smiled.

'Very well, just one,' she said, taking the pencil and seeing Madame's eyes light up.

'For a spring wedding?' Madame suggested. 'Yes?'

Sarah looked down at the blank pad on her knee, then swiftly, with a few strokes, outlined the tall, slim elegant figure of a woman wearing a sleeveless gown with straps over the shoulders. The skirt had godets from the waist flowing to the floor, there were pearls around her throat, and to accompany this was a tightly fitting jacket with tiny pearl buttons to the waist, while the long tight sleeves ended in a point at the wrist to match the base of the jacket. On her upswept hair a small coronet of pearls and orange blossom.

'Ivory and silver brocade,' Madame whispered.

'Worn with the jacket as a wedding dress, take the jacket off and it becomes a separate evening gown…' They were both lost in their imagination when the sound of a bell rang through the apartment, and they both started.

'Oh, give it to me – *vite, vite,*' Madame said, stuffing the pad behind her and plumping up the cushion as Sarah got to her feet.

Then there was a tap on the door and Hortense, her eyes glowing with pleasure, opened the door to be followed by a tall good-looking man of middle age who came over swiftly and took Madame's hands in his.

'Excusez-moi,' he said to Sarah, kissing his mother on both cheeks. 'Maman, Maman – what is this I hear?'

Delighted at witnessing this emotional meeting between mother and son, Sarah put a finger to her lips at Hortense, and tiptoed to the door.

'Ah, wait – *un moment–*' Madame said. 'I

would like you to meet my son Gerard, this is Mlle Sarah Roberts; Sarah, my son Gerard–'

'Enchanté, Mam'selle.'

And Sarah looked up into a pair of the darkest eyes she had ever seen, eyes which burned and glowed like coals in his handsome face.

The hand which took hers was warm and firm. 'Monsieur,' she began.

'Mademoiselle,' and he took her hand and pressed it to his lips with a slight half-bow.

Oh, thought Sarah, these Frenchmen–

'Now,' Madame said firmly. 'You shall meet again, but now–'

Sarah smiled. *'Bonsoir,* Madame,' she said. 'Monsieur–'

'Bonsoir, Sarah.'

And Hortense saw her to the door.

'Bonsoir, Mademoiselle,' and as the outer door closed behind her, Sarah made her way to the lift and thence up the stairs to her room.

Later that night, Gerard Puligny closed the door of his room behind him, and switched on the light. The dear old familiar room looked exactly the same as when he had left it, as it had always done since he was a boy.

For he had been born in his mother's room – that spacious apartment next door, but this had been his room, the small one off the hall, the room where he had spent his boyhood, where he had dreamed his dreams as all small boys do, his sanctuary against the outside world.

Crossing over to the bed, turned down by Hortense and ready to get into, he took off his shoes and lay flat against the huge pillows. He was more shocked than he had thought he would be at seeing his beloved mother. She had obviously been very ill, more ill than he had realised by the telephone calls and letters. Frail – but then she was getting on in years. Seventy-five, but she still had many more years in her yet. If they could build up her strength – and in normal times that might have been possible, but now with the serious political situation as it was, she had been knocked sideways, first by her illness and then by the gradual slackening off of business at the fashion house.

Well, he was back now, and in charge of things, although how much time he would have in his position as a senior army officer on urgent call was doubtful. But he must look on the bright side. At least he was back in Paris.

After a day at the War Office, he spent the evening dining with his mother, having called Birgitta, his mistress, to tell her he had arrived safely. She had been with him throughout his three years in Algeria, and although he had mentioned her to his mother in the early days, he had sensed his mother's disapproval and had never mentioned her since. She had been so fond of his wife who had tragically died so young, and it is not, he thought, as though I am going to marry Birgitta and bring her into the family. Birgitta was an Austrian and worked for the Embassy, but as far as his mother was concerned, that was close enough to Germany as to be impossible. So Birgitta was filed away with his other secrets – and there were many of those. State and otherwise.

His mother seemed to have been cheered more than somewhat by his presence.

'Now, tell me,' he said. 'About the salon. Has it been doing well?'

'Wonderfully well,' Madame said. 'One of our best years until these war scares, and now that they become more serious–'

'You will have to go into production making army uniforms,' he teased her, and she shot him a look, wondering if he was serious, then playfully tapped his arm.

'Oh, it's lovely to have you home.'

'Gaby still with you? And what happened to the other little English girl – what was her name? Does this new girl replace her?'

'Nicole? No, she left to go back to England, but she and Sarah spent some months together; she taught Sarah as much French as she knows.'

'Sarah Roberts … what an English name!' he smiled.

Madame put down her coffee cup. 'She is the girl Freddie sent – you remember – did I not tell you?'

He frowned. 'Freddie?' and his mind worked swiftly. 'Lady Freddie?'

'Yes, she is the daughter of her lady's maid, Mrs Roberts.'

'Oh, I see.' And the penny dropped.

'May I?' and he extracted a cigarette from a silver case.

'Of course,' Madame said. 'Here is an ashtray.'

'Do you hear from her?' he asked, lighting his cigarette. 'Lady Freddie?'

'Not often. Only recently when she telephoned me about the girl, and then again to hear how she was getting along.'

'I see.'

'She had done some time at Gallen's in London, Sarah, I mean, and I must say, she is excellent, Gerard. So talented – if only there had not been this war scare I am sure I could have settled her in here quite nicely.'

'Well, we shall see,' he soothed her, knowing as he did, that it would not be long before their whole world would be turned upside down.

'Why don't you ask her to lunch on Sunday – Mlle Sarah Roberts? I'd like to hear more about Freddie – she had a son, had she not?'

'Yes, he must be twenty-three or four now; he is in the Royal Air Force, Freddie says, and then, of course, Freddie had two daughters after the war.'

'Really, how time flies,' he said. 'Yes, do that, Maman – more coffee?'

Sarah was delighted to receive an invitation to lunch once more with Madame. She dressed herself carefully in the new navy dress she had made with the white collar and matching jacket, and wore a navy pillbox hat quite straight on her dark hair with a tiny question mark of a slim feather at the back. With navy high-heeled shoes and white kid gloves, she was sure Madame would approve.

As did Hortense when she opened the door, leading her into the drawing room where she found Madame seated on the button-back sofa and her son, Gerard, standing by the fireplace.

He came forward to greet her, bending low over her hand, and she smiled at Madame in greeting.

'*Bonjour,* Madame, Monsieur–'

'Please sit down, Mam'selle; may I call you Sarah?' She was pleased to find that he spoke faultless English.

'Of course,' said Sarah, and he handed her a tiny glass from a silver tray, '*Merci,* Monsieur,' feeling very sophisticated and cosmopolitan in such surroundings.

'You look very well today, Madame,' she said putting her glass down on the side table.

'Thank you, *ma chérie* – it is my son who always cheers me,' and she smiled at him over her glass.

Lunch was a long affair, soup followed by a light omelette, then veal, deliciously cooked in cream with a mushroom sauce, and tiny vegetables which were freshly delivered every day from Normandy farms,

Madame told her. Sarah wondered if Hortense did all the cooking as well as looking after Madame, but as she had quickly realised the French approached food in quite a different manner from the English. Food was to be eaten slowly, savoured and enjoyed as one of the principal pleasures of living.

There was tarte tatin to follow, as light as a feather, and Sarah made up her mind that come what might, despite her luggage, she would take a large one back home to her family.

All during the meal, Madame and her son talked of everyday things – something the French were very good at, Sarah discovered. Never at a loss for words, they discussed everything from the state of the fashion world, to art and the political situation, to finance and government building – even to education, bringing Sarah in from politeness and wanting to hear her views.

At the end of the meal, Gerard suggested that he and Sarah take coffee in the drawing room while Madame rested for a while. He was such easy company that Sarah had no qualms or nervousness at being with such an exalted man, knowing that at home she would have been tongue-tied in such a man's company.

'So tell me,' he began, seating himself opposite her by the fireplace. 'Are you enjoying your stay in Paris, Sarah?'

'Very much,' Sarah said. 'I simply love it – I feel so at home here, and Madame is so kind and encouraging. I shall be sorry to go home when the time comes.'

'And when is that?' he asked, knowing that it could be much sooner than she thought.

'Well, I should have gone home for two weeks starting next week, but I am staying on for a few days to see how things pan out – also, with Madame's illness–'

'Yes, of course,' he murmured. 'So you live at Kirby Hall, do you? You were brought up there?'

'You know it?' Sarah was surprised.

'Yes, of course, although I have only been there once, but I remember it well; a lovely old house. The two families used to be friends, Lady Freddie's parents and mine, years ago. We used to meet in Provence in the summer where we both had houses – and great fun we had too.'

'That must have been wonderful,' Sarah said wistfully, trying to imagine it all.

'And Lady Freddie – you call her that, too?'

'Yes,' and Sarah smiled.

'Is she still as charming? She was quite *ravissante* when she was younger–'

'Yes, she is lovely,' Sarah said. 'It is thanks to her that I am here.'

He raised inquiring eyebrows.

'When she realised that I loved design and the fashion world, she suggested to Madame – your mother – that I should come here for a spell.'

'So, that's how it was,' Gerard said. 'And tell me about your family?'

'We live at First Lodge on the estate,' Sarah said. 'My mother used to be Lady Freddie's nursery nurse, she was only fifteen when Lady Freddie was born, and she stayed on with the family. Lady Freddie's maid, really,' she said, thinking about it.

'And your father works on the estate?'

'Yes, he was invalided home in the war; he really comes from London, but he stayed in the country because he likes it. He used to be the groom, but they don't keep horses now – well, only one.'

'And have you brothers and sisters?' he asked.

'Yes, two brothers, both quite a bit older than I am, both married.'

What a nice man he was, Sarah thought.

‘Were you an only child, Monsieur?’ she asked politely, since personal questions seemed to be the order of the day.

‘Yes, I was, unfortunately – well, in some ways. My father died when I was thirteen and my mother’s family brought me up while my mother started the business and kept it going.’

‘That must have been very hard for her,’ Sarah said.

‘Yes … well, Sarah,’ and he got to his feet. ‘I have enjoyed talking to you, but I must see Hortense before I leave. When did you say you were due to return home?’

‘I am not sure, but I would like to be back for my birthday – my twenty-first birthday – on the ninth of September.’

‘Your twenty-first birthday,’ he said. ‘How wonderful. Yes, of course you must be back for that – your family will want to give you a party, I daresay–’

Sarah dimpled.

‘I expect your mother was delighted to have a daughter after two boys,’ he said. ‘I know I would have been–’ thinking of his little daughter who had died so tragically.

‘Yes, they have been wonderful to me,’ Sarah said. ‘Allowing me to come to France – the best parents in the world – well, considering I was adopted.'

'You were adopted?' he said, half his mind still on Lady Freddie.

'Yes, wasn't I lucky to find such a good home?' and she smiled up at him.

'You certainly were,' he said slowly, and bent down to take her hand. *'Au revoir,* Mademoiselle, *à bientôt.* I think I can hear Maman – yes, here she comes.'

Walking with the aid of a stick and Hortense holding her other arm, Madame came into the drawing room, and Sarah got up.

'Sit down,' Madame Lisette said. 'I hope you will stay for some tea – although it looks as if Gerard must leave us; are you going, Gerard?'

'Yes, but I shall be back later this evening,' and kissing her on both cheeks, he left them.

'Now–' Madame Lisette said, when Hortense had gone leaving them together. 'Let us get down to work, eh?' and pulled out the design drawing from behind the cushions, smiling like a naughty child who was up to no good…

Chapter Twelve

Gerard walked slowly into his room, his hands trembling slightly on the door handle as he opened the door.

He sank into the chair at his desk, his heart pounding as he tried to make sense of what he had just heard. It was not difficult to work out the timing factor, he realised; the girl, Sarah, would be twenty-one in September so she would have been born just nine months after – and he dropped his head in his hands.

That meant that she would have been conceived around Christmas time in 1917 or New Year 1918…

He sat back, reliving that time, the most momentous in his life, never knowing that there could have been repercussions – or had there?

How beautiful Freddie had been as a girl; she had totally captivated him that summer before the war, the last time the two families had spent together as neighbours and friends in the south of France. They had danced and gone swimming beneath the Provençal skies, the air scented with lavender and thyme, at night the stars hung so low you felt you could have reached out to touch them ... the world had been their oyster.

Freddie, with fair golden hair, and deep blue eyes that laughed all the time, her mouth provocatively meeting his, his arms holding her close, they had gloried in their love thinking – knowing – it would last for ever, come what might...

But fate intervened in the shape of a telegram calling Freddie's father back home, and Sir Edward Kirby returned to England taking his wife and daughter Freddie with him.

A war with Germany was imminent...

He couldn't believe she had gone – the days were empty and soon he and his mother returned to Paris. Once the war started he was in the army and had made it his life ever since.

No one could have described the loss he felt, the emptiness, the feeling of betrayal, when the news came through of Freddie's engagement the following year and subsequent marriage to Richard Drummond. He told himself she had not been prepared to wait for them to meet again after the war. And when, in 1915, the news came through his mother of the birth of Freddie's son, he finally came to terms with himself, and tried to forget her totally.

His mother heard from Lady Freddie from time to time, but he never asked about her. Not until two years later when he was sent to London on War Office business did she intrude into his thoughts again, and resisting all efforts to use common sense, he rang her at home in Kirby Hall.

Who would have known the far-reaching effects of that telephone call, he wondered now.

Christmas was just over, and it was before New Year started, those strange few days in limbo, days when time seemed to hang still, as though waiting for a sign to start a brand new year of hope and promise. On learning from the housekeeper that her Ladyship was in London in Edwardes Square, he telephoned her there, and at the sound of her voice he knew that, despite valiant efforts, she could still move him as no other woman could.

'Gerard – oh, Gerard,' and he thought she sounded near to tears.

'Can I – may I see you? Please, Freddie–'

'Oh, darling, of course you can! Where are you?'

'At my club but we will meet wherever you say.'

'At the Hyde Park Hotel,' she said. 'This evening, six-thirty.'

Never had time gone more slowly than when he was waiting in the foyer for her, but when he saw her, he rose to his feet, almost mesmerised.

For she was still beautiful. She came towards him, swathed in furs, hands outstretched, eyes glowing with delight at seeing him again. It was a glorious moment. He bent and kissed her on both cheeks and she took his arm.

What bliss it had been – those two days.

They had dined and afterwards taken a stroll. It was cold, but neither of them seemed to mind, Freddie in furs, he in his greatcoat, but it could have snowed for all they cared.

Later, over coffee, they talked – had not seemed to stop since they met each other.

No, he was not married – yes, young David was well, and staying with his grandmother, while Richard was in Palestine.

'How long has he been out there?'

'Six months,' she said.

There was a long silence. 'Why, Freddie?' he said at length. 'Why? I thought you loved me.'

'I did – I do – oh, how much! But you see – my father didn't want me to marry a Frenchman…'

'I don't believe it,' he said. 'I always got on with your father. I liked him.'

'Oh, darling, he liked you too, but as his only daughter he wanted me to marry an Englishman; there was a war coming, and Richard – well, Richard is a dear–'

'Do you love him?' and the words came out harshly.

'No, not in the way I love you, but I like him, I respect him, and we get on well – he is like a friend.'

His mouth had curled. 'That's a poor excuse for a marriage–'

'Perhaps,' she had said.

So she still loved him–

That night he took her home and left her at the door of the house in Edwardes Square, promising to see her again the next day, the day before New Year's Day.

They had talked and walked in the park, had lunch, and then, by tacit agreement – he was never sure how it happened; in fact he thought it was Freddie – they booked in at the Hyde Park and spent the night together…

Never had he experienced such joy, and he was sure she never had. They belonged together – he had always known it.

'Freddie, Freddie, you are not going to leave me again–'

But in the morning over breakfast, she was adamant. 'Gerard, I will treasure the memory of this night as long as I live,' and he had turned a troubled face to hers.

'But – after the war–'

'If anything happens to Richard, well, perhaps, but if he comes through it alive – and I hope he will – I shall stay with him, Gerard.'

'But how can you? You don't love him–'

'He is my husband, and little David's father – that's the way I see it – don't be cross with me, don't spoil it, Gerard, I shall love you as long as I live. You do know that, don't you? But we belong to different worlds.'

'I don't understand you,' he had said, through frozen lips, his heart like lead.

They sat facing each other over the coffee cups, seeing no one but themselves reflected in each other's tragic eyes.

'And please, Gerard, don't try to get in

touch with me–' she laid a gentle hand on his arm. 'Promise?'

'If that's what you wish,' he said stiffly.

'It's for the best – really – you will see it one day. Promise?'

'I promise,' he said, knowing the bottom had fallen out of his world.

'Don't come with me,' she had said as she got up and pulled her furs around her, and made for the exit doors. She stopped, pulling her gloves on, and half-turned, as if for a last look.

He got up and followed her swiftly, asking the doorman to call her a cab.

She turned to him. 'It was wonderful,' she said. 'Heaven,' and he could see her eyes brimming over with tears… It was almost more than he could bear…

But he never had got in touch with her. He had promised. But was this child – Sarah – the result of that wonderful meeting all those years ago?

He got up and stood by the window looking out, but saw nothing. It stood to reason. If Richard had been in Palestine and Sarah born in September then Sarah–

Was his daughter, he thought. She could be. What more natural than that Freddie would ask her beloved maid to adopt the baby. Finding herself pregnant, she would want the child, he was sure of it, as a legacy of their love. There was no way she would be prepared to get rid of it. But what explanation had she given Richard when he came home? What possible excuse could she make?

He sighed from the depths of his being. Well, knowing Freddie, she had plenty of ways of getting round a man...

He was sure of it now, as sure as he had been of anything in this world.

But why had she sent Sarah to Paris? Was there some meaning to it? Was it to tell him? To let him realise that he had a daughter? What was the reason behind it? For he was sure there was one.

He thought of his wife, Alicia. A pretty and rather delicate girl who reminded him of Freddie, except that she had not Freddie's self-assurance nor her passion nor exuberance. They had a baby daughter, who was just two when she died. That terrible influenza epidemic, in which both of them lost their lives.

No. He might have had success in the army, but you couldn't say he had been successful in love or marriage...

But he had a daughter. He was sure there

had been something about that girl from the start. She looked French–

Suddenly he walked over to the small round table where sat four family photographs, of his parents and himself taken when he was a small baby, and another of his mother as a young girl. She was wearing a dark pinstripe tailored dress with a deep white collar. Looking straight into the camera, the same shaped face, the dark hair, the eyes – this sepia snapshot of his mother looked just like Sarah of today. Why had his mother never noticed it?

Because you see in a photograph what you want to see, he had been told. Was that it? Was he imagining things?

And another thing. Her talent – did she not take after her grandmother, Madame Lisette? The same flair for design, for fashion – yes, he was sure. The only certain thing was that she was nothing like her true mother, Lady Freddie. But why would the woman, Freddie's old nanny, have wanted to adopt a child at her age if she already had two sons unless Freddie had prevailed upon her?

Why had Freddie sent her to Paris?

Round and round went his thoughts, but he always came back to the same thing in the end.

No – Sarah was his daughter but ... he would never know for sure. He could never ask Freddie – they hadn't spoken for twenty years – but it didn't alter the fact; he was both exalted and deflated by turns, and the more he thought about it the more sure he became – Sarah Roberts was his daughter.

That night he relived the whole of those two days with Freddie – and by the morning accepted the fact that his feelings had not changed, by some wonderful, remote and obscure chance, he had a daughter...

There was nothing he could do about it. He could not acknowledge her as such, could not tell his mother and he would never know for certain. He was sure Freddie would deny such an accusation – and besides he could never ask her. Happily married, as he now knew, with a grown-up son and two daughters – how could he disrupt her little world? No, he must keep it to himself.

He only knew one thing for certain: having found her, he had no desire to let her go. He wanted to keep her safe in the bosom of his family, even if she never learned who she really was – he knew, and that was all that mattered...

Back in England, Robbie was shocked and heartbroken to learn that Sarah had postponed her return home. She feared for Sarah's life if she stayed in France and felt that however much she liked Paris and Madame Lisette, there was no excuse not to come home. Sarah's explanations over the telephone were reasonable enough, she sounded quite confident about her decision, told Robbie not to worry, and that she would telephone often. It was only for a short time, after all.

Robbie eyed the three letters from David sitting on the mantelpiece with misgiving – he had obviously thought she would be arriving home soon.

Oh, I can't worry any more, she thought wearily, what with my beloved Sarah in France, Hilda's baby due, and poor Tom in such pain with his legs.

When the telephone call came from David the next day, she had to tell him of Sarah's decision, and could hear that he was as shocked as she herself at the news.

'Well, Robbie,' he said. 'I suppose she knows what she is doing–'

'Just tell her to get herself home,' Tom ordered.

'Tom, I can't do that,' Robbie said. 'She's

old enough to know her own mind – you know what it's like when you're young – you see no fear.'

On his return to base from London, David put in a telephone call to Madame Lisette's salon, and got through to Sarah right away.

'Sarah, darling, what are you playing at? You've got us all worried – your poor mother–'

'David, it's only for a short time. Madame Lisette is ill, I must stay and help her, and there is a big wedding in September. I must stay for that, and Madame Lisette … oh, I can't explain, but I'll be all right, I promise. I'll come back home just as soon as I can–'

'And you will miss your birthday,' he said. 'I had a special present for you.'

She blushed furiously. 'Oh, David, you mustn't spoil me–'

'Look,' he said hurriedly, 'I've got to go but I'll phone you again. You take care – I love you, Sarah–' and the phone went dead.

Sarah put her hands to her burning cheeks. Dear, dear David–

The following Sunday morning, as Robbie and Tom sat in the kitchen of First Lodge, they awaited the promised speech by the prime minister, and as Big Ben struck the last strokes of eleven o'clock they learned, as did the whole nation, that from midnight, 3 September, Britain was at war with Germany...

Tom looked across at Robbie and Robbie looked back at him. There seemed nothing to say. This had nothing to do with the fever and patriotism of the last war – this war would be different, a war that affected soldiers and civilians alike, women and children. Robbie knew she had to be strong, come what may.

'Well,' she said. 'That's that. I never thought it would come to pass–' and thought of Sarah out there in France. Oh, why hadn't she come home! And saw by Tom's stricken face that he was thinking the same thing.

At that moment they both automatically ducked as the roar of planes deafened them, but they were gone in a moment and, hurrying to the door, they saw them disappearing into the distance. Robbie walked to the gate, where a policeman stood.

'Ours,' he said. 'On reconnaissance, making for the Channel, I expect.'

God help us, Robbie thought.

In France, Sarah received the news of Britain at war with mixed feelings. Guilt mainly – that she hadn't gone home for her birthday, fears for her family, for the future of Britain and France. Would the Germans really march into France as everyone said?

'Could I possibly have a telephone call to England?' she asked Gaby. 'My family will be worried.'

'Of course, *ma cherie,*' Gaby replied. 'But I don't rate your chances of getting through…'

Paris was surprisingly quiet, considering, and in the days that followed, it soon became apparent that many men had been called up, public buildings – the Obelisk and the Marly Horses on the Place de la Concorde – had been sandbagged, and the Café de la Paix was filled with German emigrés and all sorts of strange people. But, compared with London, had Sarah known it, the blackout in Paris was nowhere near as daunting.

There was a sense of optimism everywhere, victory was taken for granted, and no one was in any doubt that the Germans would starve sooner rather than later.

So the preparations for the wedding went on undisturbed, and a grand affair it was too. Sarah sent photographs home to Robbie and, the atmosphere being as it was in England with the constant threat of air raids which did not materialise, they began to wonder if there really was a war on. The fighter planes, however, kept a strict vigil over the Channel, the noise of aircraft overhead was constant. Several times the warnings sounded until people got almost used to them – and ignored them – taking more and more chances as the days went by.

At the beginning of October, the wedding safely over, fate played once more into Gerard's hands.

It was noticeable that Madame Lisette was not improving as much as he had hoped. The excitement of the wedding had kept her going, but now she lay listless, wanting Sarah's company more and more. It was as if she kept going by listening to stories of how the workshop was getting on, although Sarah kept it from her that the business was going rapidly downhill. She loved to sit and watch Sarah sketch, but the big shock came when Hortense, who had served Madame so loyally for fifteen years, announced her intention of leaving.

Her daughter, who was married to a

farmer with a smallholding near the Belgian border, had just heard that her husband had been called into the army, and with four small children to look after and feed, with no help and having to run the farm single handed, Hortense felt she must go to her.

'Of course you must go,' Madame Lisette said. 'I shall miss you, you have been a good and faithful servant for such a long time, but now you have a duty to your family.'

Hortense, showing her feelings for once, wept openly, and Madame shed a few tears too. If only, Gerard thought, he could prevail upon Sarah to stay. It was decided that Hortense should go at the end of the week and, while Sarah was thinking about making plans to return home – after all, the wedding was over, there was nothing to keep her in Paris – Gerard made his decision.

He returned from the War Office at the end of the day, and went in to see his mother. The last thing he wanted was Hortense to leave, but there it was. They would have to make the best of it. But all was not lost, yet…

'Maman,' he began, taking her hand in his, and noticing how thin and birdlike it had become. His mother had always had such strong and capable hands. 'I've had an idea. Sarah has been very good to you while you have been ill, and I wondered what you thought of the idea of my taking her out to dinner, as a special treat. After all, she has missed her birthday at home–'

'Oh, that's a splendid idea,' and Gerard could see that his mother was pleased.

'Friday, tomorrow perhaps,' he said, 'it will be Hortense's last evening, but all is well – Mimi is going to come in every day as usual, and I have been busy making plans.'

'Dear Gerard,' Madame said. 'We shall have to get used to doing without her–'

'Leave it to me,' Gerard said.

He telephoned the salon later, and asked to speak to Sarah.

Surprised to receive a telephone call from him, she thought at first that something had happened to Madame. 'Oh, Monsieur, it is not Madame–'

'No, no,' he assured her, 'but I have something to ask you.'

Sarah waited, wondering what was coming next.

'I wonder whether you would like to come out to dinner with me on Friday evening,' he suggested, and Sarah's heart took a leap.

She couldn't think of anything she would rather do.

'It is my way of saying thank you for all your kindness to my mother,' he said.

'But but there is no need–' Sarah began

'If you are agreeable, I would be delighted. After all, it will be a sort of birthday treat before you leave us,' and thought as he said it that he would be absolutely devastated when she did so.

'What do you say?'

'I would be delighted,' Sarah said. 'It is very kind of you, M. Gerard–'

'Please call me Gerard,' he said. 'I should like us to be friends–'

'Then thank you, Gerard,' she said.

'It is a pity that Maman cannot join us, but she is really not up to dining out just at present.'

'Of course,' Sarah said.

'So if you would be ready at eight o'clock – would that suit you?'

'Yes–' she sounded a little doubtful.

Sensing her hesitation, he said, 'Put on your prettiest dress. Come down to the apartment so that Maman may see you before we go–'

'Yes, yes, I will.' Her eyes shining with excitement, she began almost counting the hours until Friday evening.

She knew she would never look better than she did for her evening with M. Gerard. The dress was sleeveless, midnight blue georgette, long, falling to her ankles. She had made it in her spare time, for practice as much as anything else, never dreaming she might have an opportunity to wear it to dine in Paris. The *pièce de résistance* was the evening coat, full length with a large collar, made in the same colour, but in grosgrain, so that it stood out around her. Both materials she had managed to buy in the market at knockdown prices, offcuts from famous couture houses. She knew she could wear such a coat for years ahead, should she get the chance of going out in the evenings. She put on her long earrings, rejecting a necklace, and then went over to the drawer where David's present lay in its box, having arrived a few days ago by special delivery from a Paris jeweller. A slim, gold bracelet, quite plain, with an inscription on the inside which read TO SARAH FROM DAVID WITH LOVE.

She smiled to herself as she fixed the safety clasp, then looked at herself in the mirror.

The starry eyes stared back at her. If only

David could see her now ... he wouldn't believe it was the same girl…

'My dear, you look absolutely wonderful! *Ravissante!*' Madame Lisette said at the sight of her. 'Doesn't she, Gerard?'

'Thank you, Madame,' Sarah said, but Gerard couldn't take his eyes off her – it was the proudest moment of his life. His very own daughter!

The taxi took them a short distance from the Champs-Elysées and stopped outside a small restaurant that bore the name LA FLORENCE. Gerard escorted her inside, where the head waiter greeted him before beckoning another waiter to take him to a quiet and discreet corner table. M. Gerard was obviously held in some esteem, Sarah decided and, sitting opposite him, realised not for the first time what a handsome figure of a man he was. Of course, he must be around fifty, but he bore himself well, with an upright carriage, and an air of importance – that, she thought, must be the army training, although he was very much like his mother, who carried herself well.

The restaurant was beautifully appointed, very quiet, with low red lamps on each table, and the menu when it appeared was given to Gerard, she was happy to see, while another smaller one was given to her. It was almost frightening in its complexity, and she looked up to find his eyes on her, smiling indulgently.

'You have not to worry at all,' he said. 'Are you happy to leave the decision to me?'

'Oh, please, M. Gerard!' she said.

He gave the order, and the wine waiter appeared, and while all this was going on she looked around the room realising what a privilege it was to eat in such a superb restaurant. It must be quite famous.

The napery was snow white, the glasses positively shone in their brilliance, the service by two waiters serving from a small trolley at their side. An assortment of food, samples of things with tastes she had never had before, and then there was white wine which she sipped slowly, knowing she was unused to drinking, but there was plenty of water.

Gerard took his eating very seriously, and was absorbed in enjoying the hors d'oeuvres eyeing her from time to time. 'What do you think? Do you like?'

'Delicious,' said Sarah, having no idea what on earth these unusual tasty bits were.

The waiters had cleared away the first

course and were preparing to serve the fish course, when Gerard leaned across at her.

'You look quite beautiful, Sarah,' he said. 'Your lovely dress – and is that–' nodding towards her bracelet '–is that new?'

She blushed. 'It was a present – it arrived the other day–'

'Oh, I see,' and he smiled across at her.

The waiters placed the fish plates in position, and began to serve as Gerard spoke, with one eye on them, one on Sarah's arm.

'From a special friend?' he asked.

'Yes,' and Sarah smiled, looking down.

'A boyfriend! And you have had to leave him behind, *quel dommage!*' he smiled sympathetically.

'Let me see–' and she reached her arm across the table. 'Very pretty,' he said. 'And engraved too – what does it say?'

Her face was rosy pink. 'To Sarah from David with love.'

'Ah. That is his name?'

'Yes…'

A problem, he was thinking. She will never want to stay in France if she has this boyfriend at home. *Quel dommage* – but he smiled across at her.

'Does he live near you?' he asked politely,

helping himself to butter.

'Yes – well, no, not really. He is in the Royal Air Force,' she said.

'Ah, one of your brave young men,' he said. 'Is he a pilot?' he asked.

'Yes,' she said proudly. 'He flies Spitfires.'

He was very impressed. 'Where did you meet him?' he asked casually.

'We grew up together – his name is David Drummond – he lives at Kirby Hall–'

He stopped, the fork half-way to his mouth.

'David Drummond? Lady Freddie's son?' and it was as if the blood drained away from his heart.

'Yes,' and Sarah smiled at him but he didn't see her. Instead he saw suddenly what all this was about and anguish seared his soul. It was as if a knife pierced his heart.

That was why Freddie had sent her to France! To get her out of the way – there had to be a reason, he had known it all along. Suddenly the food felt like ashes in his mouth and he put down his knife and fork.

'A little rich,' he said, but his mouth felt stiff.

This child was being manipulated, first by one and then the other. Oh, Freddie,

Freddie – did you never think what the outcome might be? And now, I too…

But all his soldier's training came to the fore.

'And now, I promise you, the best meal La Florence can provide,' and he raised his glass to her.

'To you, Sarah! *Bon santé!*'

And as those lovely brown eyes met his over the rim of his glass, he felt like weeping, a father's tears…

Chapter Thirteen

If Sarah thought Gerard had become somewhat subdued towards the end of the meal she was right. His mind was in tumult, but being the gentleman he was, he had no desire to spoil her evening, and by the look in those soft brown eyes, he knew she was having a wonderful time – enjoying every moment.

It was only afterwards, after seeing her on her way home, that he went to his room and collapsed into the easy chair, staring into space.

Poor little thing – and Freddie – how could she have so manoeuvred things, but she had been desperate and got away with it. He had to admit he was glad Sarah had come to Paris, otherwise he might – most definitely, not – have learned that he had a daughter. But the implications and danger of David and Sarah being in love were too awful to contemplate. And, he told himself, some time they would have to know. They must be told. He could see Freddie's point – not only was she enhancing Sarah's career by sending her to Paris, but she was also keeping her out of David's way. But the confrontation had to come some time. What did Freddie plan to do about that?

As he saw it, Sarah must remain in Paris. At least, she must remain as far away as possible from young David Drummond. If she returned to England there was little chance of seeing a great deal of him as a Spitfire pilot, but still, love will find a way – they were young and knew nothing of the awful circumstances surrounding them.

Sarah must stay in France…

It was almost three in the morning before he finally went to bed, and thought he had worked things out to the best of his ability. If he could prevail upon her stay and be with his mother in her time of need, would that be sufficient to keep her in Paris?

He decided to leave a note under Sarah's door which she would be sure to see when she left the apartment in the morning. It would be to the effect that he wished to see her – could she possibly call into his mother's apartment before she left? The next day was Saturday, and he guessed she went to the salon, at least in the morning. If not, maybe she would go shopping – he hoped at least she would turn up before lunch time, for he was due at the War Office at two p.m. and would be busy there for the next few days. It was imperative that he see her and put his idea to the test.

He left the apartment and climbed the stairs to Sarah's room, slipping the large white envelope under the door where she would be sure to see it.

He was awake at seven having set his alarm so as to be sure to be about whenever Sarah came, which she did around eight-thirty.

Dressed, and looking as immaculate as ever, he smiled at her.

'*Bonjour*, Sarah, come in.'

'*Bonjour*, Gerard, you wished to see me?' a look of apprehension on her face. She was sure Madame had taken a turn for the worse.

He led the way into the drawing room. 'No, it is not Maman. She is sleeping peacefully – I wanted to talk to you; were you on your way to the salon?'

'Yes, I am due there at nine-thirty, we have a special order to finish.'

'Sit down, Sarah – would you like coffee? Mimi is in the kitchen–'

'No, thank you, I had breakfast.'

He made himself comfortable and adopted a relaxed manner.

'Sarah, I expect you were planning to go home shortly, yes?'

She nodded.

'I will come straight to the point, I am going to ask you to do me a special favour,' he said, watching her face carefully to see her reaction. 'Would you be prepared – to think about – staying on for a while?' and saw her eyes glow, then become concerned.

'Oh, Gerard–'

'It is selfish of me to ask you this, but my mother is really not too well, the business as you know is declining, which I know is worrying her – how many staff have you at the moment?'

'Just four, and one of those is about to

leave,' Sarah said.

'Well, my proposal is this: would you be prepared to stay on and be with my mother in a totally different capacity? You would be paid a salary as companion to my mother and you could work in the salon during the morning to help with your training, and be here for the rest of the day. She rests in the afternoon, but it is the evenings she would be alone and it is a lot to ask of a young woman, but I am sure you would have plenty of free time – there are many people we could call on if you wish to go out. She is very fond of you, you seem to instil some life into her, and I cannot bear to see her going downhill. Mimi is here, and I will be some of the time, but I shall be going away until Tuesday myself and it is at times like that that I would like you to be around–' He realised he was rambling on and she must be a little confused.

She was silent. 'Well,' she said, at length. 'You have taken me by surprise. It is not an idea I ever contemplated – although it is a delightful one. I expect my mother would be worried, and I suppose I should go home, but–'

'I am not going to put pressure on you, it must be your own decision. As things are at the moment, it is fairly quiet – let us hope it remains so,' he said, no word of his doubts as to what might happen, or his fears – but he would see she was safe if it was the last thing he did…

'You could move down to the spare room here,' he said. 'There is no point in keeping that room upstairs – you would be much more comfortable here – and there is always the doctor who is an old friend, and a retired nurse living near by if things get difficult, but then I hope my mother will gradually get well again with you to keep her company. Hortense leaving was a shock to her, and if you go too–'

'Of course I will stay for a while,' she said. 'After all, at home things will be bad in the couturier trade, and I should have to find some sort of war work, I expect – it is just that my family will be expecting me.'

'But if you like the idea,' he stressed, 'could you not think about it?'

'Of course I will,' she said. 'And I am very tempted to say yes straight away, but I must let my family know.'

'It is a good thing that you are of age,' he said, knowing he was turning the knife, but he was desperate, and desperate men took desperate measures–

'You wish to know fairly soon?' she said.

'Yes, I do. I must be certain in my mind.'

'Then yes, I will,' she said. 'Personally, I am happy to be of service, I am very fond of your mother, she has been very kind to me and taught me a lot. I will talk to my mother on the telephone and explain things to her.'

'And David?' he was about to ask, but stopped himself. Better not make that an important issue.

What are we playing at, he thought. Both of us, myself and Freddie? We are really only putting off the evil day when they have to be told, he thought sadly.

Sarah telephoned Robbie in the afternoon, and heard Robbie's excited voice. 'Oh, Sarah, I'm glad you telephoned – Hilda has a baby daughter – yesterday – and we were getting so concerned because it was late.'

'Oh, that's wonderful! Give her my love – is she well, and the baby?'

'She is beautiful. She weighed six and a half pounds and is fair like Laurie – and guess what they have called her? Editha!' she said triumphantly. 'Hilda said she had always loved the name, she read it somewhere – and since it is a little like mine – isn't that nice?'

Thank goodness, Hilda's baby might take some of the edge off her not going home.

'Yes, that's lovely, Mum. Give her my love – er, why I rang was to tell you that I won't be home straight away,' and as she had expected, Robbie was outraged.

'What are you thinking of, Sarah?' she said. 'You must be mad! Darling, we miss you, and we want you safely home. Out there in that Paris–'

'Mum, it's all right, really, otherwise I wouldn't stay, but Madame has been so kind to me, and she really is quite ill and depressed.'

'Then let her get a proper nurse!' Robbie said hotly. 'It's not for you – a young English girl,' but then stopped short. What if Lady Freddie was still up to her tricks? She had wanted Sarah out of the way; was David being difficult? Who knew what was going on behind the scenes?

'Well,' she said grudgingly, 'you know best. But you will be home at Christmas, won't you?'

'Of course I will. Perhaps even before that.'

'Then take care of yourself; all our love,' Robbie said, and put down the phone. How would she explain to Tom? He would go through the roof.

So Sarah moved her few belongings from the tiny room on the sixth floor, and moved down to the comparable luxury of Madame's apartment. She would leave for the salon early in the morning, leaving Madame in the care of Mimi and old friends who paid her visits quite frequently, and would return home in time for lunch with Madame. She would draw and sketch for her, for she enjoyed that immensely, and keep her in touch with the salon, which now she never visited.

But in spite of her frailty, Madame was in good spirits. Just having Sarah around seemed to put new life into her, and as the days went by, she seemed to grow a little stronger. Sometimes in the afternoon when Madame rested, Sarah went out and explored Paris, but most of her evenings were spent indoors, and it was then that she felt at her loneliest.

She knew from his frequent telephone calls that David was busy now. Over the Channel a constant vigil was being kept, and she found herself longing to see him sometimes, looking forward to Christmas when she was sure he would have some leave.

One Sunday she met Pierre again as he was passing through Paris. He was in uniform, and looked very handsome. It was a brief visit, but they laughed and talked and he was delighted that she had stayed in Paris – he had telephoned on the offchance. Sarah waved him goodbye at the station wondering if she would ever see him again, but she promised to write.

In the run-up to Christmas, Paris seemed much as it ever was. Theatres and *thés dansants* and music-halls were open. There were many revivals of famous plays, and *La Traviata* was at the Opéra Comique and Josephine Baker and Maurice Chevalier at the Casino de Paris…

In December Gerard took her to a grand pre-Christmas dinner with turkey and oysters – which she had never tasted – and champagne. This was Christmas just as it ever was, Gerard assured her, but Sarah could not help but wonder what it was like back home, and began to feel a little homesick.

Gerard, sensing her mood, told her of his arrangements to see that she got home for Christmas.

'I have pulled a few strings,' he smiled at

her. 'I have a flight booked for you–' and Sarah gasped.

'A flight!' she cried. 'I've never flown–'

'You will love it,' Gerard assured her. 'It is the best way to get you back without problems. A flight from Paris to Northolt and thence by car to London, where I am sure someone – your brothers? Your father? – will be there to meet you, or you could hire a car. I am sure it can be arranged.'

Her heart fluttering with excitement, Sarah stared at him.

'I have had to use special papers and get permission – there is a war on,' he said drily '–but no matter. The flight is booked for the twenty-third of December and you will return on the twenty-seventh – is that all right with you? You will have five days with your family–' and how I will miss you, he thought, but in fairness, she deserves it. Let us hope the young man ... but it was useless to hope. Gerard knew if he requested Sarah back at a set time, she would be there. She wouldn't let him down, but it was the least he could do, to get her home in time for Christmas.

'I shall drive you to the aerodrome myself,' he said, 'and give you the necessary papers. You will be quite safe – perhaps you would telephone your parents and tell them what time you will arrive in London. I have all the timetable worked out for you, and you will do the same in reverse on the day you come back.'

'Oh!' Sarah gasped. 'I can't imagine–'

'You will find it very exciting,' Gerard assured her. 'Like a wartime mission, eh?'

Sarah and Madame Lisette went over the details many times to make sure she had got it correctly, and when the time came for her to go, Madame Lisette kissed her goodbye and there were tears in Sarah's eyes.

'Oh Madame,' she cried, taking both her hands. 'I shall be back soon–' and found herself hoping she would be.

Gerard was as good as his word, driving her to the military base where a small camouflaged aircraft waited on the runway, and Sarah found herself escorted to the plane, her heart thumping wildly, as she took her seat with four other people who seemed to have done it many times before. In no time they were airborne over the Channel, and after a bumpy ride of little more than an hour the plane landed at Northolt. There was plenty of protocol there, but presently an airman in uniform took charge and assured her that a car was waiting to take her to Paddington in London.

How strange it was to be back in England! The driver asked no questions and deposited her and her small suitcase at Paddington, where a seat had been reserved for her on the Allington train. With little time to spare, she found the train and her seat, and sat back, somewhat bewildered as the train pulled out of the station, crowded with troops, and out into the green countryside of England.

Paris seemed a long way off – it was another world.

Seated by Laurie's side, she stared about her with disbelief at the changes that had been made. To be sitting beside Laurie in his own car was almost unbelievable, to be driving along roads where previously she had driven in the pony and trap was all very strange and new to her. The shops were boarded up, and the windows of the houses were criss-crossed with black sticky tape to prevent shattering.

'Oh, Laurie, it's awful,' she said. 'Everything is so different; I hadn't imagined it like this – there wasn't a war on when I left home.'

'No,' Laurie said seriously for once. 'It's a bugger, isn't it?'

'Will you have to go?' she asked him, dreading his answer.

'I expect so, eventually, the reserves and the single ones go first, then married ones. I am qualified in the job I do, so I suppose I'll be sent to a transport unit. Anyway, we won't think about that at the moment.'

'I was delighted to hear about the baby! A little girl – you must be pleased. It's just such a shame that there is a war on.'

'Don't tell Hilda that – funnily enough she doesn't seem to worry – the war news seems to run off her like water off a duck's back. I'm pleased really, except she doesn't seem to realise the seriousness of it all. Mum worries more than she does.'

'What about Donnie?'

'There's another funny thing, they both want to join up straight away. Ginny wants to join the ATS and Donnie the Air Force, except I don't think they'll take him because of his eyes.'

'I didn't know he had bad eyesight.'

'Well, it's not good enough for flying, but he'll probably make the ground staff.'

Oh, the world was changing before her very eyes, but the biggest shock came as they neared Kirby Hall, for a huge red poster blew in the wind across the entrance with the words KIRBY HALL, with arrows pointing up towards the Hall, and bold signs leading this way and that towards stables and the outhouses and to the long paths leading to the farm and there was one to the greenhouse: GET YOUR VEGETABLE SEEDS HERE–

THIS WAY, THIS WAY, they said. THIS WAY TO THE WVS ... THIS WAY TO THE INFORMATION CENTRE – DOCTOR'S SURGERY – RED CROSS–

'Oh, Laurie!'

'Well, they've turned Kirby Hall into a reception area, it was not considered suitable for a hospital and they needed a convenient base for various organisations and since her Ladyship is not in residence–' he said with a slight sneer which Sarah did not fail to notice – 'she has given it over lock, stock and barrel to the government for the duration, for them to use at their discretion.'

It didn't look like the same place.

'Mum and Dad will be all right though won't they?'

'Oh, sure, they'll be all right,' Laurie said as they turned into the drive beneath the scarlet banner. Sarah could see Robbie standing there holding Laurie's little boy on her hip at the door of First Lodge. Grey-haired now, she looked older and Sarah felt her throat constrict.

'Oh, Laurie, she looks so old–'

'Well, she is getting on a bit, and she's had a lot of worries.'

'Well, then, I'm glad I came home.'

She got out of the car and saw Robbie's eyes light up as she hurried forward to greet her.

'Sarah, Sarah! You look wonderful! Doesn't she, Laurie, oh it's lovely to have you home.'

Sarah hugged her, blinking back the tears, then Tom appeared, using a walking stick, in the kitchen doorway, and she hurried over to him.

'Oh, Dad, Dad – it's so good to be home.'

She put her arms around him and kissed him and could feel through his shirt his heart pounding.

She forgot France at that moment – put all thoughts of it behind her, it was another world.

Once inside the familiar kitchen she glanced automatically up towards the mantelpiece where the Blue Girl with her painted rosy cheeks still stood. She went over to her and then saw the golden greetings telegram addressed to herself. With a quick glance towards her mother and a racing heart she ripped it open.

MY DARLING – WELCOME HOME – ALL MY LOVE – DAVID

She folded it slowly and slipped it into her coat pocket.

'It's from David,' she said.

But it was hard to hide the special glow with which she examined everything and asked questions, her deep brown eyes smiling at them all, genuinely delighted to be home.

Robbie stood little Tommy down and he stayed, finger in his mouth, holding on to Robbie's apron and surveying Sarah with big blue eyes.

'Don't you remember me, young Tommy?' said Sarah, going over to him and lifting him up. Oh, he smelt so sweet, his clothes had the soft smell of Lux flakes and baby soap.

'So, how are things out there in France?' Tom asked.

'Pretty much the same as here, Dad. Everyone waiting for the next move.'

'They said we fought the war to end all wars when I was over there,' Tom said.

'Now don't start, Tom,' Robbie said, dishing up the mashed potatoes and trying to keep the peace. 'Now you sit next to your Auntie Sarah, Tommy,' who was still gazing at her, 'Hilda will be down in a minute or two, she's seeing to the baby.'

When Hilda came down she was carrying the new baby in a pristine white shawl, her dark eyes shining with pride and pleasure.

'Oh, let me see her!' Sarah cried, lifting away the shawl to take a peek at the sleeping infant.

'I brought her down for you to see; she's just had her feed,' Hilda said. 'I'll put her to bed now, you can see her again tomorrow.'

'Oh, she's beautiful!' Sarah said.

They seemed to talk all through the meal, asking questions about France while Sarah wanted to know what was going on at home. The time went so fast and it was a while later that, with the curtains drawn and the whole of the outside in darkness, Sarah went to the window.

'Careful,' Robbie warned. 'We mustn't show a light after dark – haven't you noticed the blackout curtains?'

'Aren't they grim?' and Sarah made a face. 'Do you really have to have those?'

''Fraid so.'

'It makes everything look so depressing. Perhaps you could find some pretty material and use the blackout material as lining and that will make them thicker and warmer for the winter. How on earth do you manage to find your way about – to get up to the Hall without a lamp-post? It's nowhere near so bad in Paris.'

'All lights are extinguished,' Tom said. 'Torches only, and they have to be pointed towards the ground. It's a bit rough, I tell you.'

'It's a nightmare, and dangerous,' Sarah agreed.

'Headlights on cars have to be covered with black paper so the minimum light can be seen through a narrow slit; you can buy these black paper masks anywhere,' Laurie said. 'Just enough to see and be seen by. I tell you, it's dicey driving at night especially if it's foggy, that's the only thing that worries Hilda – my driving in the blackout.'

'Yes, we have that in Paris, but somehow in a city it's not so bad.'

That night when she went to bed, Sarah dreamed of Kirby Hall and First Lodge the way they used to be, but on waking the next morning, knew it for what it was – a dream. No doubting what lay outside – stark, cold reality. Would life ever get back to normal?

She shivered, and, putting on her dressing gown, went downstairs.

It was Christmas Eve, and Laurie had gone to work, but Hilda and the baby and Tommy were spending the day at First Lodge. Tom was already up and about, and outside there was a hive of activity. Sarah could scarcely believe her eyes, there were people everywhere, walking up to the Hall, along the paths, there was a porter at the gate directing everyone and a long queue waiting to be seen at the Information Centre.

'What's that for?' she asked Robbie.

'Being rehoused; people coming down from London in case of raids, they feel it will be a safer place, I don't know, I'm sure. Then there are the wives and sweethearts of serving soldiers from the camp. They all want to be near their loved ones – it's only natural – and everyone wants to avoid the big cities. 'Course it's early days yet, no one knows what will happen, but everyone is expecting the worst as you can imagine.'

'Where is Lady Freddie – and Sir Richard?'

'In London, I expect. They'll only move out if things get hot. They've sent the two girls to an aunt in America.'

'Already!'

'Well, I expect they know more than we do what's likely to happen and they won't be taking any chances.'

She sounded a little bitter, which was very unlike her. Poor Robbie – she had not had an easy life; work, always work, with never a break–

'Well,' Sarah said, taking her mother's arm, 'you must tell me what I can do to help. I must make the most of every moment–'

It was a happy household that Christmas; a Christmas tree and fairy lights, presents for everyone and having the baby and little Tommy there made it such a festive occasion. There was nothing like children to make a Christmas, Robbie thought.

In the afternoon of Christmas Day there was the King's speech, which they all listened to very seriously, but it was around six in the evening when the telephone rang.

Who would it be but David, thought Robbie grimly, and watched Sarah as she ran to the telephone.

'David! Happy Christmas!' she almost sang into the receiver. 'Where are you?'

'Can't tell you that, my darling, and not much chance of seeing you – but what's this I hear, Robbie said you are going back to France?'

'Yes, I am, just for a while.'

'Why, Sarah? Why on earth would you go back to Paris?'

'Because – oh, there are many reasons which I can't explain to you now, but really it's because, well, I am useful there, Madame Lisette is ill, and has lost her staff and her housekeeper–'

'But that's not your problem, Sarah.'

'I know, David, but I've explained it all in a letter to you. Are you still in the same place?'

'No, been moved, can't tell you where – oh, Sarah, I wish you'd come home, I should feel happier if you were in England.'

'Well, it won't be for long – but David, do take care.'

'You too,' he said, 'I've got to go Sarah, there's a queue waiting.'

'David – I'll be back as soon as possible.'

'I wish I could see you – bye–'

And Sarah put down the phone, tears springing to her eyes. Dabbing them with a hankie, she sniffed hard, and returned to the sitting room.

'It was David,' she said, blowing her nose.

'Are you going to see him over Christmas?' Robbie asked, trying to keep the desperation out of her voice.

'No, not possible, unfortunately,' Sarah said, then smiled brightly. 'Right – where is that lovely box of chocs?'

Chapter Fourteen

There was no doubting Madame Lisette's welcome when Sarah returned to Paris. She had waited patiently for the taxi bringing her from the aerodrome, and now held out her hands in welcome.

'Ah, *ma chérie*, you have come back safely. I have thought about you so often.'

Sarah kissed the elderly lady on both soft cheeks. 'Madame–' so pleased to see her again, and to note that she looked much the same as when she had left. It was like coming home. So had she felt when she saw Robbie again.

A war reminded you of how much you loved people close to you.

'And you must tell me all about it,'

Madame said. 'Go and tidy up, for I want to hear about your family, and what is happening in England.'

It was reassuring to find her so lively.

'Is Gerard at home?' Sarah asked. She looked forward to seeing him again.

'Alas, not,' Madame answered. 'He is being kept very busy lately. Something is going on, I am sure.'

Once back into her routine, Sarah settled down. She saw little of Gerard, who called in briefly to see his mother, and seemed relieved that Sarah had returned safely to Paris – not that he had ever doubted her return – but it had to be said that it had occurred to him once or twice that she might stay in England. But now there were more important things on his mind.

'There are rumours flying around that the Germans are about to invade us,' Madame said drily. 'I have heard that they already tried but failed.'

What Gerard knew, and what was keeping him more than usually busy, was that Hitler had decided that 17 January would be the day chosen to invade Belgium and Holland to make it possible to launch an assault from that direction on Great Britain. He was about to give orders to his army commanders to move the troops into position when fate intervened.

On the 10 January, a lone German military plane on a domestic flight lost its way and made a forced landing in Belgium. The pilot and a passenger, Major Helmut Reinberger, a staff officer in an airborne division, was carrying important documents on Luftwaffe operation details, including secret instructions for the proposed invasion of Belgium.

Belgian soldiers surrounded the two men, and the major attempted to destroy the papers by setting fire to them, but he was foiled when soldiers extinguished the blaze. In the interrogation room, the papers lay on a nearby table, and he made a second effort when he stuffed them into a stove, from where, despite receiving burns on his hand, a fast-moving Belgian officer managed to retrieve them.

Enough of the burned papers remained to reveal plans for a German assault on Belgium. They were immediately dispatched to senior officers in the Belgian army.

Belgium had no wish to enter the war, and at first believed that it might be a put-up job all round to persuade Allied forces into Belgium; so the arguments and repercussions went on.

The Germans decided to postpone their January invasion, all in all, so France breathed again, thus enabling Gerard to spend a few hours at home with Madame. They had recovered from this threat, but Hitler was going to do it some day. The question was – when?

Gerard came to Sunday lunch, and asked Sarah about her trip home. There was no doubt she had enjoyed herself enormously, and knowing that she would not mention David to him, he perforce had to ask her if she had seen her friend. 'Your fiancé?' he teased.

Sarah blushed. 'Oh, no, Gerard, he is not my fiancé, but I spoke to him over Christmas. He is very busy–'

'I imagine,' Gerard said gravely. 'Doing a wonderful job – and I expect he was not best pleased about your return to Paris?'

She smiled. 'He was disappointed, but I explained to him in a letter – he will understand.'

'And your parents?'

Sarah waded in and told him. About the Hall, and the changes that had been made there.

'So, Lady Freddie is not in residence?' he

asked in an offhand manner, smiling at his mother as he did so.

'No, they are away; she is in London, I think. The two girls have been sent to America apparently to stay with relatives, so my brother said.'

'Ah,' he nodded.

'Well, Maman,' he said, 'much as it grieves me to leave such pleasant company, I must return to base. I am not sure when I shall call in again, but I shall telephone you first–' and he kissed his mother on both cheeks.

'*Au revoir,* Sarah.'

'*Au revoir,* Gerard,' she said. She always missed him when he left, felt sad that he was not there. He gave her a feeling of stability, that all was right with the world – he was such a warm-hearted man…

In the weeks that followed, the war situation centred on Norway as the Germans prepared for their big offensive, and Allied attention was focused on Sweden and its iron ore, without access to which the Germans would find themselves in a critical situation.

The French knew by now that it was only a question of time – invasion of the Low Countries was a certainty, and thence to

France, where the British Expeditionary Force was biding its time.

The business of LISETTE was just ticking over; many people, taking advantage of the lower prices on offer, sought to have things made, but there was no question of fashion competition. Wealthy Parisiennes, after all, still had to dress well, and be seen to dress well. They were not going to be put off by threats and bullying from Germany. It was up to them to present a calm exterior, to show they were not afraid. France would be standing long after the Germans had been annihilated…

They were confident but wary, after all, was not Germany on their very doorstep – at least Great Britain had twenty-one miles of Channel water between them – but that counted for nothing in these days of modern warfare…

Gaby and Sarah and one assistant managed to keep the business going. Sarah was able to report to Madame, and that way she kept tabs on the business. That she longed to get back in harness was all too evident, but even Sarah realised now that she never would. She was far too old, even if she recovered completely. Her day was done. From certain things she said, Sarah was sure that she saw her, Sarah, as her successor – she had built such hopes around her. Sarah was a good dressmaker, but there were others just as good. Where Sarah scored was in the design, the styling, the ideas – and Madame knew it. She was just like herself when young.

Sarah, meanwhile, learned all she could. Not only about the actual making of the clothes but the business itself, the risks one took, the chances. It had to be the most exciting trade in normal times, she admitted. But even now, just ticking over, she still found it absorbing.

As the days wore on, the evenings lightened and in Paris the trees began to show their pale green buds; there was a touch of spring in the air.

David wrote often and Sarah replied to him, but one day in late March he telephoned her.

He sounded tired, not his usual self, and Sarah caught her breath.

'David, are you all right?'

'I'm fine. What about you?'

'I'm very well – busy–'

'Sarah, please come home I long to see you–'

'Me too,' she said. 'It's been so long.'

'You should never have gone back – I feel I have lost you.'

'Of course you haven't lost me!' Sarah cried. 'I shall be coming home soon, I am sure of it.'

'But suppose–'

'Suppose what?'

'Suppose you have difficulty in getting back–'

'Oh, never, M. Gerard will see that I am safe–' and he would, she was sure of that.

'Will you promise me that you will come home very soon?'

'Of course I will,' she assured him. 'Madame Lisette seems reasonably well now.'

'Then you must come home,' he insisted. 'There is no reason for you to stay, is there?'

'Well, I like the work, and I like to think I am doing a useful job and as long as all is quiet–'

'But for how long?' David insisted.

'You mean–'

'Yes, something will happen, and I'd like you to get out before it does.'

'Look, David,' she said gently. 'I am guided by M. Gerard; he is on top of things, and as soon as it gets – awkward – he will arrange for me to go home. There is no rush–'

'But I want to see you,' he said. 'There is just no chance with you over there.'

Sarah had pangs of guilt.

'I'll be home soon, David, I promise–'

'Take care, Sarah.'

Oh, he did sound depressed, Sarah thought, as well he might – she imagined what his life must be like, on duty all the time with perhaps never a moment – it must be a nerve-racking business, and, she thought, that if he were doing an ordinary job, or was in England in the army – she would have gone home like a shot. But knowing she never would see him, or hardly ever – perhaps she was being selfish – and of course, she loved him but they were both young, and there were so many hurdles – if she flew home to him, what would Lady Freddie say about it? Would she be opposed to their becoming engaged – for it was obvious that that was what David had in mind and her heart glowed – dear David – she wished he hadn't chosen flying as a career, but then he loved it, it was what he wanted to do...

David, based in Scotland, had been on

almost continual duty over the North Sea, providing air cover for the large convoys being threatened off Montrose, intercepting enemy marauders, following Intelligence information that German navigational beacons were more than usually active.

The weather was very cold flying at dusk and dawn over the Firth of Forth in gales and strong winds, knowing that bitter winds would greet them on their return, the landing flares giving them a warm welcome as the men made their way back to the dispersal hut.

Then, unexpectedly, David's squadron was moved to Dyce, near Aberdeen, where he found many Norwegians who had escaped somehow or other from under the German noses, and who told them the only British fighters still flying were being operated from a frozen lake, but best of all as far as he was concerned was meeting again an old school chum, now a squadron leader.

At first sight, in the mess, he could hardly believe it.

'Bill!'

There was no doubting their exuberance at seeing each other again. They had a good crew, anyway, but to meet an old buddy was just the tonic David needed. Dyce was a new airfield, with the promise of its being one of the best in the future, but at the moment it was anything but. Muddy, soft underfoot after the heavy rains and snow, which made take-off and landing more difficult. Added to the general unrest was the fact that people were dissatisfied with Neville Chamberlain's government, and when the first British civilian was killed in a German air raid on the Orkneys, this alone alerted everyone to what would undoubtedly happen in the future. There would be no stopping the Germans now.

Then the flying began in earnest. British bombers returning from night operations were landing at any airfield they could on the coast to avoid flying back to their bases further inland so that the coastguards were kept on their toes day and night.

Chamberlain's Conservative government had resigned in April, to be replaced by a national coalition government led by Winston Churchill – and the Germans wasted no time. They had invaded Denmark and Norway, operating from captured airfields in Norway, which led to an increasing number of planes in the area, particularly against the Navy at Scapa Flow including many minelayers. David's squadron flew out from the base in appalling weather and British bombers joined them on the field to step up support in Norway.

Weary and exhausted, the pilots met briefly in the dispersal hut before being ordered to go up once more.

Then the trouble broke out again between the government Ministers, many people deciding that Winston Churchill should be Prime Minister. He was the obvious choice, but there were those who thought Lord Halifax would be better.

While the British Parliamentary crisis was coming to a head, France was also undergoing political problems. Paul Reynaud was convinced that the French Army needed a stronger commander-in-chief than General Gamelin. He went as far as to say that if France continued to suffer the kind of military leadership that General Gamelin provided then Hitler would win the war. This was challenged by the Minister of War, M. Daladier, who was a personal friend of Reynaud's.

Altogether, the domestic situation of Britain and France was in turmoil, and Hitler seized his chance.

The air was hotting up even more, and

there were rumours that David's squadron would be moved. Then Bill came in with the news that they were sending some new personnel to the station which would include some WAAFs; this raised a great cheer in the mess.

Bill grinned at David, but although David gave an answering smile, his thoughts, as always, were with Sarah.

Then came the news that they were to be transferred to Hornchurch in Essex from which they would fly out to protect the English Channel ports.

He was getting closer to France, David thought…

Awakened early by gunfire, Sarah left her bedroom and on her way to the kitchen was confronted by a distraught Mimi.

'Mam'selle! Mam'selle! *Les Boches – les Boches* – they have invaded Belgium, Holland and Luxemburg! *Mon Dieu!* We are finished–'

Mimi had no English at all, but no one could have mistaken the fast French *patois* as, still muttering to herself accompanied by not a few hurried crossings across her meagre bosom, she hurried into the kitchen to prepare Madame's breakfast.

Sarah had to admit to a feeling of slight fear – what would happen now? France would be next, and then what?

She hurried along to Madame's room, but a peep around the door showed her Madame still fast asleep. She suffered from disturbed nights and took pills which caused her to sleep late.

It was 10 May – a lovely sunny morning and no wonder Mimi was distressed: she had a son in the army somewhere near the Dutch border. Sarah decided to take the air on this lovely morning and see what was happening outside.

The streets seemed more crowded than usual, and she took a bus to the Place de l'Opéra where women were buying from the outside stalls of the Galeries Lafayette as though nothing like a war was going on at all. Inside, she ordered coffee and croissants and sat looking around her. What was going through their minds – these women who must realise by now that the phoney war was over? The real war had begun. And what of her? What now? The time had come for her to leave. I must get home, she thought. I must leave France – the time has come at last.

Leaving the store, she took a bus to the

Gare du Nord, where she bought a *Paris-Midi* – but the news was scant: LA BELGIQUE ET LA HOLLANDE RESISTANT A L'ENVAHISSEUR – while scores of young men stood about with luggage looking anxious. She heard a porter say: 'Brussels was bombed twice this morning,' and outside found the streets crowded. She walked back slowly and bought a *Paris Soir* which seemed to have more news. Disturbing news. 'Several French towns bombed – Nancy, Pontoise, Lille and Lyon…' and she felt the need to hurry.

There could be no reason for her to stay on now. She must get home to her family. Would the German troops get to Paris? It seemed impossible; the French had staked so much on the Maginot Line, and the Belgians their fortifications over the Albert Canal. Who could have guessed that troop-carrying gliders would swoop out of the sky and land right on top of the fort? Leaping from their gliders the troops proceeded immediately with the instructions which had been given them – what else could they not do – these magnificently well trained soldiers?

French and British installations had come

under attack too. Troops who hitherto had indulged in the phoney war were roused early as news of the bombings spread, and they were quickly formed up to await instructions.

General Rommel, in charge of the German 7th Armoured Division, sent a note to his wife: '*Everything wonderful so far.*'

Hitler had forecast a Nazi Millennium.

The whole world was theirs for the taking.

Chapter Fifteen

Inside the War Office, Gerard Puligny de Montfort was pulling a few strings with difficulty. Useless to tell himself now that something should have been done before, his own personal problem could equate with France's own; he had not foreseen the swiftness of Hitler's operation.

For Sarah must return home, and at once. There would be difficulties, but they must be surmounted. Much as he hated the thought of her going, it was beyond him now, her journey must be made as safe as possible. Useless to say she might be in as much danger in England, perhaps even more, but he owed it to her to send her back to the bosom of her family. Heaven knew what Maman would say – but he would have to deal with that later.

It seemed that Germany had set out to do what it had failed to do in the First World War, to annihilate France and crush Britain.

With the defences broken on the Belgian and Dutch frontiers, who knew where they would strike next? Their army manoeuvres on a grand scale were accompanied by colossal air attacks. They were bombing major cities and the French army, previously considered the finest army in the world, was now on the point of collapse – while in London top military officers were appalled by the rapidity and magnitude of the German rampage across northern France. Not only that, but the British Expeditionary Force could well have their backs against the seawall on the coast.

Things had escalated far beyond what would have been thought possible or probable, and Gerard had to think hard. Perhaps if both the British and French had had stronger governments and leadership they would not be in this mess now. But it was no use crying over spilt milk. He had to plan, and plan carefully. No point in taking chances, going the obvious way towards Boulogne and Calais. He would have to take precautionary measures probably towards the south. Already Rheims and Lille had been bombed – where next? He could not believe the rapidity with which the Germans were gaining control. He must waste no more time.

Inquiries showed that all available seats on aircraft were taken, and long queues were forming of people seeking permission to leave France. Telephone communication between the countries for civilians had been stopped, but everywhere there was talk of the wonderful job the RAF were doing – for the German bombardments were heavy, their onslaught on Le Havre and Rheims very severe. The Dutch Government had resigned – a ferry boat carrying injured men had been bombed – the rumours and stories abounded.

He would take Sarah personally – he owed her that much. If only he could manage to get her a seat on an aircraft going to England as he had done before at Christmas – and how far that seemed away! It was so peaceful then, no one would have believed there was a war on, but with false papers he would see that she found transport back to England. As for himself, with an assumed identity he should be safe enough; he certainly could not travel far with his normal rank.

Sarah returned from her walk somewhat chastened, for there was an atmosphere that could not be denied. Cars, French and Belgian, were going through the streets with suitcases and mattresses on top, several shops were closed – and she heard people talking. Why, when they were so near, did the German bombers not bomb Paris?

It was an ominous sign.

Returning late that morning, and inserting her key in the door of the apartment, she had a sudden feeling of foreboding, but told herself it was the result of her walk, and hearing and seeing so many disturbing things, but at the moment of closing the door, the doctor emerged from Madame's bedroom, looking very serious.

'*Bonjour,* Mademoiselle,' he said, putting his small case on a chair. 'I am glad you are here.'

'Is something wrong?' Sarah asked. 'Madame–?'

'I am afraid so. Madame has suffered a

heart attack. Fortunately I was in the surgery when Mimi telephoned.'

'How is she? Is she all right?' The anxiety showed in Sarah's face.

He shook his head. 'She is very ill. Unfortunately, I cannot remove her to the hospital, it is full of emergency cases, so I have taken the liberty of sending for a nurse – and, of course, you will be here, yourself, Mam'selle?'

'Well, I was on the point of returning to England,' Sarah said doubtfully, 'but if Madame–'

'Yes, I do understand. We live in worrying times, but I think Mimi has telephoned for her son, and I am sure he will be here when he is able. But in the meantime, I have given her a sedative and some medicine, and she must be kept very quiet indeed. No news of any kind, that would only disturb her.'

'I see,' Sarah said. 'What can I do to help?'

'Stay with her, as long as you are able, see that she takes her medicine, keep her warm, and let her sleep. I shall be here again tomorrow. If she takes a turn for the worse, of course, then I shall have to find room for her somewhere or other. Although she is very ill, I am hoping she will pull through. Rest is the most important thing.'

'I understand,' Sarah said. 'I will do all I can.'

'Go in and see her,' he said, picking up his bag, 'I will call again tomorrow.'

Sarah tapped on Madame's door, and went in. Mimi was sitting by her bedside, and got up when Sarah came in. She looked relieved.

'Mademoiselle – you saw the doctor?'

'Yes, he has just left,' Sarah said, taking one of Madame's almost lifeless hands.

'Madame Lisette – how do you feel now?'

The deep-set dark eyes looked into hers. She was obviously trying to keep awake following the doctor's sedative.

'Oh, Sarah, I am sorry,' she whispered.

'Oh, you mustn't say that!' Sarah said. 'We must do all we can to get you better.' She smiled. 'I expect Gerard will telephone soon.'

'What is happening?' Madame asked. 'The wireless seems to have shut down – and I don't know anything that is going on ... there is nothing in the newspapers – I don't understand–'

Just as well she didn't, Sarah thought grimly. How to keep the news from her?

'Did you go for a walk?' Madame asked. 'What was happening? Are the streets quiet

– what did you hear of the war?'

'Now, Madame,' Sarah soothed her. 'You must not worry – everything is fine.'

'But they are not saying anything on the wireless–'

'Well, I expect they are being careful, not wanting the Germans to know what is going on behind closed doors.'

And Sarah hoped this inane excuse would do for the time being.

'Let me tell you about my little walk,' she said, seeing Madame was about to drop off. 'It was really lovely out, the sun was shining, and when you are better–'

But Madame's eyes were closed and she slept, while Sarah went on talking softly. Studying her face, she could see just how ill she really was. She was ashen pale, the deeply sunken eyes had dark blue shadows, and she seemed to have got thinner – pinched around the mouth. She looked so ill.

Sarah, not by nature a pessimist, knew that this could be the beginning of the end. Madame was far too frail to bear another attack.

When she woke, Mimi gave her a light soup, which she made an attempt at eating, and towards seven, Gerard came home. She was dozing lightly, and he looked stricken when he saw her. Poor man, Sarah thought. All the worries he has to face, and now this – to say nothing of trying to get me safely back to England.

'Gerard,' she said, putting a hand on his arm. 'She will be all right; the doctor is coming in again tomorrow and he says we must keep her very quiet.'

He turned anxious eyes to her. 'Oh, Sarah,' he said. 'At such a time – but I am so glad you are here.'

'So am I,' she said, 'and you mustn't worry about me. I shall stay until she gets better – I couldn't leave her now.'

'But, child,' he said. 'You must get back–'

'Oh, I will, I will,' she said, 'but let's not think about it now. You have enough to worry about.'

The look he gave her was enough to bring the colour into her cheeks and she got up swiftly and went over to the cabinet feeling her heart pounding for some reason. No one had ever looked at her like that, not even David.

Then Madame opened her eyes, those dark eyes so like her son's.

'Gerard,' she whispered.

'Maman–'

Sarah tiptoed out of the room and went into the kitchen to find Mimi.

The nurse arrived soon after Gerard had left and said she would be moving in. She would be quite happy on the *chaise-longue* in Madame's room – she was used to elderly patients – and would be on hand when Madame woke.

Sarah was very relieved. Even so, she meant to stay with Madame in her hour of need; she couldn't leave her now.

Gerard contemplated his next move. Whatever Sarah had said, however much she meant it, he knew that he could not take advantage of her. His mother was old, and ill – but Sarah must have her chance in life, too. The most important thing was to get her home, and safely.

He thought briefly of young David Drummond, who as far as he knew, was based in England. Great though the dangers were, the British contingents of the RAF based in France were fighting greater odds. It was becoming more and more obvious that ground battles could not be won without air support, and he thought again of the English bomber squadrons based around Rheims, which had received a battering only the night before. The stockpiling of equipment from Great Britain had been going on since the year before, but much good it did now, and he wondered how bad the destruction was. He would be better to use a smaller airfield – but where? Over four hundred British combat aircraft were based in France, from Hurricanes to Blenheims, and had been since September the previous year, but they were based in out of the way spots, often with no accommodation so that pilots slept in village halls or farm buildings and were continually being moved about because of the German bombers.

It was useless to think of her going by sea, even though he had a few contacts. It was an extremely hazardous crossing and would be considerably longer now that the northern ports were under fire. No, it had to be an aerodrome – and he cursed himself again for leaving it so late. No one, he consoled himself, had foreseen the swiftness of the German onslaught, from every direction.

He made his plans accordingly, he would drive towards the west thus avoiding the Channel ports and just prayed that he would find the right connections.

It was midnight before he had completed his new plans, outlandish though they were. A high-ranking British officer was leaving the next afternoon on a small plane bound for London, it being thought safer than at night or early morning. If he could get Sarah there by two p.m. she was promised a lift. But no help was forthcoming for the journey to the aerodrome, which was buried in deep countryside. The small landing ground hidden in Brittany had been his only chance.

He would leave Paris mid-morning, and must telephone Sarah first thing. It was a speedy move, but he knew he could take no chances. She must travel light, a small travelling bag. Anything else she must leave in Paris.

Sarah was alarmed when the telephone rang at six-thirty. But it was Gerard with instructions for her to leave, and he sounded so serious that she knew there would be no point in her arguing.

She was up at seven, packed and ready to leave by nine o'clock. Going into the kitchen where she found the nurse comforting Mimi who was in tears, her heart sank as she stared at them both.

'What is it?'

'Madame Puligny passed away early this morning … I am sorry,' the nurse said.

'Oh, no!' Sarah's hand went to her mouth.

'But she was–'

'It was to be expected,' the nurse said. 'She was very poorly, and it is for the best. She could not have lasted much longer.'

'Does M Puligny de Montfort know?'

She shook her head. 'No. I was unable to get hold of him.'

'He telephoned me early on,' Sarah said, then realised she must say no more, perhaps her leaving and means of transport was to be kept secret.

Poor Gerard, surely she wouldn't be able to leave now.

'May I see her?' she asked.

'If you wish,' the nurse said and took her into Madame's bedroom for the last time.

Madame looked much as she did in life, beautiful even in old age, the hooded eyes now closed, and Sarah wept uncontrollable tears. It was the first time she had seen a dead person, and the sorrow she felt was also compounded by the shock. Surely, she would wake up soon, those dark eyes studying Sarah or smiling with affection?

'Come along,' the nurse said, putting an arm round Sarah's shoulders.

They had reached the hall when Gerard came in, dressed in casual clothes. Sarah hardly recognised him, and one look at her tear-drenched face told him all.

'I am sorry, Monsieur,' the nurse said. 'Madame passed away early this morning,' and saw his drained face, the distress the news caused him. 'I did telephone you, Monsieur.'

'Yes, I am sure you did, thank you,' and without another word went into his mother's room.

When he came out, he was composed, and went straight over to Sarah.

'My dear Sarah, you must not upset yourself.'

Sarah held back the tears.

'Come, let us go into the kitchen where Mimi will make us some strong coffee.'

He took her arm, and smiled down at her sadly, but she stopped.

'I cannot go now,' she said. 'Not today.'

'Of course you can,' he said firmly. 'There will be no better time. There is nothing more you can do here.'

'I am so sorry, Gerard.'

'Well, perhaps it is for the best.' Knowing what he did, in a way he was relieved that his mother would not be exposed to whatever Paris had in store for her.

'Death is always difficult to deal with, even when it's expected, and my mother had lived a long life, and a very full one.' Sarah remembered his wife who had died so young and the small daughter. Tragedy had already dealt him a bitter blow.

She sat in the kitchen drinking her coffee while Gerard was discussing a plan of operation with Mimi and the nurse.

When he came back into the room, he was purposeful and brisk.

'Now, Sarah, there is no time to waste,' he said. 'Are you packed? The car is outside, and I shall tell you on the way what the plan is.'

Her dark eyes were wide with apprehension; she hated to be leaving him, much of her heart was in this wonderful city which had been so kind to her; she felt she was deserting it in its time of need. To say nothing of leaving Gerard...

'Is this all?' he asked as she emerged carrying her raincoat with a small suitcase.

'I shall be back for the other things,' she smiled at him and he gave her again that heart-searching look before picking up her case and leading her out to the car.

The car, a small Peugeot, made its way out of Paris westwards on a road Sarah had never been on before. She was curious to see the preparations made for the war effort, sandbags everywhere, boarded-up shops, villagers who stood around in small groups, anxiety on their faces. It was not until they were well out of Paris that Gerard relaxed and talked to her.

'I have got you on a small plane going to England. There is one other passenger, and I suspect it will land in Kent, probably Manston, somewhere like that. The pilot will have to decide when and where. I honestly do not know nor could I plan what will happen to you after that, but passage will be cleared for you, all the papers are in order, and at least you will be home,' and he thrust a hand inside his jacket and came up with an official manila envelope.

'Inside you will find details of your time in Paris; if asked, although it is written there, you have been my personal assistant,' and he turned to her and smiled. *'N'est-ce pas?'*

'Oui, c'est vrai,' she said.

'I hope the journey will be comfortable, but I can't guarantee it, it is a small plane. You won't mind the bumpy ride, will you?'

And please God that's all it will be, he thought. Please keep her safe – guilt flooding through him that he had left it so late.

Now they were in open countryside, long, long roads, lined with poplars, all was quiet

– a village or two, where dogs lay sleeping and gladioli grew in tiny front gardens, churches with lovely spires or Norman towers.

'Tell me about your life in England,' Gerald said suddenly. 'I want to picture you when you return home. Your mother's pleasure – your father – how pleased they will be to see you.'

'Yes, it has been a long time.'

'You will come back,' he said. 'Paris will be your second home.'

Yes, she thought. It will ... and then from out of the skies a plane zoomed, flying low almost as though the pilot was going to attack them. Gerard recognised a German plane and knew a moment's fear – had the news of what he was doing got out?

The plane came in again this time spattering the roadside with bullets before flying off into the distance.

'From what I am given to understand, they do quite a lot of this sort of thing,' Gerard tried to reassure her, although feeling somewhat shaky himself, and was reminded that Le Touquet had been bombed only the night before.

Well, he was committed now, no turning back.

They had been driving for an hour, past one small town which had evidently been at the mercy of a bombing attack. The scene of devastation was all around them. The place was deserted, the market square strewn with shrapnel, the First World War memorial pitted with machine gun bullets, a row of shops razed to the ground.

Press on, he told himself firmly.

'And what are you going to do when you get back?' he asked, with more assurance than he felt, while Sarah was shocked by the shots and bomb damage. What lay in store? And had to admit to a feeling of trepidation. Everything was all right as long as Gerard was with her, but what about when he left?

After another twenty miles, he slowed down and pulled up in a field, where he stopped and took a map out of the pocket of the car.

'Ah,' he said. 'Now, where are we – and how far is it now? The small airfield is quite buried, so I am told, so we might have some difficulty finding it, but unless I am mistaken, it is not far off now.'

Reassuring himself from the map, he handed it to Sarah. 'Now, as I see it, some five miles on is a turning to the left. It is wooded, and the very narrow path widens until we come to a small *bois,* with tall trees, and a small flat area which is big enough for a small plane to land and take off.'

Sarah studied the map, roughly drawn and in French, but the directions were clear.

He started up the car again. 'So–'

There was nothing to be seen for the five miles but wide open countryside, not even a small cottage, but Gerard knew what he was looking for. He slowed down before turning into a rutted path just wide enough to take a car. He drove slowly over the rough road, taking it carefully, for a quarter of a mile or so before coming to a small, flat grassy field, which he bumped the car over before coming to a halt by a small clump of trees. Sarah was amazed to see under the trees a small aircraft, camouflaged and almost perfectly hidden. Gerard got out of the car, and came round to help her out then took her hand.

In the small clump of trees was a tiny hut, like an outdoor privy, and going towards it, Gerard knocked on the door. It was opened by a young man in civilian clothes who grinned at him and saluted.

'You made it, sir,' he said, and Sarah, realising that he was English, felt a great sense of relief.

'Are you game, miss?' he asked cheekily, and she smiled back at him.

'Stay there,' Gerard said, and went inside, coming out with a tall middle-aged Englishman, who greeted her formally.

'The pilot has to leave almost immediately,' Gerard said, while the young man ran towards the plane.

I cannot believe this, Sarah thought. Are we really, three of us, going to travel in that little plane. She took a deep breath, and thought, in for a penny, in for a pound, as the roar of the little engine started and the man ran towards the plane.

'Come,' Gerard said, and ran with her to the door of the plane. She turned to him, her heart in her mouth, her dark eyes meeting his, and impulsively threw her arms around his neck, as he held her tightly.

She broke away, and made a move towards the door, but Gerard held her arm. 'Remember me,' he said, and kissed her on both cheeks, taking from his pocket a folded pad of tissue paper which he gave to her.

She looked down at it in her palm, and then at him, her eyes brimming over.

'*Au revoir,* Gerard,' she whispered, '*au revoir*–' and stepped up into the plane.

He slammed the door tight and waved as

the plane made a move forward and bumped over the field, and looking out of one of the tiny windows, Sarah saw him gradually disappearing from sight. The Englishman sat beside the pilot, while Sarah sat in an uncomfortable bucket seat. Cramped it was, but Sarah undid the small package before the plane finally left the earth to soar up into the skies.

Looking down into the palm of her hand, she saw the tiny red enamelled Cross of Lorraine ... the symbol of the Free French.

Gerard was never to know if they really meant to get him. If it was a personal thing, or just a practice trip against some poor French villager. It all happened so swiftly – he did see the three German Stukas – and they seemed to be heading his way, but when his car was found, riddled with bullet holes, he was lying dead inside, his face turned to the skies.

Chapter Sixteen

When the telephone rang Robbie jumped. As a family, they received so few telephone calls these days, and she dropped her knitting and hurried over to it.

There was a lot of noise going on, but she could hear a girl's voice, a voice she recognised, and her heart leapt.

'Sarah? Sarah?'

'Mum, it's me – I'm home!'

Robbie was choked and held back the tears. 'Where are you? Are you all right?'

'Yes, I'm fine, I'm in Paddington, at the station; can you hear me?'

Robbie's tears spilled over. 'Yes, oh, Sarah darling, you're sure you're–'

'Yes,' Sarah said firmly. Time to tell of her journey later. 'I'll find a train and make my way, so expect me when you see me – OK?'

There would be no transport from the station, Robbie knew – no pony and trap now, and with Laurie called up no car, and no taxis; petrol was rationed, but it didn't matter. Sarah would find a way home even if she walked the mile and a half, and she glanced up at the mantelpiece where several letters from David sat awaiting Sarah's return. Many times Robbie had wanted to destroy them, but couldn't bring herself to do so. They were Sarah's property, it was up to Sarah what she did with them.

'Wonderful, see you later, and mind how you go,' Robbie said now, hanging up the receiver and letting the tears fall. Oh, the relief – the blessed relief – she was all right, Sarah was safe – then pulling herself together took down David's letters; five of them, and put them in the dresser drawer. She didn't want Sarah to see them as soon as she arrived home. Time for that later. Then she hurried upstairs to get Sarah's old room ready. Tom would be over the moon – he would be home soon, limping his way back from the lower field.

The first thing Sarah was aware of was barrage balloons, hanging in the sky all over London, a sea of them. She thanked God she had only a small case – enough to get oneself about in these crowds, there seemed to be thousands of people going this way and that, the station murky with smoke, airmen, soldiers, WAAFs, girls in ATS uniform, slick pageboy hairdos beneath their small caps, unobtrusive lipsticks and sturdy legs in their army issue stockings and polished brown shoes – was that what she was going to do? The thought passed through Sarah's mind – but she pushed it away and found the time of a train to Allington – a fair delay – but she would have a sandwich and coffee to tide her over, knowing that her mother would be preparing a meal fit for a homecoming. To be on terra firma again after that terrifying plane ride was enough to make one feel glad to be alive.

The advertisement boards everywhere grabbed her attention. DON'T KEEP DAD – KEEP MUM and another EVEN WALLS HAVE EARS – but the difference between London and Paris could not have been more noticeable. She had read somewhere that Paris was a feminine city, and she recognised now that this was true. Even in war, there was a certain frivolity about it, a nonchalance, a light-hearted air, or light-headedness perhaps – but London was so dark, so grim-faced; she reminded herself that British humour was the best in the world. That was certainly something Paris lacked.

On the packed train she found the humour; seventeen and eighteen to a carriage, ten seats; mercifully she had one – and the strap-hangers, young men and women going off to war, their brand-new uniforms sitting oddly on them, their belongings stacked high in the corridors with even more young men, the jokes they bandied about to hide what must have been excitement or trepidation about the new life that was ahead of them.

Glancing out of the window, she could see there were no more signs to tell you where you were and, as the train pulled out of the wayside stations, no signposts to guide travellers on their way. Rows and rows of vegetables grew in long narrow front gardens; no doubt everyone was digging for victory – the corrugated iron shelters protruding above the earth as though from a prehistoric age.

She had put off thinking about Gerard – or trying to – those last moments when she had felt so drained, so empty, so wretched that she could, for two pins, have refused to leave – tempted to say, 'I am not going – I am going to stay with you.' But–

And Madame, dead; she could hardly believe it, even now. It was difficult to imagine, as Gerard said, that everything that was happening was all for the best. She almost felt like an alien here, going home, but thrust the thought of Paris from her. This was her home, where she had lived for twenty years, Paris had been but a little episode in her life, and she could always go back, after the war.

It was strange getting out at Allington station – it seemed so small, and the very air smelt different. Fresh, clean air, after all, it was miles away from London, and it made all the difference. She breathed deeply; she had imagined that there would be no transport available, not even a bus, at least not one in sight, and she began walking home.

It was so strange – she had walked this way to school every day, thought nothing of it, meeting friends on the way, walking in twos or threes. What were they doing, now, those girls? The cottages she passed were quiet at early evening, she could see lines of washing in backyards, some houses had sticky tape on the windows to prevent them from shattering – the fields, with neat rows of vegetables, which disappeared into the distant horizon; but best of all was the scent

– there was nothing like it. Not a perfume, as in Paris, but the fresh English scent of flowering blossom trees, late cherry trees, lilac – surely there was never a scent as lovely as real lilac after rain. She caught again the haunting smell of a balsam poplar that came every May time, and, closing her eyes, she breathed deeply, then swung her case with renewed energy and made for home…

Well, of course, Robbie was outside waiting for her on this spring evening, her father Tom sitting on the bench outside the front door. Her breath caught in her throat as she dropped her case and ran straight into Robbie's arms.

'Oh, Mum! Mum!' How could she have stayed away so long. Then she ran to her father – how old he looked – such a change in him, and a fear went through her – but he wasn't anywhere near as old as Madame Lisette – and there was Kirby Hall, with its banner proclaiming its help and shelter, a bit ragged after a few months' weathering, and then she was inside First Lodge with the smell of roast lamb and rosemary and the familiar sounds and sights of home.

'Oh, you look so pretty!' and Robbie stood, arms folded and looked at her. How proud she was of her, this daughter who had actually lived in Paris, and through a war, too, elegantly dressed, travelling about on her own, flying, can you believe, as if she had been doing it all her life.

'Well, come on in,' she said at length, 'you must be exhausted. Tell us how you got home. We had some anxious moments, I can tell you, sometimes we thought we would never–'

'Now, Edie,' Tom said, 'the girl's tired out. Sit you down – let her take her time – she's back home for good now.'

Sarah flopped into the basket chair by the big black stove, her father's chair – and smiled at them both.

'Oh, it is good to be home, but I shall sleep tonight, I promise you,' she said, grinning at them.

A sound came from upstairs, a child's voice, and she started.

'Who's that?'

Robbie smiled. 'It's little Tommy, Hilda and the baby, they're staying with us now, just for the duration. With Laurie away, they had to give up the flat over the garage, you see, and we have the room.'

'Oh, that's lovely!' Sarah cried, and went towards the stairs, where Hilda, carrying baby Editha and holding Tommy's hand, made her careful progress down.

She smiled her gentle smile. 'Hallo, Sarah, say hallo, Tommy, this is your Auntie Sarah.'

Sarah whipped the little boy up into her arms – oh, but he was a handsome little boy, just like Laurie, and he regarded her with Laurie's blue eyes.

'Do you remember me?' She hugged him then put him down.

'And little Editha…'

Baby Editha looked like her mother, those serious dark eyes, and a tuft of hair on top of her head, dressed all in white, a tiny pink smocked dress, and little white bootees, tied with pink ribbon.

Sarah kissed Hilda warmly. 'Oh, it's good to be home,' she said, and meant it.

There was wine, in her honour; perhaps they imagined that she lived daily on wine in Paris, and the excellent roast potatoes and lamb with rosemary, and fresh vegetables, followed by champagne rhubarb and custard.

After dinner Hilda, having put the children to bed, insisted on doing the washing up.

'You two sit and talk,' she said and Robbie looked at her gratefully.

'She's a good girl,' she said to Sarah.

'And where is Laurie?' Sarah asked.

'The army – REME somewhere in Yorkshire, I think.'

'And Donnie, and Ginny?'

'Donnie is in the RAF, it's what he wanted to do, ground staff, and Ginny, well, she's got a job in Reading. Changed her mind about joining up, I think the new little house won – she loves it – a place of her own.'

'I shall go over and see her,' Sarah said.

'Oh, she'll be over. 'Course, they've had to give up their car – no petrol, you see – anyway tell us about your journey, we were so upset when you didn't come back when you said.'

Sarah took a deep breath.

'Well, first of all, I'm sorry to tell you that Madame Lisette died yesterday – no,' she amended, 'early this morning–' was it really today, she wondered. It seemed a lifetime ago.

Robbie was shocked. 'This morning? Today? But how–'

'Well, Gerard had already arranged for me to come home, and it took a bit of doing, I am sure, but he had managed to get a flight – I'll tell you about it later, but last night, Madame had another heart attack, and –

well, this morning, she died.'

'Oh, Sarah, love, I am sorry, you were very fond of the old lady, weren't you?' Truth to tell, she had sometimes been a little jealous of the affection Sarah had for Madame.

'Yes, I was – she was very good to me, I wanted to stay, but Gerard insisted that I came. Perhaps he knew she was going to die, I don't know, but the Germans were on the doorstep, I believe now, from what I've heard, and he insisted I get away.'

I should think so, Robbie thought privately.

'Well, I am glad he did,' she said. 'This Gerard – this is Madame's son?'

'Yes,' Sarah said and Robbie could see by her expression that he meant something to her. He must be old enough to be her father, she frowned. I hope she didn't really fall for him. Those Frenchmen can be fascinating, so I'm told, specially the older ones.

'So, then how did you manage to get away?'

And Sarah told them, word for word, while Tom, his eyes fastened on his beloved daughter, listened with fascination as the tale unfolded.

'And you say this officer was being flown

back and you were on the same plane?' He was proud of her and worried sick at the same time. If he had known…

'Then how did you get back from the aerodrome?'

'A young airman gave me a lift into London as far as the Embankment, and I took a bus.'

'Well, I don't know,' he said, lost for words, thinking of all she had done in the past twenty-four hours. 'You see, we didn't get any letters for some time, did we, Edie?'

'No,' she said, 'and not being able to telephone – oh, it was awful – one or two letters filtered through, but they were old ones, posted in March.'

'I got two from you,' Sarah said, 'but of course, to phone was out of the question, so I couldn't let you know–'

The moment is now, Robbie thought. 'Oh, by the way,' she said casually, 'some letters arrived from David Drummond – I put them – yes, here they are–' as if the thought had suddenly occurred to her, and handed them to Sarah, and saw her face flush deep with pleasure.

'Oh, thank you–' and held them close to her. 'Well, I'll read them later. I did write to him. I hope they got through,' and she sighed. 'Well, I think I'll go up to bed now – I'm whacked.'

'Your bed is ready, darling,' Robbie said, and Sarah went over and kissed them both. What dears they were, and how lucky she was to have such understanding parents.

'Good-night, both of you,' she said.

'And don't bother to get up early – you sleep late,' Tom said as she disappeared up the stairs.

'You should have thrown them away,' he said disapprovingly when he heard Sarah's door close.

'Tom, how could I? They are Sarah's letters, she has a right to them–'

'But she hasn't,' Tom said. 'Has she?'

There was the sound of distant gunfire, but Sarah was used to that, as upstairs, she kicked off her shoes and lay on the bed, opening David's letters in date order. Oh, poor David, with no news from her, and apparently worried sick – she must get in touch with him right away – tomorrow, first thing. He was unable to say much about what he was doing, but by the time she came to the last letter she could see that he must be exhausted, and worn out with arduous flying duties. She had no idea where he was stationed, but figured out that it was somewhere in the south. At least he had left Scotland, she was certain. His last letter assured her of his undying love, and his wish to see her as soon as possible. Had she received the bracelet he sent her? Well, she had, and had written to him thanking him, but he couldn't have received the letter. He had still not forgiven her for staying on, that much she read into the letters. Well, she was home now, and tomorrow she would try to get in touch with him and let him know she was safe. He wanted to see her more than anything in the world – it was the thought of her that kept him going, and flushed with the joy at being home again and hearing from David after all this time, she found the prospect of seeing him again exciting. Now she was wound up and not the least bit sleepy.

What would she do with her life now? She had to do some kind of war work, that was certain, and really, it was not the time to think of it then, but she found herself unable to sleep. Getting up off the bed, she ran a bath, and afterwards stepped into her old dressing gown which still hung on the back of the door. Another world, she thought.

Oh, she did wish she knew how Gerard had got on driving back to Paris. How would she know? Was he even now, back at the War Office, helping to design some plan to keep the Germans at bay? She realised that she missed him more than she missed Madame. He was a special person, and she would write first thing in the morning – perhaps the letter would get through – she would send two, one to Gaby at the salon and one to Gerard.

Opening her handbag, she took out the folded tissue paper to expose the little red Cross of Lorraine, and pursed her lips to hold back the tears. The emblem of the Free French – well, she would join the Free French, there was perhaps something she could do. They had their headquarters in London, that much she knew. Turning the brooch over, she pinned it on to her dressing gown, and going over to the mirror to see it she saw herself, a dark-haired girl, a little tired around the eyes; but her brown eyes were warm, her skin smooth, her hair shone; would David find her much changed?

She longed to see him again, remembering the blue eyes, eyes that reflected the blue of the skies, his tall figure, wide shoulders – and shivered slightly.

She unpinned the brooch and removed her dressing gown, sliding between the sheets and finding even in this warm spring evening a hot-water bottle between the sheets.

She must sleep, or she would be fit for nothing in the morning, and tucking herself down went through the incredible events of the day…

She was downstairs early – Tom had already gone to work, but Robbie was there, and Hilda and the children.

'Morning!' she cried.

'Oh, you're up!' Robbie said, pleased. 'I thought you would sleep late, you looked so tired last night.'

'I slept well, that's more to the point, and you young fella-me-lad, how are you?' but little Tommy edged into his mother's side.

'How about a boiled egg?' Robbie asked. 'You're lucky we keep chickens – some people never see a new-laid egg.'

'I'll bet,' Sarah said, 'but not for me, just toast, if I may. Oh, you've got a toaster – I'll see to it–'

'Don't you want a cooked breakfast?' Robbie asked. She hoped Sarah wasn't going all French on them.

'No, thank you, I've got out of the way of it,' Sarah said.

'What do you have over there then?' Robbie asked suspiciously.

'Coffee,' and Robbie looked worried. 'Oh, we've no coffee,' and Sarah laughed.

'I'd rather have tea, anyway. We'd have toast then French bread, perhaps jam, croissants–'

Robbie looked disapproving. 'Well, that's not much to start the day on,' and Sarah smiled.

'I'm still the same old me, Mum,' she said, and winked at Hilda who showed her broken tooth in a sweet smile.

Tommy put out a tentative hand and touched the little brooch which she had pinned to her cardigan.

'What's that?' Robbie asked, pouring from the big teapot.

'The Cross of Lorraine, the emblem of the Free French,' Sarah said, trying to sound as practical as she could. 'Gerard gave it to me when I left – wasn't that kind of him?'

Robbie frowned again. Surely, now, it couldn't be, surely she hadn't fallen for this middle-aged Frenchman – why did he give her a brooch? Glancing down, she saw the slim gold bracelet that David had given her for her birthday.

Oh, Sarah, she thought, I wish you could be like other girls, and meet a proper man – an ordinary man.

Having written her letters, three of them, one to David, and two to Paris, Sarah went for a walk round Kirby Hall with Hilda, sometimes pushing the pram, or taking Tommy's hand. It seemed so strange to be back; nothing had changed, yet it was all so different.

Hilda was a sweet girl, shy, gentle, no wonder Laurie had fallen in love with her, and a true mother. Sarah hated wars that set young families apart from their loved ones, and remembered so saying to David, who had appeared slightly shocked.

'Do you hear from Laurie?' she asked Hilda.

'Yes, he writes, telephoned once when he arrived at the camp. He's in Catterick, that's in Yorkshire.'

'Oh,' Sarah said. 'I'm glad you are staying with Mum.'

'Yes, she's lovely, your mum,' Hilda said, and her eyes were shining.

'Well, I suppose I shall have to turn my mind to something, I can't be idle, and if things get worse, they will call women up I suppose.'

'I think so,' Hilda said gravely.

'Come on, Tommy, let's run back to the house,' Sarah cried, taking Tommy's hand. It was only a short distance. His little legs flew along, and they arrived breathless and laughing at the door of First Lodge as Robbie appeared in the doorway.

'Just in time,' she said. 'It's David on the phone.'

'Oh!' and Sarah ran.

'David? David?'

Robbie sighed. Now what, she wondered.

Chapter Seventeen

When the news came that the German forces had made enormous headway in France and captured Arras and Amiens, David Drummond was frantic with worry. The British troops would be forced to retreat to the Channel ports and what chance then of a safe passage for Sarah? She had left it far too late, and he blamed the Puligny de Montfort family for encouraging her to stay on. He was sure Sarah would never have stayed unless she had been urged to do so. They should have forced her to get home whatever her feelings about staying. Not only that, but the German advances put a heavy burden on Fighter Command, and they were stretched to the limit as it was.

And then came rumours of the British troops making their way towards the Channel ports, trapped in their thousands, marooned on the beaches, waiting for anything that would get them back across the Channel. Little ships and big ships, ferryboats and cargo ships, it was a desperate battle against all odds when David's squadron took to the skies again and again to do battle against the Heinkel bombers and Messerschmitts, the skies buzzing with the sound of machine-gun fire and the scream of planes zooming out of the clouds. On the second day he came out of the briefing room and took off once again, could see Calais and Boulogne below him and the Messerschmitts on his tail, as he fired all eight guns at the Stuka he could see ahead of him; then he saw the Messerschmitt hurtling towards the ground – someone in the squadron had scored a direct hit. He knew that he would have to return to base and refuel before going up again – you only came alive when you reached the ground, up here it was a nightmare from hell.

They flew another patrol two hours later and after a few hours' sleep, he was up again early and out again to do battle with the German Luftwaffe who seemed to have an inexhaustible number of planes, though he knew himself they had shot down twelve the day before.

Two days of this and he was exhausted, had hardly left the coast when he saw the Heinkel making directly for him, guns blazing. He knew that he had been hit in a wing and the petrol tank, then the cockpit caught fire and he knew he must bale out – not an easy thing to do from a Spitfire, and saw the Hurricane pilot waving to him as he chased the Heinkel. He baled out, his parachute opening. But he could see the Heinkel plunging towards the ground, black smoke pouring from it as it plummeted.

Well done, he thought, to his fellow pilot whoever he was, thanking God he had landed on British soil, even in a field of turnips, as the farmer came hurrying towards him to escort him back to the farmhouse for checking in case he was a German in disguise. He seemed to be bruised all over with a painful ankle. After clearance, he was driven back to Hornchurch, where examination showed that he had extensive bruising and a twisted ankle, but no more than that.

He was, however, grounded for six hours, after assuring them that he felt fit enough to go up again, and at that point decided to ring First Lodge, to see if by chance Sarah had arrived home. He dare not think of his reactions if she was still in Paris.

The telephone was answered almost at once by Robbie, and a great wave of relief surged through him when she told him that Sarah had arrived home the day before.

'Could I speak to her, Robbie?'

'Well, David, she is not here at the moment, she has gone for a walk – but I think I can see her coming back – yes, it is, hold on–'

Well, what could you do? she thought. What was the point of putting off the evil day, for that's what it would be, and the sooner the break came the better.

'It's David,' she said, handing the telephone to Sarah.

'David – David! How lovely to hear you!' and the tears sprang to her eyes, as Robbie joined Hilda and the children outside.

'Sarah, I can't believe it! I thought I would never see you again, life has been so hectic–'

'I can imagine,' she said, 'I've thought of you so often – you are all right, aren't you, David?'

She didn't say 'you sound absolutely worn out, as indeed you must be'.

'Yes, I'm fine, but you–'

'David, I'm home now, so–'

'Any chance of my seeing you?' he asked.

'Well, I'm free, but it's up to you, you don't get much time to yourself.'

'I could get to London, but I don't know when. It would have to be just a brief meeting, the time is precious, also I'm not sure that I want you to come to London; there may be–'

'Now David, if you can make it, so can I. Will you have far to come?'

'Er – no,' he said. 'I'm not sure when, but I must see you – I have something very special to ask you.'

She flushed rosy red – she guessed what it could be.

'Look, Sarah, I mean it, I'm desperate, tired of being so far away from you – let's put it like that – we've wasted lots of unnecessary months as it is.'

'I know.'

'Did you miss me?' he asked, lowering his voice.

'Of course I did.'

'Look, I've got to go, there's a queue behind me. I'll ring you in a day or two. I hope … it'll be short notice. I'm afraid, take care.'

'You too,' she said, and heard the phone click as he replaced the receiver.

'Well,' she said, 'that's that,' as Robbie came back into the kitchen.

'How is he?'

'He sounds awful, he must be exhausted, but I think he might get to London soon and I've said I will go up and meet him.'

Robbie frowned. 'Oh, Sarah there might be raids–'

'Look, Mum, if I can travel back from Paris, then I certainly can get to London, and besides, we never know what might happen–'

'That's what I mean,' Robbie said grimly.

'Well, I'm going to see him, and that's that.'

Her chin set in a stubborn line, and Robbie wondered yet again, as she had a thousand times – what would become of this sad romance? Where would it end?

It was two days later that David telephoned her, and Sarah had almost been sitting by the telephone waiting for his call.

'David?'

'Sarah, darling, just a brief call. Could you meet me in London tomorrow, around twelve outside Swan and Edgar's in Piccadilly? We can go to St James's Park – I won't have long – I have a few other things to do–'

'Of course I can.' Her eyes were shining and her breath coming fast.

'I thought that might be the most convenient meeting-place. I'll explain when I see you. We don't want to be in town long, in case of–'

'I know, I know – I'll see you then, outside Swan and Edgar's in Piccadilly at noon. Don't worry if you are late.'

When she hung up the receiver her dark eyes were dancing as she twirled round with the exuberance of youth, and ran over to kiss Robbie.

'I'm going to see him, David, Mum – oh, it's so exciting!'

So that's how she really feels about him, Robbie thought – no doubt about her excitement at the prospect. Should she let Lady Freddie know? Was it her duty to let her Ladyship know? Someone had to do something – but then she decided. She would keep out of it. Bad enough to be an onlooker in this little charade – let alone a participant.

'What will you wear?' she asked – as if it mattered in the slightest. No one bothered to dress up these days of clothes rationing – too much risk of being caught in an air raid, and wondered if Sarah had seen the newspapers that the Germans were already in Paris. If she had, it hadn't dampened her ardour.

'A mac, I should think,' she laughed, looking up at the overcast skies.

It was drizzling as she set off for the long walk to the station, but her step was light as she retrod the ground she had walked a few days before. Now, she was on quite a different errand, an exciting errand, for she knew – or rather suspected – what David was going to ask her, and she was not surprised. All this time he had waited for her while she was in Paris – wasted time, as he said, especially when you were doing the job he was doing–

Paddington was packed as usual, and almost fighting her way through the crowds she made for the underground, and bought her ticket for Piccadilly. When she emerged she found the rain had stopped and the sun was shining, it was going to be a fine day.

London was so different in wartime. Many more people than she remembered, mostly in uniform and people it seemed from all over the world. Passing St James's church she saw that they had a soup kitchen; everything that could be done for civilians and men and women in uniform – but it could not have been more unlike Paris and she wondered, as she did often, if Gerard had got back safely.

The windows of the shops were sometimes blacked over, although others were taped against bomb blast. A pathetic attempt had been made to put merchandise on view, there was so little to be had, but then London had never had the gift of window dressing as Paris had. Frenchwomen took their wearing apparel much more seriously. Now people were dressed in workmanlike clothes, women wearing navy trousers because of the jobs they did, bus conductors – clippies they were called – ARP personnel, again in navy blue. There were sandbags everywhere and on everyone's face a sober look of resignation.

She found Swan and Edgar and was

surprised to find their window display quite interesting, featuring underwear made of pink spotted organdie, French knickers and cami-knickers and slips: WHAT THE WELL-DRESSED FRENCHWOMAN IS WEARING – the notices read, and she smiled as a hand touched her shoulder, and turning, she saw David, tall, handsome in his RAF uniform, the pair of rings on his sleeves denoting the rank of squadron leader, his silver wings on his chest.

'Oh, David!' and despite the passers-by he took her into his arms and held her close; they might, she thought later, have been in the Gare du Nord where greetings and farewells were quite spectacular.

When she raised her head from his embrace, he kissed her swiftly on the mouth, and hurried her away from the crowds on the corner and along Piccadilly.

They fell into step, he holding Sarah's arm firmly, walking purposefully as though he hadn't a moment to lose. Taking a sidelong look at him, Sarah could see how thin he was, pale, with dark shadows beneath the blue eyes – and she could have wept when she imagined what his life must be like, up there in the skies, fighting their battles with no sign of any let-up.

He stopped in his tracks when they reached Green Park station where there were not so many crowds.

'Let me look at you,' he said, and took her in his arms again. 'You are the most beautiful girl in the world, and now I shall give you lunch, but it will have to be quick for I have a lot to do today and I'll explain later. Do you mind a quick lunch?'

'Of course not,' Sarah said stoutly, and he led the way into a small café near the park, where they sold snacks and coffee.

They settled for ham and tomato sandwiches – the days had not yet arrived when Spam came on the scene – and sat eating them without being aware of what they were doing, as they stared hungrily at each other across the table.

'I am not going to ask you how Paris was, for presumably you loved it or you wouldn't have stayed on.'

'But, I–'

'Never mind,' he said. 'You're home now,' and looked at the lovely face in front of him. 'Sarah, will you marry me?'

She was taken aback at the suddenness of his proposal.

'David!' She hadn't expected it to be quite like this, with the emphasis on speed.

'I meant it – I want to marry you more than anything in the world. I always have.'

'Sshh,' she said, softly, laying a hand on his arm. 'David, it really isn't as simple as all that. You really don't know enough about me to ask me to marry you. We come from entirely different worlds, you and I.'

'Sarah, darling, that's old hat, and I do know you. We grew up together – remember? What more can you know about a person than that? We played together, rode together – lived in the same house, almost–'

'Oh David, David!' she cried. How could she explain? Her life had been totally different: he the son of wealthy parents, she the daughter – and adopted at that – of his mother's servants. Things might have got easier on the class-war front since the war began, but they certainly had not reached those proportions.

'Anyway,' he said, 'I am not interested in your reasons for not marrying me, only that you want to marry me. Do you love me, Sarah?'

'You know I do,' she said softly. She always had, hadn't she? There had never been anyone like David.

'Well, then,' he said triumphantly.

'But you don't think perhaps we should

have some time together, as a couple I mean, to really get to know each other?'

'I don't see how that's possible, if we are always to be apart,' he said stubbornly. 'I have spent all this time away from you, and you from me. I want you beside me. Some of the chaps have their wives nearby and that's what I'd like you to do, for us to get married and you move in with me – we could get digs wherever I am stationed. Oh, Sarah,' and he took her hands across the table – 'what is the point of living separate lives when we want to be together? We need to be together – for the rest of our lives, however long that may be.'

Poor David, he sounded desperate – and she ached with all her heart to accept him, but did he really know what he was doing? In peace-time, she was sure, it never would have been possible. His mother would have manoeuvred things so that he met a nice girl of his own class, who would make him a suitable wife.

'And your mother,' she said softly. 'What do you suppose she would say? I can't think she would welcome it, David.'

'It has nothing to do with my mother. It is my life. Anyway, she wouldn't object if it's what I want.'

'Now, David, you know what I mean – and your father–'

'Well, he's not here at the moment, and I certainly don't intend to wait for his return from the States – or whatever mission he is on now. Anyway, Mother is at home in Edwardes Square for a few days; that's why I thought it would be a good idea to get the whole thing settled,' and Sarah's heart sank.

'You are going to see her today, to ask her?'

'I am going to tell her,' he amended. 'I shall tell her I am going to marry you and I won't brook any opposition. If you are right, and she does disapprove, then so be it. We'll marry anyway. You are over twenty-one – oh, Sarah, I can't take no for an answer. I love you so much–'

The blue eyes burned into hers, there could be no doubting his genuine feelings. After all, she felt, why should Lady Freddie object? It was true she was not of the same social background, but she was talented in her own right, and had a career to fall back on after the war, although as David's wife, she knew she would not be called on to work. It just wouldn't do.

'Do you want to marry me, that's the important thing?' David said. 'Sarah?'

'Of course I do,' she said. 'I would be thrilled to marry you, I think I've loved you ever since I was a little girl, although I never dreamt the day would come when you would ask me to marry you.'

'Then it's settled,' he said. 'I shall go and tell Mother – and no matter what, and I mean it, Sarah, it will make no difference to us – we shall get married. What do you think your parents will say? Will they approve, do you suppose?'

'I should think so,' Sarah dimpled. Robbie had never done anything to encourage the friendship, indeed sometimes she seemed to disapprove, but that was only because she had Sarah's happiness at heart and didn't want to see her get hurt. When she knew how David loved her, she would go along with it.

He smiled into her eyes. 'So, shall we consider ourselves engaged, Sarah?'

And she smiled back at him.

'Yes, David,' and he took her hand across the table and kissed it.

He had a special errand to do at his bank in Knightsbridge and, leaving Sarah at the tube station, went along to see the bank manager.

He emerged half an hour later having

obtained from the vaults the very special something that he had made an appointment for. His grandmother's ring, which she had bequeathed to him for his twenty-first birthday, for his bride, she had said. It had been her own engagement ring, and her mother's before her. A striking opal surrounded by diamonds, it rested now safely in his pocket.

It belonged to Sarah now, and even if she didn't like it, it was hers – and he would buy her another when the time came. Some people he knew were superstitious about opals, but he had no time for that nonsense himself.

If he was honest he had to admit that his heart was beating a little faster when he reached Edwardes Square and made his way up the path to the front door. It was opened by Mrs Reading, his mother's housekeeper, who was delighted to see him.

'Mr David! Is your mother expecting you? She said nothing to me – but you're lucky, she is in.'

'I want to surprise her,' David said, 'and I haven't very long, it's just a fleeting visit – where is she?'

'Upstairs in the drawing room,' she said,

'and I'll put the kettle on – it's nearly teatime.'

She was right, his mother gasped when she saw him, and walked towards him taking him in her arms. 'David, my dear, dear David.'

He kissed her warmly. 'Mother, how are you? You look wonderful.'

She stood him away from her. 'I wish I could say the same for you; you look tired – oh, David, this terrible war, your father away, and you, and I am missing the girls. I just came down to London for a few days.'

'I know, Mrs Reading told me. I telephoned her yesterday, and I'm afraid I can't stay long, I've got to get back.'

'Then sit down, darling, we must make the most of it; has it been very awful?'

He nodded. 'At times, yes, still, it's a job that has to be done. I came really, mother, to speak to you about something – something important,' and she sat very still, but when she turned to look at him her eyes were very bright.

'Yes, darling, what is it?'

Mrs Reading came in with the tea things which she set down on a small table. 'Excuse me – will you pour, Milady?'

'Yes, yes,' she said. 'I'll pour,' and

proceeded to do so, handing a cup to David.

'Well?' she said and smiled at him.

'Mother,' he said, and all his rehearsed speeches went out of his head. 'I have just seen Sarah – Sarah Roberts – and I have asked her to marry me–' and saw his mother's eyes close for a moment as she leaned back against the sofa.

Then she opened them. 'Sarah?' she said. 'Robbie's Sarah?'

'Yes, Mother,' he said patiently.

'But I didn't know you had been – I mean, I thought she was in Paris–'

'No, she's home, she got home two or three days ago.'

'Well, you didn't waste much time,' she said, almost bitterly.

'You must know how I feel about her, how I have always felt about her.'

She made no reply at first, then she looked at him. 'And Sarah, does she feel the same about you?'

He smiled. 'Yes, she does, I'm happy to say.'

'Well!' she said, and again. 'Well,' as though she was playing for time, and she walked over to the window and stood staring out.

Sarah was right, he thought, this is not

going to be easy.

When she turned, she came back to the table, and took a cigarette out of the box, and lit it, taking a long time to do so.

Then she blew out a long stream of smoke.

'It's just not on, David,' she said quietly.

He frowned. 'What do you mean – not on? That's a vulgar way of putting it, isn't it?'

'What I am saying is, that you can't possibly marry Sarah, you have let your feelings run away with you. It would be a most – unsuitable marriage. She is not the girl for you.'

'You mean, because she is not of our class,' he said flatly.

'That, and the fact that you are living a most unusual and unnatural life, things have got on top of you, and you are imagining something – well, that in real life, just doesn't exist.'

'What is that supposed to mean?'

'I mean, darling, in ordinary circumstances, you would never consider marrying someone like Sarah.'

'I have always wanted to marry Sarah,' he said.

'A childish dream,' she said, stubbing out her cigarette in an ashtray. 'You went from school to university and then straight into the RAF, you simply have not had time to make a judgement, you haven't yet met the sort of girl that you should marry.'

'Should marry? What does that mean? I'm in love with Sarah, and Sarah is in love with me.'

'Oh, David,' she covered her face with her hands and he thought she was weeping.

'Mother, don't upset yourself, it's not that bad! Sarah is a lovely girl, well, you know she is – how can you say someone like Sarah is unsuitable, it's a joke–'

She turned anguished eyes to his.

'David, I want you to be happy–'

'Then accept Sarah as my wife, I am not going to change my mind, so–'

'Have you asked her yet?' she whispered.

'Yes, today, I asked her to meet me in town, and she–'

'Accepted you?'

'Yes, I am delighted to say,' and his mother flopped down on the nearest chair, and covered her face with her hands.

At this, he was angry. Making such a drama out of it…

'You'd better get used to the idea, Mother,' he said, 'because that's how it is. I'm sorry, I've no wish to upset you,' and kissing her gently, left the room and let himself out.

Minutes after he had gone, Freddie roused herself and went to the telephone.

'Get me First Lodge,' she said to Mrs Reading. 'I wish to speak to Mrs Roberts.'

Chapter Eighteen

Sitting in the train taking him back to Hornchurch, David was deep in thought. All around him were people going about their business, homeward bound, office staff who worked in the city, RAF personnel, but he saw nothing of them.

He could hardly hide his disappointment at his mother's reaction. He had thought she might query his decision, laugh even, never in his wildest dreams did he imagine that she would be so devastated with his news.

David stumbled up the stairs – it was more than he could take.

So Sarah had been right then. Was this where a woman's intuition came in, or did she think, like his mother, that it really was 'not on' as his mother had so succinctly put it.

First and foremost he was shocked at his mother's reaction. If anyone had asked him he would have said snobbery was not one of her failings; she was the most easy-going, friendly woman, it didn't matter who it was. Look how good she had been to Sarah when she was small; he had always played with Sarah, she went to all their parties, she rode alongside him when they went out with the horses – and what's more, Sarah had grown up into the most charming young woman, talented, beautiful, able to hold her own anywhere, was travelled, spoke French – what more did his mother want? Was it merely because she was the maid's daughter, out of their class – he just could not believe it of his mother.

His mind harked back over the years, Sarah as a toddler – he even remembered her as a baby, one of his earliest memories, remembered bending over the pram and seeing this dark-eyed baby studying him so seriously, saw her in her little blue dresses, always perfectly turned out by Robbie; and she was never a tomboy, even though they always played together. Sarah was feminine – that was part of her charm.

Well, to hell with it. Of course, he didn't want to upset his mother, she was very dear to him, but he had his life to lead. She would just have to get used to it.

Back at the base, he made his way to the mess, where he saw Bill standing at the bar and went over to him.

'How's it been?'

'Lucky sod – we've had a hell of a day!'

'My turn tomorrow,' David grinned.

'Well, did you get your mission accomplished? Did you see her?'

He had grown used to the sight of David's girl, her picture started out at him every time David opened his locker. A grave-eyed, dark-haired beauty, was how he would have described her, and he envied David. He had never had anyone special in mind, but the new draft of WAAFS had made a difference, and perked up the flying personnel more than somewhat.

'Yes, not only did I see her, but I popped the question.'

'I thought you might,' Bill said.

David dived into his pocket, and from a buff envelope took out a small velvet box. Opening it, Bill saw a magnificent ring. He had no idea what it was, but it shone with a thousand colours in the lights from the overhead lamps. Surrounding the stone were diamonds, he knew that much.

'Phew!' he whistled.

'It's a family ring, belonged to my grandmother, who left it to me for my twenty-first birthday for my bride-to-be. Of course, I didn't know then it would be Sarah – mind, I had hopes, even then.'

'Some ring,' Bill said.

'I got it out of the bank, and next time I see Sarah, I shall slip it on her finger – can't wait – and I'm going to keep it in my belongings, so you'll know what it is if anything should happen–'

'Come off it,' Bill laughed. 'Don't tempt fate–'

'I wish I'd got it from the bank before I saw her, but I was not absolutely certain she would accept me – anyway, she has.'

'Well, congratulations, old boy,' Bill said.

Robbie's day had started badly on the morning that Sarah went to town. For a start, little Editha was not well, she had a temperature, and they were waiting for the doctor to come. Tom, also, was not well, he had limped his way down to the field, upset because Sarah was going to see David, but there was nothing anyone could do about that. Events had to take their course. Added to that, the siren went for the fourth time that day sounding its alarming wail across the countryside, so that when the telephone rang, she was almost prepared for bad news.

It was Lady Freddie, and she sounded desperate.

'Robbie, are you alone?'

'Yes, Milady.'

'Then listen carefully; David has proposed to Sarah,' and Robbie gave a small gasp. So it had come, she shouldn't have been surprised, of course that was why David wanted to see her.

'Oh, Milady!'

'You can say that again, Robbie. What are we to do? Things can't go on like this–'

There was a silence, as though, Robbie thought, I could come up with the answer.

'Robbie, are you there? What can we do?'

'Seems to me, Milady, the time has come to tell them.'

'Oh, don't!' Lady Freddie cried. 'I couldn't possibly–'

'Well, someone has to; how else can it be solved? I'm thinking of David as much as anything, because I think he really is in love with her. I'm not too sure about Sarah, but it will be a shock, anyway. Oh, it doesn't bear thinking of–'

'Well, I want to see Sarah,' Lady Freddie said doggedly.

'What for?' Robbie said, concern for her daughter uppermost in her mind.

'I want to talk to her, if I can make her see sense – tell her how unsuitable the whole thing would be, if I can persuade her to see sense–'

'I don't think so, but you could try. She is going to be very upset.'

'Oh, Robbie, I know, it is all my fault, but I never dreamed–'

'Now, Milady, don't upset yourself. It can't be helped, the damage is done now.'

'Perhaps we should have thought of the consequences before we–'

Before you, you mean, Robbie thought, and could not help feeling a little bitter.

'I'll tell her,' she said. 'When do you want to see her?'

'Tomorrow or Friday, I'm leaving here on Saturday.'

'I'll tell her, Milady,' Robbie said.

Sarah was back, and in Hilda's room watching her bathe and change little Editha when Robbie found her. The doctor had been and thought she had a chesty cold, but Hilda was to let him know if her temperature didn't go down.

'Oh, there you are,' Robbie said with false brightness. 'How is she, Hilda?'

'She's not her usual self, fretful, I'd say, and she doesn't want her feed.'

'We'll just have to keep her warm; it'll be just one of those baby things. Oh, by the way, Sarah, Lady Freddie telephoned. She would like you to go up and see her.'

Sarah frowned. 'Go up and see her, what for?' Then Sarah relaxed and smiled. 'I expect she wants to congratulate me on my engagement! David proposed! Isn't it wonderful? He was going to see her after he left me.'

Robbie wasn't given the chance to respond.

'Did she say when?' Sarah rushed on.

'Well, tomorrow, she thought, or Friday.'

'I'll go tomorrow immediately after lunch, perhaps do a little shopping, although I can't think of anything I want. What about you, Hilda?'

Hilda shook her head. Shopping in London had never been on her agenda, and anyway the shops were nearly empty.

So once more Sarah walked to the station. There was an air raid alert on, but she didn't take much notice, although there was always the possibility of a raid. You were supposed to go to a shelter, but there was no way she was going into a public shelter, they smelt so awful, damp, and earthy, and she shuddered. She'd rather take her chances, and duck for cover if she heard a plane.

She bought her ticket, and on the train thought about David and his proposal. I hope Lady Freddie is pleased, she thought – it is nice of her to want to see me, but as my future mother-in-law, I suppose that is the polite thing to do in her circle.

Thinking about her love for David, she tried to analyse it, for it was not the passionate thing that David seemed to possess. She loved David with all her heart, he was her best friend, there was no one she would rather be with; she was comfortable with him, and wondered if that was enough. The *grande passion* as the French called it was not there, not on her side, at any rate, and she wondered if it mattered. She recalled Mary Anderson, a girl from the village who had had a baby at fifteen – and when the other girls talked to her, she told them she didn't regret a moment of that quick furtive love affair behind the cow-sheds. He had been a visiting itinerant young man, doing farm work. Mary, it seemed, didn't even mind being left with his baby. If he ever gets in touch, I'd follow him, wherever he is, she said. I love him, she said, simply, and they were left wondering what it must be like to love someone like that.

Well, Sarah decided, I don't love David like that, not enough to toss my bonnet over the windmill, as they say, but I do love him, and I am excited at the prospect of being his wife. Perhaps when we really get to know each other it will be different…

Also, she had to admit, he was handsome, and came from a good family. She was a very lucky girl to be marrying into the Drummond family, and if she were honest, there was a touch of glamour about it. But that was extra – all that, and dear, dear David as well…

What was love? And suddenly she thought of and remembered Pierre – and those two brief episodes in Paris – how nice he had been – and she wondered where he was now.

And Gerard, what of him? Truth to tell, she had felt something for him, too, a strong attraction, and when he looked at her with those dark eyes, he had felt something for her too – but that wasn't love either, was it?

The train stopped at Paddington, bringing

her back to earth, and getting off the train she made for the underground to High Street Kensington.

Mrs Reading greeted her warmly, and showed her upstairs to the drawing room, where Lady Freddie sat sewing. She looked up when Sarah came in and smiled, then rose and went towards her, still with that bright blue gaze that Sarah remembered so well.

'Sarah, my dear, you look wonderful! I'm so glad you could come, I thought–' but her words faded away, and for the first time, Sarah felt that Lady Freddie was not totally in command of herself.

'Do sit down, my dear,' she said. 'Would you like some tea?'

'That would be nice, if you are going to have tea–'

'Yes,' Lady Freddie said hastily, 'of course. I'll ring the bell.'

Sarah looked at her as she went over to the fireplace, still slim and extremely pretty, with her luxuriant fair hair and those blue eyes, and caught sight of a photograph of the two girls taken together.

'How are the girls?' she asked. 'Joanna and Candida?'

'They are in America, and enjoying life enormously.'

She came back, and sat down.

'Now, my dear, you must tell me about Paris; I hear you enjoyed it very much.'

'Yes, I did.'

'And Madame Lisette, she's a darling, isn't she, but quite a martinet in the workroom, I imagine.'

Sarah hesitated. 'I don't expect you know, but I'm sorry to tell you that she died a few days ago. That's why I came home,' and saw Lady Freddie bite her lip.

'I didn't know,' she murmured. 'And Gerard – he is well?'

'Yes, he was so good to me – he took me personally to the airfield to get my plane back to England. He was so kind,' and Lady Freddie got up abruptly and went over to the window where she stood for a few moments, silent.

'Ah,' she said presently, 'here is Mrs Reading–' and came back and sat down opposite Sarah, where she poured the tea and handed her a plate for the tiny cakes.

'Home-made by Mrs Reading,' she said, 'although I don't expect you to be impressed, your mother is such a good cook,' and Sarah smiled.

She asked Sarah questions about Paris before coming to the point, and Sarah had the strange feeling that she was playing for time.

When Mrs Reading had taken the tea things away, she sat up straight and looked at Sarah.

'Sarah, my dear, David has told me–' and Sarah blushed and smiled, but Lady Freddie was not smiling.

'Sarah,' she said firmly and clearly. 'I think you are both making a big mistake.'

Sarah's first reaction was one of shock, then anger, as she realised swiftly why she had been asked to come to London.

'I'm sorry, Milady?'

'I don't want you to take this personally, you are a very beautiful girl, Sarah, with a great future in front of you–'

Sarah stopped her. 'But, Milady?'

'It is very difficult for me to say this–' Lady Freddie began.

But you are going to say it, nevertheless, Sarah thought and felt the anger rise in her again.

'You don't think me a suitable wife for David?' and there was a look in the dark eyes that should have warned Lady Freddie.

'Oh, my dear, you mustn't think that! It has nothing to do with that – nothing at all. I feel you really don't know each other that well, not enough to become engaged at any rate. The fact that you almost grew up together as children is not enough, and David is under a great strain as I am sure you know–'

She had not been prepared for Sarah's reaction. Had thought she would be malleable – understanding, agree to a postponement – at least for the time being, but this Sarah was angry, although she was taking great pains to hide it.

'You know, Sarah,' she said gently, 'a wartime marriage is not always a good thing. Young couples get carried away – by the urgency of things, the turn of events, and often do something that they are sorry for afterwards–'

Sarah sat politely, listening.

'And David – as I am sure you realise, has a very, very responsible task to do. He needs to have his wits about him, to be alert at all times, and a wife – having a wife, could be–'

'An encumbrance?' Sarah asked. She no longer feared Lady Freddie or was in awe of her. Her time in Paris had changed all that, and given her the knowledge that she was a person in her own right.

'No, my dear, of course not, not an encumbrance, but a responsibility that a young man can do without – yes, a responsibility,' and, pleased she had found the word, she repeated it.

'You don't see it as my being a help to him, a comfort, someone for him to be with. He must get very lonely–'

'Yes, of course, they all do, all fighting men get lonely, it is one of the tragic things about war; anyway, he is young–'

Sarah frowned. 'Too young to marry, you think? But David loves me,' she said quietly. 'Isn't it going to upset him terribly if you are against the marriage?'

'My dear, not against the marriage,' Lady Freddie said. 'Just that the time is not right. Perhaps–'

'But that's just what he wanted; a wife to help share his problems, to be there for him.'

And Lady Freddie gave a little tinkling laugh.

'My dear, I am sure that is what all fighting men want; think of all those brave men without wives, their children, their loved ones.'

Sitting there Sarah was wondering how David had got on the day before – had his mother said all this to him? Poor David, he must have been so upset. Perhaps she had said nothing, intending just to let Sarah know her feelings and hoping that Sarah would do the necessary thing and call it off.

Well, Sarah thought, I am not going to hurt David, although I do know that she has a point. I too have my doubts – but they are for me and David to sort out, not to be told by Lady Freddie what to do.

As Sarah sat still, Lady Freddie seemed to grow more in command of herself.

'Perhaps later on–' she said, and gave a small smile. 'Things can't go on like this for ever–' as if giving Sarah slight hope.

But Sarah was not convinced. She is going to stop this marriage in any way she can, she thought. If it is left to her, David will never marry me. She will want to vet the girl, make sure she is right in every way. I must think of David and what he wants, even though I have to accept she could be right, it could be a mistake, but I would do anything for him, he is the best friend in the world, and if that's what he wants – after all, who knows what will happen in wartime?

She got to her feet.

'Oh, Sarah,' and Lady Freddie clapped a hand to her mouth, 'Sarah my dear–'

'I don't think there is anything more to be said. I won't say anything to David about this visit. I am sure you wouldn't want me to.'

'Sarah, don't leave like this,' and Sarah was horrified to see tears running down Lady Freddie's face as she followed Sarah to the door.

'Goodbye, Milady,' she said, opening the door and going through it, hurrying down the stairs without a backward glance...

Her heart was beating uncontrollably as she made her way back to the tube station. Oh, how awful! And how rude she had been to Lady Freddie – her mother would be horrified.

Well, she thought, I am furious – how dare she, how dare she think she has a right. I can have my doubts, I am entitled, but she has none. He may be her son, but he has a right to his own life, and if he wants to marry me, well, so be it.

Almost blindly she found her way back to Paddington and the train to Allington, and not until she was in the train did she simmer down.

Of course, seriously, Lady Freddie had a point. Perhaps she was not the right wife for David; but that was hardly the issue. David thought she was and that was all that mattered.

Poor boy, she thought, feeling old enough to be his mother. What a way to treat a son.

Well, she may have bossed Mum around all these years, but she certainly isn't going to boss me. If I decide not to marry David it will be because I have made the decision, not Lady Freddie.

And sitting back in the corner seat she went over it all again, what Lady Freddie had said – exactly what she had said.

Robbie sat nursing little Editha, while Hilda did the ironing, and Tom, his trousers rolled up to his knees, massaged his legs with horse oils, all the while thinking of Sarah and what she must be going through.

Robbie was beside herself with worry. Another air raid siren had gone, and her mind was on Sarah and what was happening up there in London with her Ladyship, as well as worrying about the baby.

Looking down at the infant, she could see that she wasn't at all well; her temperature was still high, and they were waiting for the doctor to pay a second visit. From time to time Hilda turned anxious eyes to her baby, trying desperately not to worry, while a lone plane circled overhead – was it one of theirs, or ours?

It was into this scene that Sarah returned when she opened the kitchen door, and the first thing that flew into her mind was – what a different set-up from the one she had just left.

That beautiful drawing room, Lady Freddie so elegant, so – upper-class, for want of a better word, and First Lodge kitchen – her home, Robbie with the baby, Hilda at the ironing board, Robbie whose startled eyes flew to hers in anguish.

She closed the door firmly behind her – and saw that they were all anxiously awaiting her news.

'Well, that's that,' she said, going over to Robbie. 'And how is little Editha? Oh, bless her heart–' anything to delay telling them. They both thought so much of Lady Freddie: in their eyes she could do no wrong, but well, they would have to know, and she felt her fury at Lady Freddie's words rising again, despite her determination to keep cool.

'How was she? Milady?' Robbie asked. 'Did she–'

'You might well ask,' Sarah said, her temper beginning to resurface. 'To put it bluntly, she is not in favour of the marriage – thinks I am not good enough for her son, that's it in a nutshell.'

'Oh, Sarah,' and Robbie held back the

tears. How hurt she must feel to be so rejected – for that reason – but what else could she have said but the truth?

'He's too young, I am too young, we don't know what we are doing and are just not suited. Well, it's obvious what she meant.'

Neither Tom nor Robbie said anything; what was there to say?

'I mean,' and now Sarah herself was near to tears. 'Treating David as if he were a child, how dare she, who does she think she is? I don't know if she told him that, or whether she was just telling me, but she practically forbade the marriage! Honestly! David is quite old enough to know what he wants, who he wants to marry… Who does she think she is?'

The plane circling round overhead zoomed above them while silently Tom rolled down his trouser leg and Robbie held the baby closer to her protectively.

'She is your mother,' she said … while Sarah stared at her with wide eyes like those of a startled gazelle and Hilda stood statue-like – the iron half-way to the board.

'Lady Freddie is your mother…' Tom stumbled up the stairs. It was more than he could take.

Chapter Nineteen

It was as if a tableau had been frozen in time before Sarah, both hands to her ears as if she wanted to shut out the words she had just heard, flew towards the stairs and up to her room, banging the door behind her, and flinging herself down on the bed.

Robbie swiftly handed Editha to Hilda who said not a word, before hurrying up the stairs to follow Sarah. She tapped on her door, but there was no answer. Tom came out of their room looking like death, his face ashen.

He put an arm around Robbie's heaving shoulders.

'Leave her, Edie,' he said, 'leave her – she's got to come to terms with it – it's best out – just leave her alone. It's going to take a time–' and she walked with him towards their bedroom, hardly believing what she had said, that she had actually spoken those words to Sarah.

Sarah could scarcely believe what she had heard either, even now, alone to think over

Robbie's words. Lady Freddie – her mother? How could that be? She was stunned – it was like a mortal blow, for apart from anything else, she felt she had been made a fool of. That's if it were true. But why would Robbie say such a thing, if it were not? Of course, she had known from the start that she wasn't Robbie's own child, but she never even thought about it. The boys were her brothers, her father her real father – she had never questioned it.

Her legs like lead, she got up and went over to the mirror, studying herself. She looked nothing like Lady Freddie – nothing at all – how could it be? What was all that talk of Robbie's cousin? Her husband being killed in the war, going to Canada to start life afresh? It came back to her, although she never thought of it – it was a story, a yarn – made up ... how could Robbie do such a thing? Robbie never lied. She had never known her to lie so why would she say what she had just said?

The implications struck her with deadly force. She and David – no wonder she loved him, if it were true of course. Of course they were in a tizzy – David was really her brother, half-brother, and she buried her face in the pillows and wept. Poor David, poor her – they had both been made fools of. Then she sat up.

If it were true – and she still doubted it – that would have been why Lady Freddie sent her to France. Manipulating her, getting her out of the way, so she wouldn't see David.

Arms above her head, she lay there now, her heart quieter after its racketing about, and took a deep breath.

No wonder Lady Freddie was in a state – weeping – I should think so, Sarah told herself. Sending me off like a piece of unwanted baggage. Anything to get rid of me – what a nuisance I must have been to them. A threat. And if it is true, who was my father? I don't think I want to know that at the moment. So really, I am a bastard – and she wept afresh...

If it is true, I wasn't born in wedlock – oh, how could they? And Dad, her beloved Dad; had he been partner to it all?

How had they all managed to pull the wool over her eyes for so long? She had never doubted Robbie's story – why would she? It's true she had always played with the Drummond family, had received special birthday gifts from Lady Freddie, but it wasn't unusual for a lady to give presents to her personal maid's children.

What did she want of me? she wondered. It must have been Milady doing the persuading – I bet when she found herself pregnant she was at her wits' end. She would have gone to Robbie – yes, that was it. She still only half believed it, but that was how it would happen.

Milady indeed! She certainly is no lady, she thought – even if she is my true mother – but that took a lot of believing.

The biggest thing to come to terms with was Robbie. Robbie living a lie all these years, covering up for her Ladyship.

She recalled all the times she had seen David, he in blissful ignorance. Well, so was she. How happy they were together – what on earth would David say? It was even worse for him, a man, to be made such a fool of. Why couldn't Lady Freddie have been honest before it got to the stage it had now, with David asking her to marry him?

She was horrified as she imagined all the conversations taking place between Robbie and Milady, and was furious with herself for being such a silent participant. But then how could she possibly have known? Never by any suggestion by either of them had she had any idea and that was what made it so awful.

Well, she felt drained. David was uppermost in her thoughts now, she felt incredibly sorry for him, for if she faced the truth had she not been prepared to marry him?

And why not?

And what would Lady Freddie do now? She would have to tell him – Robbie had got her part of the ordeal over, she could hardly expect Robbie to do her dirty work again.

Why couldn't Lady Freddie have told David, been honest with him when he went to see her? Not only was she deceitful, but she was a coward. If she had truly loved her son, she would have told him.

Why couldn't Lady Freddie have told her the truth when she asked to see her? Surely that would have been the fairest way, although she would have had difficulty in believing her. Lady Freddie was a monster, a lying deceitful monster, and David didn't deserve a mother like her. As for her husband, Sir Richard, poor deluded man, he was nice, a sweet man – and a fat lot she had cared about him. Of course it had been in the war, but that didn't excuse it – the behaviour of a lady!

And letting her servant take the brunt of it.

Going over the events of her past life and her life since with David and what she had thought of as her true family lasted throughout the night. She was exhausted, but sleep wouldn't come. She heard Hilda come up to bed with the baby, heard Robbie come up the stairs; she thought once she whispered at her door, but Sarah wouldn't answer.

It was almost five o'clock when she finally rose from her bed, stiff and cold, so rigidly had she lain. The dawn was up and the sun coming in through the curtains; she pulled them back, seeing Kirby Hall up on the hill, with its banners and wartime signs.

Never, in her wildest dreams, had she imagined such a thing.

She took off her clothes, and changed, sluicing her face with cold water, and, although tired, knew that she had at some point to go down and face them. She went downstairs to make some tea. Everything looked different, more strange than when she had returned from Paris, and she wished with all her heart she was there now, that she had never come back...

When she reached the kitchen she saw Robbie sitting at the kitchen table, her head resting on her arms, and a great surge of sympathy went through her; she was unable to imagine what Robbie must have gone through, and she went over to her, as Robbie looked up, such anxiety on her face, her dear lined face, as Sarah folded her arms about her. 'Mum...' she said, and Robbie wept as they held each other, not saying anything.

Presently, Sarah released her, and said she would make them some tea. 'Then we'll both go back to bed,' Sarah said. 'I imagine you had no more sleep than I did. And after that, later, I hope you will tell me about it.'

She seemed to have gained in dignity, Robbie thought, what a lovely girl she was – a true daughter. She wasn't going to lose her – she knew that now.

Later that morning, Sarah went downstairs, to find Robbie in the kitchen and Tom down in the lower field. Hilda was upstairs with the children, the baby sleeping peacefully and little Tommy playing with his father's old train set.

'Did you get some sleep?' Robbie asked her.

Sarah nodded. 'Yes, I slept, although when I woke it all came back to me again and seemed more unbelievable than ever. Still, I've accepted it now, and they say that's half the battle. I can't help thinking about what you must have gone through yourself. I bet it wasn't your idea in the first place.'

'No, I have to admit it wasn't,' Robbie said, making the tea and bringing the teapot to the table.

'She was such a lovely young thing,' she said. 'Lady Freddie. Pretty as a picture, and Sir Richard was away–'

'Oh, don't start excusing her,' Sarah said, and Robbie thought how much more direct the young were these days. Calling a spade a spade; hypocrisy was just not acceptable.

'No, I'm not excusing her any more than I did then. I can only tell you that she wanted to have that baby more than anything – there was nothing I could do or say to prevent her going through with it.'

'So you would have recommended an abortion?'

'Well, what was the alternative? A baby that she could not expect her husband to accept – he had been away six months–'

'Who was my father?' Sarah asked.

'I don't know, I honestly don't know. She never said – but she must have loved him, that's all I can say. It was as if she wanted a

– legacy of his love, something to remember him by,' and Robbie turned away, embarrassed to think she had felt so romantically about it.

'Hmm,' Sarah said. 'But you bore the brunt of it, didn't you? What did Dad say?'

'Oh, he was shocked. He thought the world of Lady Freddie. Couldn't believe she had done such a thing as to get herself pregnant by someone other than her husband, and when she suggested we adopted you, he was dead against it.'

'I bet–'

'So was I, but I did think – well, it would be a little baby to look after, and you have to remember I was her old nanny, so there was no way I wanted her to give the baby out to strangers.'

Sarah said nothing for a while, then she spoke. 'Yes, I can see how it happened. I can understand all that, what I can't forgive is the secrecy – why she has carried it on so long, never telling David when she knew how he felt about me, getting rid of me, sending me to France, for that's what she did.'

'Well, it was a good opportunity for you, seeing that you had such a flair for dress design.'

'Don't excuse her, she wanted me out of the way. Well, it's over now, and it'll take me a time to get used to it, but my main worry is David. I can't bear to think of what she will say to him, the shock it will be, he will feel so foolish, as I did.'

'Not foolish, surely,' Robbie interjected.

'Yes, I think there is an element of that in it, I know that's what I felt – that I had been fooled, you had both pulled the wool over our eyes and let us get on with it.'

'Oh, Sarah, it wasn't like that, events sort of took over.'

'Well, at least I know now, but David... You will tell her, won't you?'

'Of course, I shall telephone her this morning.'

'Tell her that she must tell David immediately, it can't be allowed to go on. Deception is the worst thing,' and her pretty face looked quite grim, Robbie thought. Such disillusion – she would need to be strong to bear it.

She went over to the stove, where the kettle boiled.

'Will you want to see her? Milady?' she asked.

'See her?' Sarah cried. 'See her? That's the last thing I want to do. I don't care if I never set eyes on her again!' and once more ran out of the kitchen and up the stairs to her room.

Robbie gave a great sigh.

Well, half the hurdle had been got over – now for the other half...

'Milady, she knows...'

'Oh my God!'

At the other end of the line, Robbie could picture Lady Freddie's horrified face.

'What did you say? What did you tell her?'

'I told her the truth,' Robbie said quietly. 'And about time too.'

'How did she take it?'

'Well, of course, she was very upset, it's going to take her a long time to get over it, to accept it.'

She could hear Milady's sobs, as she spoke in a broken voice.

'Does – she – I suppose she hates me?'

'Well, Milady, it's an understandable reaction. What she hates more than anything is the deception – having been allowed to go on – with her and David I mean. She is quite right when she says you must tell David at once, lose no more time. It has gone on far too long. He is a man and you can't trifle with his affections. God knows how he will take it, I can't think–'

'Oh, Robbie, I don't think I can!'

'You will have to find the strength from somewhere, Milady.'

'I can't,' she whispered, 'I can't…'

'You must,' Robbie said in a firm voice. 'You must, Milady. It's only fair.'

Two days later, with the evacuation of Dunkirk in its fifth day, Operation Dynamo as it was called, Churchill had just returned from Paris, aware of the immense naval losses and a fighting air command sadly depleted. Trying to smooth over differences between London and Paris was an almost insurmountable task, the evacuation of Dunkirk was seen as a triumph for the British, but it was something of a disaster for the French.

With the British still holding rearguard positions, the pace of the evacuation had not diminished. There was one remaining cross-Channel route used and it was covered by Spitfires and Hurricanes. Liaison with RAF Fighter Command arranged for strong patrols over the evacuation area for the hour prior to darkness to keep the German Luftwaffe at bay, for it had been decided two more days would bring the operation to a close.

With minutes to spare, David put in a telephone call to Sarah, only to be told that Sarah was not at home. She was, in fact, in the kitchen with Robbie, but shaking her head vigorously – she couldn't speak to him now. Not now – knowing that Lady Freddie would hardly have had time to tell him already, and knowing what she knew, no good could come of talking to him. She felt guilty, but told herself it was for the best. Time enough to talk when he heard the truth – if Lady Freddie ever got round to telling it. But suppose she didn't? What then?

Sarah decided to cross that bridge when she came to it.

The fighter pilots were aware of the disorganisation owing to heavy losses and with no time to train new pilots properly, but they were sent up time and time again as reports came in of Germans massing at the Channel ports for an invasion. With so many losses the squadrons were sadly depleted.

There was an air of bravado about it all; nevertheless, it was a surreal situation, and not much they could do about it.

It was an early June evening, and the sun

was setting when David took off once again, out into the Channel, flying towards the French coast, and saw below him the aftermath of the great exodus from Dunkirk. Broken ships, the wood which littered the water below, the wreckage was indescribable. But the great salvage operation even now continued with every available ship taking on board as many personnel as they could manage. Rumours of U-boats based in Belgium were considered another threat as David ranged the skies towards St Malo with three other pilots from his squadron. He saw the two Messchersmitts coming towards him, close enough to see the great black swastikas on their wings as he opened up his fire, but not before they had shot at him, with perfect accuracy hitting the fuselage and the cockpit – then the fuel tank – he had no time to think of anything; he was already dead when the plane crashed into the sea just off the French coast.

It was five days before Sarah had news of him. There had been no more telephone calls, and she began to worry and fret.

'Suppose something has happened to him – how would I know? Would Lady Freddie tell me? Oh, surely she would let me know. I can't bear this waiting – I know he would have telephoned if he was all right.'

Sarah tried to keep busy while she awaited news, and decided to write to Gaby again, care of the LISETTE salon, since on writing to the apartment where Gerard lived, there had been no reply, and she guessed he was hardly ever there, now that his mother had gone. She was so anxious to hear how he was, and she had no address for Mimi, so writing to Gaby would be the next best thing. She walked to the letterbox in the village, and when she returned found Robbie waiting for her. By her expression she knew that something was wrong. It was written all over Robbie's face.

'Sarah–'

She braced herself. 'It's David, isn't it?'

'Yes, I'm afraid so, darling.'

'And I didn't speak to him, oh, I'll never forgive myself, poor David–' and she wept, bitters tears of regret.

Robbie held her tightly, rocking her gently until the sobs subsided.

Then she stood up and wiped the tears.

'How do you know? Who told you? What happened?'

'Mrs Reading telephoned. He was shot

down, missing, believed killed. Lady Freddie had had the official notification from the Air Ministry this morning and thought you should know.'

There was no hiding the disgust on Sarah's face.

'She didn't even have the guts to tell me herself,' she said, scathingly.

They say time heals all wounds: I can only hope so, Robbie thought sadly.

A few days later, David's friend and erstwhile school chum limped into the mess – the injury his legacy from the same sortie that David had been on; he had watched, with frozen horror and sickening helplessness, the sight of David plummeting to the sea – as he had watched so many others. He himself had been lucky; he was grounded now, at least for the time being, and a broken leg was a small price to pay for all the flying activities he and David had been on in the last few months.

When the aircraftman came to collect David's possessions, Bill had taken Sarah's photograph from his locker for the simple reason that he wanted it. It was the photograph of a beautiful girl, and he remembered David's words that the ring safely tucked in a locked box belonged to Sarah if anything happened to him, and he had given Bill the key. At the time, he hadn't wanted it, hated the thought that David might not come back.

He took it out now, and placed it carefully in his own locker. He was due for two days' leave, and would go to London. His parents were in Scotland for the duration of the war, and there would be no time to go up there. He knew where David lived in London, but had no idea where Sarah was. Better to take it to Lady Drummond. He knew nothing about jewellery, but he guessed it must be worth a great deal of money.

Tuesday saw him in a taxi en route to Edwardes Square having telephoned first for permission to see her.

A very serious-faced housekeeper ushered him in, and led the way to the upstairs drawing room, where her Ladyship sat, still as a statue.

She held out her hand.

'Lady Drummond,' he began, struck by her ethereal beauty, for here was a woman who had been dealt a dreadful blow. Her porcelain skin looked almost transparent, the blue eyes enormous in her heart-shaped face, the cheekbones standing out, her face empty of all expression.

'Please sit down, Bill,' she said. 'You do not seem to have escaped injury yourself. I do remember you came to stay for a weekend – oh, a long time ago – at Kirby Hall.'

'Yes, indeed, Lady Drummond,' Bill said. 'It was during our times at Oxford.'

'Well,' she said, 'we meet again in more tragic times.'

'I am sorry–' he began.

She shook her head. 'It was very kind of you to come and see me–'

'I had a purpose in coming,' he said, and withdrew from his inside pocket the small package.

'David left this in trust with me; said if anything happened to him, I was to – well, he didn't say exactly what – but I think he meant to give it to Sarah. He said his grandmother had left it to him for his bride-to-be–' and saw the look of horror come over her face.

She covered her face with her hands; he was acutely embarrassed. He held out the little velvet box to her.

But she drew back, and looked at him, shocked, almost horrified.

'It belongs to Sarah,' she said. 'Sarah was

his chosen bride. Would you, please, see that she gets it?'

'I've no idea where she is,' he said.

She got up and went over to the desk and taking out a card, wrote on it.

Sarah Roberts, First Lodge, Kirby Hall, Allington, Berkshire.

'And here is her telephone number. It would be better if you gave it to her personally. I expect you were one of the last people to see David alive – she will appreciate that–'

'Of course,' he said.

'Now, if you will excuse me, I am rather tired. Perhaps we shall meet again when this dreadful war is over.'

He manoeuvred himself into a standing position, wincing in pain.

'Thank you for coming, it was very kind of you–' she said, 'I hope your leg soon heals. If – when – you see Sarah, will you give her my love?' and rang the bell for Mrs Reading to see him out.

'I will. Goodbye, Lady Drummond.' And even before the door had closed he could hear the sound of her softly weeping.

Chapter Twenty

Looking back over the years, reliving them, Sarah found she was quite wide awake. Bringing back old memories had seemed to stimulate her, and the fact that she was eighty that day and going into her eighty-first year seemed incredible; so much packed into one lifetime. Seeing herself as she had been then; a dark-haired, dark-eyed beauty, William had called her after meeting her for the first time.

He had telephoned her mother, soon after David died. Said he was in London, on a short visit, preparatory to going back to his base and could he possibly see Sarah? Past connections with the Drummond family had made Robbie wary…

'Who is it?' Sarah had asked, coming into the kitchen.

'William Harper, Squadron Leader William Harper,' Robbie said, her hand over the mouthpiece.

'I'll talk to him,' Sarah said, and from that very moment had started the friendship that had turned into a lasting love.

It was arranged that he would call her, the following week probably, and he would let her know. A few days later he had told her that he would be down on Thursday morning and would be coming by road.

The first thing she saw was a small Swallow car, a yellow one, and standing beside it, a tall young man. A young man in uniform, good-looking, cap in hand, with close-cut chestnut hair and deep grey eyes and a square jaw. A man of strength and honesty had been her first reaction, and she had never had reason to change her first impression of him. As he came towards her, she saw that he still had a slight limp.

Bill Harper saw a dark-haired beauty, just like the girl in the photograph, although in real life she was warmer, a picture-postcard beauty come to life. She was everything, more than he had imagined.

Once inside the house, she introduced him to Robbie who made them tea, and they seemed to find plenty to talk about, though Robbie, leaving them seated at the kitchen table, was shocked that Sarah hadn't invited him into the sitting room.

She noticed though, that his eyes were on Sarah and not on his surroundings.

The day was fine, a summer's day, only spoiled by the incessant wail of the air raid warnings, for this was the period that presaged the Battle of Britain. The lilacs were out, and late laburnums. Robbie's garden was full of wallflowers, you could smell the scent even inside the house.

'Shall we walk?' Sarah suggested. 'It is such a lovely day,' the day tinged with sadness for what was between them – the untimely death of David Drummond.

'Do you feel up to it? What happened to your leg?'

'I gashed it,' he said, 'baling out of a Spitfire. I was one of the lucky ones, but it is much improved,' and she knew they were both thinking of David.

'Yes, let's walk,' he said, anxious to get out into the sunshine.

'We've no need to go far, it's all so pleasant, this is such a lovely time of year,' and Sarah led the way across the courtyard to what used to be a rose garden, but was now given up to rows of vegetables.

She led the way in her pretty white summer dress and white sandals. He thought he had never seen such a pretty picture, while she was proud to be standing beside him, and pleased to be meeting a friend of David's.

'When did it happen?' she asked him quietly. 'David–?'

'Two weeks ago on Friday,' he said, 'we were on the same run.'

'How awful! And – were you there? Did you see it all?' and her eyes clouded over.

'Yes, yes, I did, and I wish I hadn't–'

'Look,' Sarah said, 'there's a seat over there. Let's sit down, shall we?'

He rested gratefully against the back of the seat, stealing sidelong glances from time to time at this lovely young woman beside him.

Sarah's thoughts were mixed. She knew David and his friend Bill were quite close. Did he know anything? Had David told him? What was more to the point was – had he himself been told?

Once they were seated, he took out the small package from his pocket.

'I came on a mission, Sarah,' he smiled gently. 'To give you this.'

She looked down at the small package.

'What is it?'

'Open it,' he commanded.

She did so, seeing the magnificent opal ring sitting on its crimson velvet bed, the diamonds winking up at her in the spring sunshine.

'Oh!' she whispered, and thrust it away towards him.

Much as Lady Drummond had, William thought.

'It doesn't belong to me,' Sarah said, shaking her head.

'I think it does, Sarah. Some time ago, after David had seen you in London, he got this out of the bank, and showed it to me then. This is for Sarah, he said, she has promised to marry me. His grandmother had left it to him, for his bride. Did you know about that?'

Sarah wished the ground would open and swallow her. Feeling slightly sick, she found her voice.

'No, no I didn't – he didn't mention it–'

'Well, he wanted you to have it,' he persisted.

She felt calmer now. 'I think it belongs to the Drummond family,' she said.

'I took it to Lady Drummond. She insisted you should have it, it belongs to you, she said – oh, and she also said when I see you, to give you her love–'

Sarah's face was crimson, but William was looking at the ground. 'Oh, thank you, how kind,' she murmured.

'So, you must understand, it is the family's

wish, both of them, that you accept it.'

It was the last thing Sarah wanted, but to refuse again would surely have seemed very odd to this nice young man.

'Please take it,' he said, and Sarah, with one more glance, closed the box, and held it. It seemed almost to burn her fingers.

'Thank you for bringing it,' she said. 'It was very kind of you to make the journey.'

'David adored you,' he said suddenly – and she felt like weeping. Oh, if this young man only knew, the heartache, the misery–

'He was a super person,' she said. 'We had known each other since we were children, he was brave, handsome, everything any girl would want–' that way she didn't commit herself.

'And you, Sarah, you must give yourself time to get over it. It won't be easy.'

She got up and he stood beside her, looking down into her eyes from his quite considerable height, and he wished she had belonged to him. How much had she loved David?

'Let's go back, we'll walk slowly,' Sarah said. 'I am so glad you came; David told me he had met an old school friend.'

'Yes, bit of luck, being posted to the same squadron,' he said, thinking if he had never met David again, he would not have met Sarah.

When they reached First Lodge, he looked up towards Kirby Hall.

'I've been here before,' he said. 'Once–'

'Really?'

'I spent a weekend here – I think you were in Paris.'

'Oh,' Sarah said. There seemed to be nothing more to say.

'Well,' he said. 'Regretfully, I must be on my way,' and held out his hand.

Then he put on his cap, which made him look younger and more rakish.

RAF men always seemed to be so handsome, Sarah thought.

'So you still manage to run your car?' she smiled.

'Only now and again – can't get the petrol, but today, being special, I decided to get her out, she enjoys a run as much as I do.'

He started the engine.

'Sarah,' he said, 'could we meet again? I'll telephone you sometime – that's if you'd like–'

'Yes, that would be nice,' Sarah said. 'I'd like that.'

Just as long as we don't have to talk about David, she thought, watching the car disappear through the gates and out into the open road.

She came in feeling quite pleased with life, and told Robbie what had happened, withdrawing the ring from its box, where it shone and Robbie, despite herself, shivered. It didn't really belong to Sarah, but then who did it belong to? With David gone – she had as much right to it as anyone else, and guessed it would be worth a lot of money.

It might just help her in the future, Robbie thought, being of a practical turn of mind. You never know.

'It's beautiful,' she said, as Sarah closed the box.

'I don't want it,' she said. 'It's a sort of a bad luck thing.'

'Don't talk nonsense,' Robbie spoke sharply. 'It's a Drummond heirloom. Who better than yourself to have it?'

And Sarah, startled by Robbie's brisk tone, looked after her in astonishment.

She supposed there was something in that. Upstairs she put it away in her drawer. She had liked William Harper and hoped to see him again.

Sarah went to work at a clothing factory, for three days a week on war work, then gave a day to the House of Gallen, which had lost more of its staff but was still ticking over with a minimal amount of orders, and in her spare time she worked as a volunteer at Kirby Hall. The WVS, a morning stint at the hospital, looking after wounded soldiers. As the Battle of Britain raged and the skies were dark with planes zooming overhead. Sometimes William came down to see her, sometimes she met him in London, and as the war stormed on, she found herself fully occupied with scarcely a moment to call her own. She helped look after evacuees at the local village hall, teaching the girls from London schools about dressmaking, and her days were full.

Hilda and her two small children stayed at First Lodge while Laurie was away, even Hilda doing some voluntary work while Robbie looked after the children.

When William's leg trouble flared up again he was grounded, and sent to Oxfordshire as ground staff, which didn't please him, but it made it easier for Sarah to see him. One day he took her to meet his parents in Scotland, and since she had never travelled north before, she found it exciting, and his parents the nicest people. He had two young brothers, both at school, and a sister in the Wrens. The family home had been loaned to the government much in the same way as Kirby Hall.

There was no one more delighted than Robbie and Tom when Sarah told them that William had asked her to marry him.

Robbie almost wept with joy.

'Oh, darling Sarah,' she cried. 'I am so happy, he is such a nice man, and you deserve to be happy–' taking Sarah in her arms.

They were married in nineteen-forty-three, and set up home near William's base in Oxfordshire. Sarah had never been happier. She had never thought she would be so lucky as to meet someone as wonderful as William, who adored her. When the war ended, and the government department moved out of Falmouth Grange she and William moved in with their firstborn, Edward. There followed Hugh, two years later, and some five years later, their daughter Laura was born.

It was when Edward was two years old that Robbie telephoned her one day and said that Lady Freddie was seriously and terminally ill. 'She has asked to see you,' Robbie said.

Sarah was shocked.

'Oh, Mum, don't ask me, I can't go – it's all water under the bridge. What does it matter now? I've put all that behind me.'

'It matters to me, Sarah,' and Robbie was quietly insistent. The Drummonds had returned to the Hall, one of the daughters, Candida, living there, and Sarah had no idea how often her mother saw Lady Freddie, or if, indeed, she ever did. She knew that Milady still spent most of her time in London.

'I think you should go, Sarah,' Robbie said firmly. 'You might regret if it you don't.'

So against her wishes, her real feelings, Sarah went, combining it with a trip south to see her mother, leaving little Edward in her care.

She often went to see Robbie and Tom, despite having lots to do and the journey involved, but by now she had a small car of her own. She hardly ever thought about Kirby Hall and its occupants, never saw them. Kirby Hall, given back to its rightful owners, had settled back once more into obscurity. Sarah's feelings were mainly those of sadness at the memories.

So it was against her better judgement that she walked up to the Hall from First Lodge

– and reminded herself it was years since she had done that.

A strange new housekeeper answered the door, and, leaving her coat in the hall, Sarah went upstairs to Lady Freddie's room, her heart thumping uncontrollably.

Once inside the room, she caught her breath and memories came crowding back. In bed lay Milady, her fair hair spread around her, a pale, wan version of her former self, and Sarah was filled with a tremendous surge of mixed emotions.

How sad that it should come to this, the beauty that was once Lady Freddie; the ethereal beauty of a dying woman, was all that was left of her. Her frail white hands plucked at the coverlet, and from the dressing room came a nurse in a starched white uniform.

'Hallo, my dear, I was expecting you, but you mustn't stay long. Sit down – she will be so glad you have come, she has been waiting to see you. I'll leave you alone for a moment – I'm just next door.'

Sarah swallowed and sat beside the bed. It was too late now for memories, to be bitter, everything passes – faced with this–

'Take my hand, Sarah,' Lady Freddie said, 'and tell me that you have forgiven me–' and the unbidden tears sprang to Sarah's eyes. This was her mother – even now she could hardly believe it.

'Of course I have, Milady. Don't talk – I am glad I came–' and knew what she said was true. She would never have forgiven herself – Robbie was right.

She could hardly make out the words, but Lady Freddie was whispering again with an effort.

'I have something to tell you, Sarah. I want you to know – I think you should know who your father was.'

Sarah's heart leapt. 'My father?'

'Your father was Gerard – Gerard Puligny de Montfort–' and the effort of saying it was almost too much for her.

Sarah felt the strength draining from her, then a great wave of sheer joy flooded through her.

'Gerard, Milady? Truly?'

Her Ladyship's eyes were closed. 'He was killed in nineteen-forty–' she didn't say on the way back from taking you to safety. 'I heard from Gaby,' and opening her eyes saw the flush of delight on Sarah's face.

'Thank you for telling me.'

But the effort had been too much for her, and Lady Freddie's eyes closed.

'Leave her for a moment or two,' the nurse said.

Sarah sat by the bed, the tears streaming down her face, stroking Milady's hand as she imagined her mother must have done all those years ago.

Then Lady Freddie's eyes opened wide, and she looked at Sarah, into Sarah's great dark eyes. 'You have his eyes,' she said, and the nurse beckoned to Sarah to leave.

Sarah bent and, leaning over her, kissed Milady's cheek, and was astonished to see the tears in Milady's own eyes.

'I'll come again,' she whispered, but outside the nurse shook her head.

'I don't think so,' she said. 'I think it was only the thought of seeing you that kept her going so long.'

Sarah flew down the path to First Lodge, a path that had seen so many momentous excursions.

Robbie looked up to see her flying through the front door, her face still wet with tears.

'Oh, Mum, she is so ill, but she told me – Gerard was my father. Gerard, you remember – Madame Lisette's son. He gave me the Cross of Lorraine. Oh, Mum, I am so proud – and do you know that makes Madame Lisette my grandmother? I am so glad I came and that she told me…'

Robbie held her. She was like her own little girl again.

Lady Freddie died that night.

Just after Sarah and William had celebrated their golden wedding, William had a massive heart attack. He was in his seventies, and up to now had been hale and hearty. He was rushed to hospital where they operated, but Sarah was devastated when told that he might not live, that his life was in danger.

She stayed with him in the hospital, holding his hand, talking to him.

It was on the second day after the operation that he seemed better, and smiled at her.

'Sarah–' and took her hand.

'Oh, I love you so much,' Sarah said.

'Haven't we been lucky?' William said softly. 'A long marriage, and you know, Sarah, if it had not been for David–'

She was startled. They had hardly ever mentioned David's name in all those years.

'Sarah,' he said, 'I want you to know – that I knew – about you – and David, being–'

The blood drained from her face.

'William! What are you saying?'

'David told me – the day he was killed –

his mother had sent for him and told him everything–'

'Oh, my God! Poor David! And you never told me – why, William? Why?'

'I thought it was best left to rest. When I thought of the misery and anguish you had both been through I thought, let it rest – no good will come of it.'

'But David–' and she bit her lip. What had he gone through? He didn't deserve that – and wished William had never told her…

William had told her, she was sure, because he thought he was going to die and it was on his conscience. Had not wanted to leave this earth with a secret – yet another secret.

Secrets – she thought now, so many secrets – Lady Freddie – Gerard – David – her mother–

She got out of bed, and went over to her dressing table and from her jewellery box took out the Cross of Lorraine and pressed it to her lips. My father gave this to me, she thought, and, taking it with her, went back to bed…

The publishers hope that this book has given you enjoyable reading. Large Print Books are especially designed to be as easy to see and hold as possible. If you wish a complete list of our books please ask at your local library or write directly to:

Magna Large Print Books
Magna House, Long Preston,
Skipton, North Yorkshire.
BD23 4ND

Other MAGNA Titles In Large Print

LYN ANDREWS
Angels Of Mercy

HELEN CANNAM
Spy For Cromwell

EMMA DARCY
The Velvet Tiger

SUE DYSON
Fairfield Rose

J. M. GREGSON
To Kill A Wife

MEG HUTCHINSON
A Promise Given

TIM WILSON
A Singing Grave

RICHARD WOODMAN
The Cruise Of The Commissioner